The Price of Peace

The Price of Peace

A Novel of Ireland

JAMES B. JOHNSTON

Celtic Cat Publishing

KNOXVILLE, TENNESSEE

Celtic Cat Publishing
2654 Wild Fern Lane
Knoxville, TN 37931
www.celticcatpublishing.com

First Edition: March 2012

Manufactured in the United States of America

Frontispiece: Scales of justice, photograph
by Oleg Golovnev / Bigstock.com
Book design and production by Dariel Mayer
Front cover design by Jamie Harris
Maps by Will Fontanez

Library of Congress Cataloging-in-Publication Data

Johnston, James B., 1944–
The price of peace : a novel / by James B. Johnston.
  p. cm.
  ISBN 978-0-9847836-2-5
  1. Northern Ireland—Fiction 2. Women—Northern
Ireland—Fiction 3. Northern Ireland—Social
conditions—1969– —Fiction. I. Title.
PS3610.O386 .P75 2012
813—dc22
2011963539

In memory of my brother, Raymond,
and
to victims of the Troubles

ACKNOWLEDGMENTS

FEW BOOKS, PARTICULARLY HISTORICAL novels, are written without the help of many people. *The Price of Peace* is no exception.

From the beginning, I was fortunate to have friends around me who provided encouragement. Joe Ownby and Bill Pritchard, who read the early chapters during our travels for Kimberly-Clark, and Art Stewart who was first to critique the initial version of the manuscript.

The novel is set in Ireland and required knowledge of the Northern Ireland justice system. I'm indebted to the guidance provided by His Honour, Judge Desmond Marrinan and by John Orr QC, who allowed me to observe his work in criminal court. They answered my many questions with patience and clarity. Any errors or misrepresentations in the story should be attributed solely to the author. I'm also grateful to Kathy Mathews for her review of the final manuscript, and to George Campbell and Philip Gallagher, who provided transportation when needed for my research.

A host of people reviewed various versions of the novel and provided key input that influenced the final edition. There are too many for my ailing memory to capture all, but I appreciate the critical insights of my novel writing group (Connie Foster, Connie Green, Sue Dunlap, Joyce McDonald, Sue Orr, Frank Jamison, and our inspirational leader Darnell Arnoult), the editing skills of Alicia Adkins, KB Ballentine, and Jenna Phillips, the keen observations of Mandy Cifaldi and Dariel Mayer, the front cover design by Jamie Harris, development of the two maps by Will Fontanez, and the helpful Irish perspective of my wife, Ann, and sister-in-law, Maura.

Through all the killings, all the hatred,
all the harsh words; past all the conflicts
and obstacles, I believe the people want
peace so badly that somehow, some
way, they can get there; and I can help.

—GEORGE J. MITCHELL, *Making*
Peace, ALFRED A. KNOPF, INC.

Map of Northern Ireland showing some of the places
referenced in this book

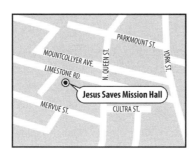

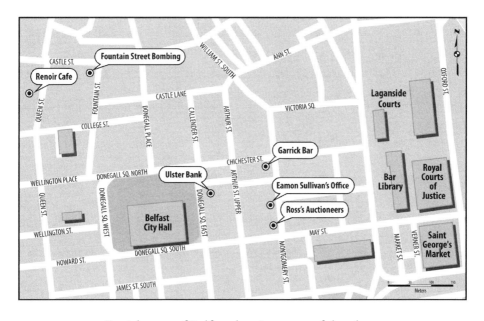

Partial maps of Belfast showing some of the places
referenced in this book

CHRONOLOGY OF IRISH HISTORY

1169–1172	Norman invasion of Ireland. Henry II declared King of Ireland
1609	Nine northern counties of Ulster 'planted' with English and Lowland Scots
1690	The Protestant King William of Orange defeats the Catholic King James II at Battle of the Boyne
1798	United Irishmen rebellion defeated
1801	Act of Union unites Ireland and England establishing the United Kingdom
1845 – 1849	The Great Famine
1867	Fenian Rising defeated
1912 – 1914	Home Rule Bill passes. Protestants arm and run guns into Ulster
1916	Easter rising defeated. Leaders executed
1921	Partition of Ireland establishes Northern Ireland and Irish Free State (Republic of Ireland)
1939	IRA begins campaign in England
1956	IRA begins Border campaign in Northern Ireland
1964	Riots in Belfast over display of Irish flag
1966	Ulster Volunteer Force (UVF) re-established in Belfast
1967	Northern Ireland Civil Rights Association (NICRA) formed
1968–1998	The Troubles
1998	The Peace Agreement
2000	All IRA and Loyalist paramilitary prisoners released

GLOSSARY

barrister: a lawyer who traditionally advocates in court.

Belfast Peace Agreement: a document signed by the British and Irish governments on Good Friday, April 10, 1998. The Agreement is designed to end the Troubles that began in 1968. A key term of the Agreement provided for the early release within two years of all paramilitary prisoners belonging to organizations observing a ceasefire.

closed-circuit television (CCTV): a camera system used in the United Kingdom for security purposes.

craic: enjoyable conversation and entertainment.

Department of Public Prosecutions (DPP): the office responsible for prosecution of criminal cases in Northern Ireland prior to June 2005, when responsibility transferred to the Public Prosecution Service of Northern Ireland (PPS). In this novel, for simplicity, only the term DPP is used.

Gardai: the national police force of the Republic of Ireland.

kitchen: equates to the American living room.

kneecapping: the use of a firearm to damage the knee joint. Widely practiced by Northern Ireland paramilitaries as a means of punishment or torture.

Loyalist: refers to someone who supports the existing union of Northern Ireland with Great Britain and who is opposed to the unification of Northern Ireland with the Republic of Ireland. Loyalists, somet-imes referred to as Unionists, are almost all Protestant.

Panadol: an over-the-counter analgesic.

parlour: the sitting room or place where visitors are entertained.

peeler: a member of the police force. Derived from Sir Robert Peel.

pictures: movies, as in "going to the movies."

potato farl: a potato pancake cut into fourths

Provisional Irish Republican Army (IRA): formed in 1969 as a paramilitary organization. Its members (Republicans) support the unification of Northern Ireland (comprised of six counties that currently are part of the United Kingdom) and the Republic of Ireland (comprised of twenty-six counties which are independent, i.e., no longer under United Kingdom control). Almost all members of the IRA are Catholic. In this novel, the Provisional Irish Republican Army is referred to as the IRA.

Queen's Counsel (QC): senior barristers or solicitors who are recognized experts in a particular field of law.

Republican: refers to someone who supports the unification of Northern Ireland and the Republic of Ireland. Republicans sometimes are referred to as Nationalists.

round of toast: one slice of toast

Royal Ulster Constabulary (RUC): the name of the national police force of Northern Ireland prior to 2001, when it was renamed the Police Service of Northern Ireland (PSNI). In this novel, for simplicity, only the term RUC is used.

scullery: a small room used for kitchen chores such as washing dishes and cooking.

solicitor: a lawyer who traditionally handles legal matters but does not advocate in court. Barristers traditionally handle advocacy.

South, the: an expression frequently used by Northern Irish Catholics when referring to the Republic of Ireland.

stone: a weight measurement equivalent to fourteen pounds.

stuffed gown: a gown with a pouch on the back left shoulder. In days gone by, the place where clients deposited money since barristers could not sue for their fees.

token: similar to a coin, but not necessarily of monetary value.

tout: a spy, typically used in reference to an informer.

Troubles, the: a thirty-year period of civil strife in Northern Ireland involving Republican and Loyalist paramilitary organizations, the police, and the British Army. During this period (1968–1998), over

3,500 people were killed and 40,000 injured by 16,000 bombings and 37,000 shootings.

Ulster Volunteer Force (UVF): a paramilitary organization founded in 1966 and named after the Ulster Volunteers of 1912. Its members (Loyalists) oppose the unification of Northern Ireland and the Republic of Ireland. Almost all members are Protestant.

PART I

The injustice done to an individual is sometimes of service to the public.

—JUNIUS

Peace is more important than all justice; and peace was not made for the sake of justice, but justice for the sake of peace.

—MARTIN LUTHER

1

September 10, 2004

It has been eleven years since she undressed in front of a stranger. A warm glow spreads across Gráinne O'Connor's cheeks. She removes her blouse and bra and clutches the light green modesty sheet to her breasts. She hands her garments to the prison official. The officer examines the clothes, sets them down, and tells Gráinne to remove all clothes from the bottom half of her body. She takes off her shoes, trousers, and underwear. As the officer examines them, Gráinne shivers and wonders what will happen next.

She has read reports in Republican newspapers about the strip searches of female prisoners. Some of them describe sexual abuse, but Pascal Bourke, her solicitor, has assured her the search will be visual only. Prison staffs have no authority to conduct body cavity searches. Still, fear penetrates.

Gráinne tenses as the officer approaches her.

"It's okay. Relax. I'm just going to look in your mouth and do a quick visual check of your body."

"Why do you have to do this?"

"It's routine. We look for explosives, weapons, drugs, anything that might endanger the staff and inmates. You'll get used to it. You'll have a full body search after every visitation, even if it's with the bishop."

The humor relaxes Gráinne, and she's relieved when the officer tells her to dress. A second reception officer records her name and national insurance number. He notes that she's forty-eight, Catholic, a widow, and her parents are next of kin.

Gráinne doesn't anticipate having many visitors, because Pascal has advised her she'll only be at Maghaberry for a few days, until she makes her first court appearance. To be on the safe side, she has brought enough clothing to last a week. The officer lists her possessions, clarifies what she can take with her, and places the rest in a property box labeled with her name. He notes her weight as ten stone and her height as five feet and four inches. He explains the rules, gives her a prison number, and takes her to her cell.

When she gets to the landing on the top floor, the guard tells her she can have a shower. Gráinne declines. She can't face undressing again. She's happy she has her own cell with a toilet, but when the door clicks shut with the finality of a spring-loaded mousetrap, Gráinne's heart races. She sits on the edge of the bed and takes deep breaths. Her anxiety eases as she looks around the cell. It's about ten feet by seven feet. The walls are bare, but there's a small window, a washbasin, and polycarbonate mirror. Beside the bed, there's a locker and wardrobe, a desk and chair, bulletin board, and bookshelf.

Gráinne rests her head on the pillow. It's thin and soft so she lies with her hands behind her head, staring at the ceiling. She thinks about her confession to Father Casey and his question about why Eamon Sullivan was the first to be killed. She's pretty sure she never told him that. Pascal is concerned that Father Casey wasn't Father Casey. If that's true, Gráinne wonders who he was.

The bed's uncomfortable. The mattress sags in the middle, and the thin blanket provides little protection against the chill night air. Gráinne sleeps fitfully. At some point during the night, she finds herself thinking about Brigid Maguire. Usually, thoughts of Brigid fill Gráinne with anger. Brigid is out of prison, instead of serving her sentence for murdering Gráinne's husband and child. But tonight there's no anger. Instead, Gráinne wonders whether Brigid occupied this same cell.

Far away from Maghaberry, in a secluded farmhouse across the border in the Republic of Ireland, Brendan McArdle watches blue smoke rise from his peat-fed stone fireplace. The farm has been his safe house for almost thirty years, since he was forced to go on the run from the British army and Northern Ireland police. It was built before the Famine and still has the original stone flag floors.

Although the house is small, its location is perfect. The narrow, winding roads and thick, blackthorn hedges provide protection from prying eyes. The British army and police are forbidden from entering the Republic of Ireland. There are numerous places to hide explosives and weapons, and Brendan finds it easy to cross the border undetected. Unlike many of his comrades, he has managed to avoid arrest and imprisonment for his Republican activities.

He puts fresh tobacco into his pipe and tamps it down. As is his habit before retiring, he switches on the radio to catch the late-night Northern Ireland news. The lead item interests him.

"A forty-eight-year-old woman will appear in Belfast Magistrates Court on Monday, September 20th, charged with the murder of two former Provisional IRA members. Eamon Sullivan and Kevin O'Neill served time in the Maze Prison and were released in July 2000, under the terms of the Belfast Peace Agreement. Sullivan was murdered in March 2002. O'Neill was murdered in March 2003."

Although not named in the statement, Brendan has no doubt the woman is Gráinne O'Connor. He lifts his blackthorn walking stick and whistles for his collie, Roscoe, to take one last evening stroll. The air is invigorating, the fields bathed in soft moonlight. Brendan replays Gráinne's confession to him two months earlier on a beach at Newcastle, County Down. It had been a stroke of genius for him to dress up as a priest, and he did well to get her to confess. But his emotions are mixed. There's huge relief at the arrest of Gráinne. He feels safer. He knows Brigid Maguire is definitely safer. But the feeling is tinged with the guilt of having deceived Gráinne. When he thinks about what she has endured this past ten years, he feels regret.

The Belfast Magistrates Court on Oxford Street is part of the renovated Laganside Courts, opened in 2002. An unmarked van brings Gráinne to court shortly before 9 a.m. She wears a light gray pantsuit, a white blouse, and a pair of low-heeled black shoes. She's surprised to see many members of the media outside the building.

Gráinne's escort takes her directly to a holding area where she's greeted by Pascal. He's dressed in a tailored charcoal suit with a gray and white striped tie.

"Your case is second on the docket, so I expect we'll begin sometime around ten o'clock. It's creating quite a stir in the public and the press. The court is packed. The judge has scheduled it early to accommodate the media. But don't worry. The hearing will be brief, and we'll ask for bail. Your parents are seated, and I've explained to them that your appearance before a magistrate is just the start of the judicial process. It makes the charges official. I've arranged for you to meet with them after the hearing."

The court is located on the second floor of the complex. The corridors are like a hall of fame for magistrates and judges. Prominent are a large photograph of the Lord Chief Justice, Basil Robinson, and a collage of the magistrates and judges murdered during the Troubles.

A hush falls over the room as Gráinne enters, escorted by two security staff. Despite Pascal's warning, she's shocked to see so many people. Evidently, the public is engrossed by the news that a forty-eight-year-old widow could have killed two former IRA volunteers. They have a good sense for why she might have done it. But, if she did do it, they are curious how she did it.

Gráinne sits in the dock to the right of the magistrate's bench and immediately looks for her parents. She's hesitant to return their smiles, unsure how the public and media might interpret it. Instead, she gives them a nod of recognition. The court clerk announces the entrance of the magistrate and everyone stands. Gráinne's surprised to see the magistrate is a woman.

David Ingram, representing the prosecution, and his solicitor, Graham McIlhenny, sit in the second row facing the bench. Pascal sits in the third row beside Herschel Solomon, senior defense counsel. The clerk calls the case, and Ingram addresses Magistrate Ruth Cantrell.

"Your Worship, this is a complex case. The defendant, Gráinne O'Connor, is charged with the premeditated murder of two individuals: Eamon Sullivan and Kevin O'Neill. The prosecution will present evidence that Mrs. O'Connor hired a third party, Hugh Barr, to commit the murders. Given we are dealing with two murders, and the murders involve a third party, and the third party is now deceased, we respectfully ask Your Worship to adjourn the case to allow adequate preparation by prosecuting counsel."

"Has defense counsel any objection to an adjournment?" Cantrell says.

Solomon stands. "Your Worship, defense counsel has no objection to an adjournment. However, given that Mrs. O'Connor has no criminal record and is a widow as the result of a 1993 IRA bombing in which she also lost her only child, we respectfully ask that the defendant be released on bail."

Cantrell turns to Ingram. "Does the prosecution have an objection to bail?"

"Your Worship, we want to make you aware that the two people murdered by Mrs. O'Connor were convicted of the bombing that resulted in the death of the defendant's husband and child. While the prosecution sympathizes with the defendant's loss, two of the other convicted bombers, Brigid Maguire and Sean Lynch, reside in Belfast. The fifth bomber, Brendan McArdle, lives in the Republic of Ireland. Our concern is that they, too, may become targets of the defendant."

"Counsel, does this mean you're objecting to the request for bail?"

"We're simply making Your Worship aware of the risks in granting bail."

"In other words, you're placing the burden on me. Fine, bail is granted on a surety of £3,000. The case is adjourned and committed to a future sitting of the Crown Court."

2

September 22, 2004

DETECTIVE INSPECTOR RORY HIGGINS kisses his wife good-bye. After placing his fully loaded Walther 9-millimeter pistol under his right thigh, he drives his Mitsubishi Galant down the driveway of his Holywood home. He has a meeting with Martin Mulligan QC to review the evidence against Gráinne O'Connor.

Rory's boss thinks of him as a jigsaw maker, someone who sifts through hundreds of facts and fits them together so there is one clear picture. He has become good at his craft, often working on puzzles with pictures on both sides, some that are three-dimensional, some with stories within stories. He's endowed with patience and persistence. He likes to gather information and characterizes it as a silent prelude in the pursuit of truth. Once this is established, he loves the hunt. However, the masterpiece is never complete until there's a conviction.

Rory regards himself as a tallyman, a keeper of numbers and facts. Although he records much of the information he gathers on computers, it's in his grubby, well-thumbed pocketbook that he most often pieces together the disemboweled truth. Names and dates, crosses and ticks. All facts, neat, clean, and precise, not sullied with blood, rage, or righteousness.

He maintains a strong network of informants on both the Republican and Loyalist sides. He pays them around £20 per week, since he believes answers lie in the heads of people on the street. He's a custodian, not a referee. Neither side plays by rules. He used to think there were rules, perhaps honor among thieves. But he has learned that there is none. It's all a gruesome game. Both sides think he's a fool. He despises them as much for their perfidy and ease of dissembling as for their terrible wickedness.

Rory isn't sure how much longer he'll work. He has been a detective for twenty-five years. The work is dangerous, and he worries about the safety of his family. The hours are long and unpredictable. He thinks he's lucky to be married. So many marriages around him have crumbled. However, before he puts the pieces back in the box, he wants to complete one more case.

Martin Mulligan is the senior prosecutor in the Department of Public Prosecutions. He's regarded not only as an expert in law, but as someone with an uncanny ability to argue the law successfully. He has worked in the department for sixteen years and frequently handles difficult cases.

"As you know, Rory, it's not enough to believe O'Connor arranged the murders of Sullivan and O'Neill. To get a conviction, we have to be able to prove that in court."

"How can I help you?"

"The most important piece of evidence that's missing is a statement from the person O'Connor confessed to in Newcastle. We need to know if Father Casey is, in fact, a priest. If he is, we may be out of luck. I doubt the judge will force a priest to disclose O'Connor's confession. However, if he's not a priest, he'll be our main witness. I need you to resolve this issue."

"If we can't find Father Casey or he turns out to be a priest, could Sean Lynch and Brigid Maguire be witnesses? After all, in a phone call, the priest gave Lynch and Maguire a full account of his conversation with O'Connor."

"The phone call is problematic, Rory. The judge is likely to rule it as hearsay evidence and, therefore, inadmissible. We need to be able to put Lynch and Maguire's informant on the stand. To do that, we need first of all to know who he is."

"I think I may have a way to find that out."

Rory finds Father Matthew D'Arcy at home when he makes an opportune call at the rectory. He sees the surprise on Father D'Arcy's face when he introduces himself. Father D'Arcy leads Rory into his study.

"It's been a long time, Rory. Unfortunately, I'm not sure our community work made a great difference. Maybe now with the Peace Agreement we can make more progress. At least, I hope so. You still look the picture of fitness."

"Well, I'm a little heavier and not as athletic. I've lost whatever hair I had. I was surprised, Matthew, when I heard you'd become a priest."

"Not as surprised as I was when I heard you'd become a peeler. Anyway, what brings you here, my friend? I hope I'm not in trouble!"

"Actually, Matthew, I need your help. I'm trying to track down a Father Casey who met with a defendant in a current murder trial. The defendant is Gráinne O'Connor, and I understand you're Mrs. O'Connor's pastor."

"Yes, I know Gráinne very well. I've watched her grow up in the church. I married her and Martin, and have spent many hours trying to help her deal with the loss of her husband and son. She has been through a lot." Father D'Arcy pauses. When he's sure he has Rory's full attention, he says, "Frankly, Rory, I don't believe she's capable of murder."

Rory notices the edge of indignation in Father D'Arcy's voice. He's not sure if Father D'Arcy's taunting him, but he needs Father D'Arcy's support. "I hope that's true, Matthew." He lets Father D'Arcy digest these words before he continues. "According to Gráinne, Father Casey indicated he was from Dundalk. I phoned the bishop, and he gave me contact information for all the Father Caseys in his diocese. Unfortunately, they all deny meeting with anyone called Gráinne. Unless she got the name wrong, there's a possibility Gráinne was tricked by someone impersonating a priest. That's what I need to clarify."

"How do you think I can help you?"

"Can we talk confidentially, off the record, as one good Catholic to another?"

"I'm a priest, Rory."

Rory hears the irritation in Father D'Arcy's voice. "Father Casey or whoever he is called two people in Belfast and told them everything Gráinne confessed. They then told me. Matthew, I know you're a confidant of Gráinne O'Connor. I want to respect that relationship, but I think we both need to know who she met with. I can't do that without your help."

"Why is that?"

"I think you could persuade one of the two people Father Casey called to give us the name."

"And you think that because I'm a priest?"

"Yes."

Rory explains his plan. Father D'Arcy indicates he'll have to think about it and he'll only participate if Gráinne agrees to the plan. Rory understands the dilemma. If Casey's a fraud, it's not in Gráinne's interest for his true identity to be revealed. He'll become the main witness against her. However, Rory knows he has to do his job, and he's relying on Gráinne's curiosity to make the plan work.

While Gráinne pours tea for Father D'Arcy and Pascal Bourke, Father D'Arcy explains the nature of their visit. He addresses Gráinne, but knows Pascal is listening intently.

"Gráinne, you know I have doubts Father Casey is a priest of the Catholic Church. The police say they know someone whom Father Casey called right after you got on the bus to return from Newcastle to Belfast. They believe that person can confirm whether Father Casey is a priest or not. They've asked me to talk to that person, but I felt I should talk to you and Pascal first."

"Why do they want you to talk to the person? Why don't they just talk to the person themselves?"

"Excellent question," Pascal says. "Obviously, the police don't believe the person will give them the information they need without Father D'Arcy's influence. Here's the problem, Gráinne. If Father

Casey's not a priest, then the imposter could become a key witness for the prosecution, a witness against you. That's what the police are looking for. That's not a risk you need to take."

Gráinne thinks about her solicitor's advice. He has been a constant, reliable counsel. He helped her through probate following the death of Martin and Peter and with her claim against the government for compensation. She has always followed his advice. However, she wants to know the truth. She wants to know the identity of the person to whom she confided her soul. She feels the odds of someone actually impersonating a priest and doing it so well are low. She looks at Pascal. "It's a risk I'll have to take. I need to know."

Pascal meets alone with Gráinne. "You mustn't do this, Gráinne. It's a mistake you could regret for the rest of your life." He watches her wrestle with the decision. He knows she's not a stubborn woman.

Gráinne raises her head. "I have to know, Pascal."

Rory's delighted when Father D'Arcy confirms that Gráinne wants to find out if she really confessed to a priest. He calls Brigid Maguire and asks if she will meet confidentially with him and Father D'Arcy. He's relieved when she agrees. They decide Father D'Arcy's rectory is the best place to meet. It's both neutral ground and out of the public eye. Rory hopes Brigid won't alert Sean.

As Brigid parks her car at the rectory, she feels goose bumps prickle her arms. She swallows hard and wonders why both a detective and a priest want to talk to her. She doesn't have long to wait. Rory quickly answers the question.

"Brigid, apart from using his rectory, I'm sure you're wondering why Father D'Arcy's with me. Father D'Arcy is a friend of mine and, coincidentally, Gráinne O'Connor's pastor. You'll remember in my discussions with Sean and you, Sean mentioned he learned of Gráinne's confession from a Father Casey."

Brigid breathes deeply.

"Both Father D'Arcy and I know, from independent research, this isn't true. There is no Father Casey. I believe not only that you know this, but also you know who called Sean and you. We would like you to share the name with us."

Brigid remains silent, her head down. Both hands tighten around her knees. Rory waits. When there's no response, Father D'Arcy intervenes.

"Brigid, I've known Gráinne O'Connor a long time. I've watched an innocent, gentle, beautiful wife and mother destroyed by the loss of her husband and child. I've watched a life of joy change to one consumed by grief, depression, and anger. She's desperate to know whom she talked to in Newcastle. You've served your time and started a new life. Will you help her?"

Since the murders of Eamon and Kevin, Brigid has wondered if Sean, Brendan, or she would be next. It would be a relief if Gráinne were behind bars. As she thinks about Father D'Arcy's words, her thoughts turn to the bombing. They hadn't meant for the bomb to explode in Fountain Street. The target was the Chichester Street Courthouse. But they'd run into an army checkpoint, and Sean panicked. Trying to escape, he turned into Fountain Street only to find it packed with shoppers. He couldn't go forward, and with the police and army behind, he couldn't go back. Kevin gave the order to abandon the van.

It was her first mission for the IRA. She can still hear the muffled sound of the explosion. She tries hard not to cry, but the picture of Gráinne's pain during Brigid's trial overwhelms her. She sobs as silently as she can. When she wipes away the last tears, she looks at Father D'Arcy. "It was Brendan McArdle."

"My God," Rory and Father D'Arcy exclaim, almost in unison.

"How could he?" Father D'Arcy says. He doesn't expect an answer. All three sit in the silence of shock. Father D'Arcy wonders how he'll tell Gráinne her confidant was one of the bombers, the only one not to get caught and serve time in jail.

"Thank you," Father D'Arcy says to Brigid. He holds her hands for a moment.

Rory asks Brigid if she told anyone she was meeting with him and Father D'Arcy.

"No," she says softly.

"Brigid, I know this is difficult for you. I appreciate your honesty. I want you to know neither Father D'Arcy nor I will reveal you as the source of our information. Obviously, we can't control what Mrs. O'Connor will do or say. I think she'll be deeply troubled, but you've done the right thing. It'll help us move forward with our investigation of Eamon and Kevin's murders."

Brigid feels numb as she drives home. She's relieved she didn't tell Sean. Although she has begun to share her life more openly with him, this visit will remain a secret. Maybe one day, when the risks to their relationship are fewer, she'll tell him.

Brendan calms Roscoe as the tires of two police cars crunch on the gravel outside the farmhouse. "What now?" he asks himself. He's surprised when the Gardai introduce Rory Higgins. A soldier in the IRA for over thirty years, Brendan has rarely been interviewed by the RUC, and when he has been, it has always taken place in Northern Ireland. The cooperation between the RUC and the Gardai as a result of the Peace Agreement makes his blood boil. No self-respecting Republican would cooperate with the RUC.

Rory tells Brendan the RUC know he impersonated a priest when he met with Mrs. O'Connor in Newcastle.

"So what," Brendan says with a smile. "As far as I know, it's not a crime to dress up as a priest."

"You're right," Rory says, "but in the process you've become a key witness in our case against Mrs. O'Connor."

Brendan's face pales, and he feels his stomach muscles contract. He shakes his head. He hadn't figured he might become part of the murder trial. "You're expecting me to testify in a court that's not a legitimate Irish court. You must be crazy."

Rory's counterpart from the Gardai intervenes. "I think Detective Inspector Higgins is saying either you provide a detailed, written statement of your conversation with Mrs. O'Connor or he'll obtain a summons to force you to testify in court. It's your choice."

"I live in the Republic of Ireland. This is a Northern Ireland issue. I can't be compelled to do either."

"Unfortunately for you, that's not so," Rory says. "The United Kingdom and the Republic of Ireland have certain responsibilities as members of the European Union. You have a choice: cooperate voluntarily, or be forced to do so under European law."

Rory lays a prepared statement on the table. Brendan scans it briefly and tosses it back on the table. "I'll review it with my lawyer."

"Just remember, we're trying to get justice for the families of your murdered comrades," Rory says before he leaves.

The Gardai escort Rory to the border. As he drives north to Belfast, he knows he's in for a long and difficult ride with Brendan.

3

October 2004

GRÁINNE MAKES HER FIRST APPEARANCE in Crown Court 12, the largest of the courts on the fourth floor of the Laganside complex. She notices immediately that the atmosphere is much more austere than at her preliminary hearing in the Magistrates Court.

Senior and junior counsel wear gray wigs and sit in the center section of the court, facing the judge's bench. Senior counsel for both the prosecution and the defense wear black silk gowns with high collars and sit in the front row. Junior counsels wear stuffed gowns and sit in the second row. The solicitors for the prosecution and defense occupy the third row.

Gráinne sits in the prisoner dock at the back of the room facing the judge's bench. Her family is in front of her to the left, while the Sullivan and O'Neill families sit in front of her to the right. The press box and public galleries are full. Only the jury box is empty.

The court crier enters and calls the court to order. Everyone stands as Judge Harold Sinclair enters. He, too, wears a gray wig. His red robe is trimmed in white ermine. Although he wears half-moon spectacles, he looks younger than his fifty-four years. He has been a High Court judge for four years.

Judge Sinclair has gained a reputation for being well-prepared, cool-headed, and a sound legal scholar. He's regarded as fair and independent, but cautious in setting precedents. This aspect concerns Pascal, for the defense strategy will test to the limit Sinclair's willingness and ability to handle arguments not previously considered by the court.

Judge Sinclair motions the court clerk to read the charges.

"This is case number 4052: *Regina versus O'Connor*. The defendant is charged that in or about February 2002, she entered into a contract with a third party, known as Hugh Barr, to murder Eamon Sullivan, a solicitor. Sullivan was found shot to death in his office on Montgomery Street on March 1st, 2002. Further, the defendant is charged that on or about February 2003, she entered into a contract with Hugh Barr to murder Kevin O'Neill, a taxi driver. O'Neill was found shot to death on the Limestone Road on March 2nd, 2003."

There's a noticeable stir as the clerk finishes. He turns to Gráinne and asks, "How does the defendant plead to count number one, the murder of Eamon Sullivan?"

Gráinne raises her head and looks directly at the clerk. "Not guilty."

"How does the defendant plead to count number two, the murder of Kevin O'Neill?"

"Not guilty."

Judge Sinclair addresses prosecution counsel. "Does the prosecution wish to enter a statement at this time?"

Martin Mulligan stands. "My Lord, the prosecution requests an adjournment so that it may continue to prepare the case against the defendant."

Sinclair turns to Herschel Solomon. "Mr. Solomon, any objection?"

"M'lord, the defense has no objection to an adjournment, but respectfully asks that the defendant be released on continuing bail."

"Mr. Mulligan, any objection?"

"My Lord, the prosecution has no objection."

Later in the afternoon, Father D'Arcy visits Gráinne in her home. She looks relaxed as she shows him into the parlor. "Well, Gráinne, how did it go today?"

"Very well, Father, and very quick. The case was adjourned until sometime in November. I think it'll be a slow process, but that's okay."

She tells Father D'Arcy about the judge, the lawyers, and all the formality. Then she makes a pot of tea. Father D'Arcy thinks he could do with something stronger. He has put off this day for as long as he could. When they're settled, he tells her he knows the name of the man she met in Newcastle.

"Well, Father, who?" she says.

"Gráinne, this is going to be difficult for you. I think by now you know the person you met with wasn't Father Casey. He was, as we suspected, not a priest. The person was Brendan McArdle, the same Brendan McArdle who was responsible for the Fountain Street bombing. I'm sorry."

"No. It can't be," Gráinne cries. "You mean I poured out my soul to that bastard, to the animal who planned the murder of my family? My God! How can that be? How could I be so stupid? What was I thinking?"

Father D'Arcy waits for a moment. "There's no way you could have known. He was dressed as a priest. He spoke the language of a priest. He obviously could play the role. I can't think of a greater evil." He watches Gráinne's growing confusion.

"What am I to do? What does this mean?"

"There's nothing you can do about the past. What's important is that you remember everything you said to McArdle. According to Pascal, the prosecution will try to use McArdle as a witness against you."

"My God! You mean the person who murdered my husband and son, and who never stood trial, will now testify against me. I must be dreaming."

"Gráinne, we don't know. He may not want to come to Northern Ireland and risk his own arrest. We'll have to wait and see. It's just a possibility. In the meantime, try to recall everything you told him. The more you remember, the better your counsel can represent you. This isn't the news I'd hoped to bring you."

"I understand, Father. I'm not upset with you. I'm angry with myself. I should've listened to Pascal."

Before he leaves Gráinne's home, Father D'Arcy prays with her words of hope that mask his feeling of misgiving.

4

September 5, 2005

ALL THE ADJOURNMENTS NECESSARY to give both sides time to prepare arguments are complete. Over the past year, Pascal has combed the evidence provided by the prosecution. He and his defense team have met regularly with Gráinne to prepare their challenge to the prosecution's case.

Solomon, the senior counsel, is forty-nine and known as an accomplished barrister. He has a reputation for being creative and shrewd. His bird-like face, mottled like an elephant's hide, testifies to years of pressure-filled court battles. William Litton, the junior counsel, is in his early forties. Like Solomon, his specialty is criminal law.

Pascal had warned Gráinne that Litton has a nervous disposition. He tends to clear his throat and has a slight facial tic which occasionally causes him to stammer. However, she's more conscious of his bobbing Adam's apple and the small tuft of hair under his bottom lip. She finds he's more confident than he appears. He's compassionate and astute. She imagines his skill is in preparation of the argument rather than oral presentation.

Many aspects of the case fascinate the public. Foremost is the charge that a forty-nine-year-old woman who lost her husband and son in a bombing hired someone to get revenge. How did she do it? What is the evidence against her? What will be her defense? There's an underlying sense of sympathy for her. Many see her as a victim. But the purists say, "Murder is murder, and if she's guilty, she deserves punishment."

Within the legal community, barristers and judges would give their eyeteeth to have this case. There are few cases with more visibility. The battle between Martin Mulligan and Herschel Solomon will be watched with interest.

Court 12 is packed as the trial of Gráinne O'Connor begins. The opening by defense counsel takes everyone by surprise. When Judge Sinclair asks counsel whether they're ready to begin jury selection, Solomon stands.

"M'lord, the defense respectfully asks that the case against Mrs. Gráinne O'Connor be dismissed."

Judge Sinclair raises his eyebrows. "On what grounds, Mr. Solomon?"

"M'lord, as you are aware, the people of Northern Ireland have endured thirty years of violence. For a period of time in political trials, we've had to suspend trial by jury due to intimidation of witnesses and jury members. In other words, because of the Troubles, there are aspects of Northern Ireland's judicial system that are unique in the United Kingdom. The Peace Agreement of April 10, 1998, is another example of something that is unique to Northern Ireland. Not only does it seek to put the Troubles behind us, but it addresses important aspects of life going forward. Two of the most important sections of the Peace Agreement deal with 'Victims of Violence,' and 'Equality and Justice.' I'll come back to these in a moment.

"There's also a section in the Agreement called 'Prisoners.' This relates to the people who created the victims of violence. It's not a long section, but it's a most important one. In fact, most observers believe there would be no Agreement were it not for the provisions of this section.

"Simply stated, the section provides for the early release of all prisoners whose incarceration is related to the Troubles. As M'lord knows, the release of prisoners was completed in July 2000. Now, M'lord, you may well ask how the early release of prisoners applies to the case before you. I want to come back to my earlier reference to 'Victims of Violence' and to 'Equality and Justice.' These two areas, I believe, are applicable to this case.

"First of all, let us never forget that the defendant, Mrs. O'Connor, is a victim of the Troubles. Mrs. O'Connor lost her only son Peter in the February 27th, 1993, Fountain Street bombing. Peter was fourteen.

She also lost her husband, Martin. To be accurate, Mrs. O'Connor lost all her family because of that bombing. Her world collapsed. Her life hasn't been the same since. It may never be the same. Now, what does the Agreement say about Mrs. O'Connor?"

Solomon walks purposefully to the defense table. Litton hands him a sheaf of papers, and Solomon flips the pages until he finds what he needs. "Let me quote just two lines from the document: 'We must never forget those who have died or been injured, and their families,' and, 'It's essential to acknowledge and address the suffering of the victims of violence.' Mrs. O'Connor is still suffering from the impact of the violence committed against her family, and yet, she sits here charged with the murder of two men who were convicted of murdering her child and husband, two men whose sins were wiped out under the provisions of the Peace Agreement.

"Think of this. Kevin O'Neill was released from prison after serving only six years of a thirty-year sentence. Eamon Sullivan was released after only six years of a ten-year sentence. Is this how we remember the families of those who died? Is this how we acknowledge and address the suffering of the victims of violence?"

Martin Mulligan intervenes. "My Lord, I don't see that this dissertation on the Peace Agreement has any relevance to the case before the court."

"Overruled, Mr. Mulligan. For the moment, I'm prepared to let Mr. Solomon have some latitude. Proceed with your argument."

"As I stated, we must not forget that Mrs. O'Connor is a victim of violence. But, secondly, and this is important, Mrs. O'Connor is not being treated with the equality and justice foreseen by the signatories to the Peace Agreement. How is it that Sean Lynch, who was sentenced to life in prison for the murder of Mrs. O'Connor's family, is now walking the streets of Belfast as a free man? How is it that Brigid Maguire, who was sentenced to fourteen years for the murder of Peter and Martin O'Connor, also is free? How is it that Brendan McArdle, who planned the bombing and provided the materials for the bomb, has never spent a day in jail and, under the terms of the Peace Agreement, may never spend a day in prison? At the most, he might spend two years.

"The answer, M'lord, is the Peace Agreement provides for this. It's designed to wipe the slate clean, to give perpetrators of violence a fresh start, to put our terrible violent past behind us. Is Mrs. O'Connor, a victim of the violence the Peace Agreement seeks to heal, not entitled to the provisions of the Agreement? Should she not be treated equally with the perpetrators of violence? Is the Peace Agreement less applicable to Gráinne O'Connor than to Brendan McArdle, Sean Lynch, and Brigid Maguire? M'lord, I don't think so. If these three perpetrators of violence now are free as the result of the Peace Agreement, why is the defendant, a victim of their violence, not free? M'lord, I respectfully ask that the charges against Mrs. O'Connor be dismissed in accordance with the intent and provisions of the 1998 Peace Agreement."

A collective sigh greets the conclusion of Solomon's lengthy motion. There's a quiet murmuring in the galleries as the public wonders how Judge Sinclair will handle this unexpected motion. The court clerk asks for quiet.

Judge Sinclair isn't easily rattled. At least, if he feels disturbed, he's not known for showing it. When the murmur subsides, he looks at the senior prosecutor, Martin Mulligan, and asks him if he wants to respond to the defense motion.

"My Lord, the prosecution didn't anticipate this motion. I think we all need time to review the provisions of the Peace Agreement. Let me say that, although it's been some time since I studied the document, I doubt the Agreement has any application to this case. The crimes for which the defendant is charged were committed three and four years after the signing of the Agreement. Secondly, I'm not sure the Crown Court is the proper court to hear arguments on this issue. However, that's a matter for My Lord to decide."

When Mulligan sits down, Sinclair asks Solomon if he has any other comments or questions.

"M'lord, in reference to the point made by Mr. Mulligan, I want to reiterate that although the Peace Agreement was signed over seven years ago, many aspects of the Agreement are still being worked out. I note, for example, the decommissioning of weapons. That was supposed to happen at the time the prisoners were released, but it still isn't in effect.

Secondly, the Agreement calls for the devolution of policing and justice. This is still in the talking stage. What I'm saying is that, in reality, the Peace Agreement is a work in progress, something that's not bound by time.

"I believe the Fountain Street bombing, which happened long before the Peace Agreement, is central to this case and, therefore, Mrs. O'Connor is subject to the provisions of the Agreement. However, as Mr. Mulligan has noted, that's for M'lord to decide."

Judge Sinclair addresses the barristers and solicitors for both sides. "As has been noted, we all need time to review the defense motion and the application of the Peace Agreement to this case. Today is September 5th. I ask counsel to let me have written representations by Thursday, September 8th, at noon. I'll make a ruling on the motion on Monday, September 12th. The court is adjourned until then at 9:30 a.m."

Gráinne's parents drive to her home off Stranmillis Road. She and Martin had picked the area because of the proximity to Queens University and it being relatively unaffected by the Troubles. It's a safe area to raise children. The house is compact and cozy, with three bedrooms and a bathroom upstairs, and the kitchen, scullery, and parlour downstairs. Gráinne uses the smallest bedroom as a study. She has left Peter's room pretty much as it was on the day he was killed.

The kitchen is where she spends most of her time, that and the scullery. Although the parlour is the nicest room in the house, it's mainly used for visitors. A soft couch lines the wall that separates the room from the entrance hallway. Two single chairs flank the bay window.

Nobody feels like eating, so they settle in the parlour where the evening light is best. The room is simply decorated. A photograph of the Pope and a picture of the Virgin Mary hang on one wall. A picture of the Sacred Heart of Jesus hangs in an alcove.

Gráinne wonders how her parents are holding up after the emotion of the day. Her father has just turned seventy while her mother is two years younger.

"Did you know Mr. Solomon was going to ask for the charges to be dismissed?" her father says.

Gráinne smiles for the first time since they left court. "I sort of did. Pascal, Herschel, and William had long discussions about the Peace Agreement and its relevance to my case."

"It was the last thing I expected," her mother says.

Gráinne's not sure how the trial will go, so she doesn't want to say too much. "They're pretty sure Judge Sinclair won't want to deal with such a novel argument, but if I understand the strategy, they may be laying the groundwork for an appeal if the worst happens and I get convicted."

"Amazing," says her mother. "Anyway, the adjournment's a nice surprise. If the weather holds this weekend, we should make the most of it."

Not far away, in a street off Malone Road, Harold Sinclair sips his first brandy of the day. When he comes home from work, he likes to sit with his wife in their sunroom and unwind with a drink before dinner. Since he works most evenings, this gives them time together during the months the court is sitting.

"Rough day?" she asks.

"No, but it was a very interesting day. Not what I'd anticipated. The defense wants the charges dismissed. They're arguing that the defendant is covered by the terms of the Peace Agreement, and that the Peace Agreement wipes the slate clean for perpetrators of violence. What they're trying to say is that, if the people who murdered Mrs. O'Connor's husband and son were given a fresh start and released from prison, she shouldn't be facing the possibility of a prison term."

"Wow. And how did His Lordship handle that?"

"I've promised a ruling next Monday."

"What you're telling me is you're going to be busy for the next few days. Am I right?"

"You're dead on, my dear."

5

September 10, 2005

Shortly after noon, Brendan places his last bet at Ladbrokes on Crowe Street in downtown Dundalk. His money's on the favorite for the two o'clock at Doncaster. He walks the few blocks to his car at Roden Place, near St. Patrick's Cathedral. He's looking forward to the first slow burn of Jameson whiskey and his meeting with Marie O'Neill.

Brendan likes the four-star Ballymascanlon House Hotel because of its location in North Dundalk. Situated on the Carlingford Road, forty minutes north of Dublin and one hour south of Belfast, it's ideally suited for urgent business. The Terrace Bar overlooks an eighteen-hole golf course. During the week the bar attracts business clientele, but on this rainy Saturday afternoon it's crowded with golfers glad to find a place of warmth.

Marie is sitting at a small table by the window facing the bar. She's wearing a white top, slacks, and a black leather jacket. Brendan guesses she must be in her fifties, but it looks like she knows how to take care of herself.

"It's good to see you, Marie. You're looking well. I only wish Kevin was with you. I can't wait to hear what happened at Gráinne O'Connor's trial."

"You're looking well yourself, Brendan. The bachelor life must be agreeing with you. It's none of my business, but whatever happened to you and Eileen? You were a pair from when you were teenagers."

Brendan doesn't want to talk about his wife. "I remember Leonard Cohen wrote this song about civil conflict. I think often of the lines 'I took my gun and vanished. I've changed my name so often; I've lost my wife and children.' At least we had no children, but thirty years on the run; she just got tired of it. Never knew when I'd be coming home, always wondering if I was alive. I don't have to tell you about that kind of stress. You know what it's like. We were no longer in love. We just grew apart. I can't blame her."

"I'm sorry."

Marie waits a few seconds before asking Brendan if he's divorced.

"Not bloody likely. We're still Catholic. I just live in sin."

Marie laughs. Kevin had recruited Brendan as an IRA volunteer in 1969. He'd watched him grow from a street soldier providing intelligence on the movement of British troops, to setting up ambushes and preparing explosives. As the struggle moved from one year to another, and volunteers were arrested and imprisoned, Brendan showed an uncanny ability to avoid arrest and quickly assumed increasing responsibility and leadership in the organization. He was a terrific support to her while Kevin was in prison.

But Brendan couldn't accept the Peace Agreement. He saw it as a betrayal of everything that had been fought for and sacrificed for thirty years. Instead, he formed a breakaway dissident IRA group to continue the armed struggle. He understood Kevin's support for the Agreement. It was his ticket out of the Maze Prison after six grueling years. Despite these differences, Brendan has kept in touch with Marie in the two and a half years since Kevin's murder. She's an excellent source of information about what's happening in Belfast.

"Tell me about last Monday," he says. "I hear the defense wants the charges dismissed because of the Peace Agreement. Surely that won't fly."

"I hope not. Solomon's a shrewd bastard, and he made an interesting argument that O'Connor's a victim of the Troubles and should be treated like the prisoners who had their sentences commuted. I think it took everyone by surprise. But the prosecutor, Martin Mulligan, says there's no chance of the charges being dismissed. I couldn't stand it if that treacherous bitch gets away with the murders of Eamon and Kevin. She killed her own. I hope she gets life."

"Well, keep me informed." Brendan says. He thinks about Gráinne's loss but decides not to comment. He hopes Marie will come back with him to the farm. He orders another round of drinks before they move to the pub he calls his local. It's small and cozy, located on a back road not far from the farm. Marie's glad to see a glowing peat fire. Pints of black porter stand like sentinels, side by side on the room-length mahogany bar. A cloth-capped band performs in a corner with uilleann pipes, fiddle, tin whistle, and bodhran. The music alternates between jigs, reels, and haunting Republican ballads.

Brendan enjoys the craic. Living alone, outside Dundalk, he misses opportunities to reminisce with his Belfast cronies. The bar talk turns to the early days of the Troubles and Brendan takes the floor. "In 1968, when the Prods attacked our homes, I knew it was only a matter of time until we got burnt out. So I said, 'Granny, we must leave or we'll die.' She looked at me like I was daft. 'I can't, Brendan,' she said. 'I've not paid the paperboy.'"

Marie laughs, even though she had heard the story before. "That's the way it was back then," she says.

Brendan's face turns serious. "The night I became a volunteer, Kevin told us the struggle would be long and difficult. I think he quoted Padraig Pearse's statement that Ireland unfree would never be at peace. I think he got that right!"

That same Saturday afternoon, despite their reservations and the inclement weather, Gráinne's parents drive her to Newcastle. She hasn't been there since her confession to Brendan. But Newcastle is Gráinne's favorite haunt. It's where Martin, Peter, and she always spent the July Twelfth holidays in their caravan.

Even after she sold the caravan following the bombing, she liked to take the bus to Newcastle on Wednesdays and visit the Church of Mary of the Assumption. Sometimes she would pray and meditate. Other times she would use the quiet to work on her novel, *The Confessional*, a story about a young girl's journey from crime to contrition.

The success of the novel had surprised her. When it was released in early 2000, critics praised the novel for its insight and sensitivity. She had written the story from the point of view of the perpetrator of the crime. In her new novel, *Absolution*, she hopes to build on the success of *The Confessional*. She wants the novel to explore reconciliation and to write it from the point of view of the victim. But her focus on writing has waned since her arrest.

To their surprise, Gráinne asks her parents to drive to Tollymore Forest Park. The Park is nestled in the foothills of the Mourne Mountains. On a summer day, it's packed with tourists, but on a cold and rainy September afternoon, they may be the only visitors. They enter the park and drive along the avenue of blue-green Himalayan cedars. The mountains provide a backdrop of gray and purple. A sign in the car park identifies four trails. The Arboretum Path at a half mile is the shortest. The River and Drinns Trails are around three miles, while the longest trail, the Mountain Trail, is over five miles.

"Is there a reason you want to visit here today?" Gráinne's father asks.

"This is where Hugh Barr died."

"How do you know?"

"Pascal found out. He has contacts in the police. He says Barr committed suicide."

"Oh, my God, that's terrible," her mother says. "What is it you want to do?"

"I'm not sure." Gráinne opens her purse and takes out a death notice from the *Belfast Telegraph*. She hands it to her mother:

Barr, Hugh. Died suddenly. The dearly loved husband of Queenie. Funeral service will be held on Wednesday, 28 July, 2004, at 12.30 p.m. in the family Dee Street residence and afterwards for burial at Roselawn Cemetery—"You fell asleep without goodbye, but memories of you will never die."

"That must've been awful for his wife and family. Do you know where it happened?"

"No. Pascal says it was off one of the trails. It happened in January last year, but they didn't find his body until July."

"Was it because he killed Sullivan and O'Neill?"

"I think so. He left a suicide note, but I'd prefer not to talk about it. I'd like to go for a short walk by myself, if that's okay?"

"Are you all right?" her mother asks. "Are you sure you don't want company?"

"No. I'll be all right. I won't be long."

She takes the River Trail. Despite the rain, the ground is firm. The grade is slight. On either side, the forest is dense with larch, spruce, fir, Scots pine, and Spanish chestnut. At the Old Bridge, she crosses the Shimna River and turns right. She walks as far as The Hermitage and prays silently for Hugh Barr's soul. "Lord Jesus and Our Lady, be merciful to Hugh Barr who died somewhere in this park. I pray for his wife, Queenie. I pray for all his family. I ask this in the name of my Lord and Savior, Jesus Christ. Amen."

6

September 12, 2005

As promised, Judge Sinclair gives his ruling on the defense motion that the court should dismiss charges against Gráinne O'Connor. "I've studied the provisions of the Peace Agreement and consulted with legal scholars and experts from the Northern Ireland Office. My finding is that there's no basis to dismiss the charges against the defendant.

"Defense counsel is correct that there are aspects of the Peace Agreement which are still being implemented. It's also true that there are provisions in the Agreement which require clarification. However, the Peace Agreement makes no provision that crimes committed during the Troubles will not be prosecuted in the period after the signing of the Agreement.

"There may be a need for clarification of the sentencing guidelines that apply to persons found guilty of a political crime during the Troubles, but not convicted until after the Peace Agreement. But the bottom line is that all crimes, whether committed before or after the Agreement, and whether related to the Troubles or not, are subject to prosecution. Accordingly, I'm denying the defense motion to dismiss the charges against the defendant. Are both the prosecution and defense ready for jury selection?"

The buzz of excitement quickly subsides. Both the prosecution and defense indicate they're ready to begin jury selection. The police Special Branch have vetted the list of potential jurors to identify anyone with past criminal behavior. These are marked as "standby" candidates.

The defense can challenge twelve people without cause. Pascal is handling challenges by the defense and has reviewed strategy with Solomon and Litton. "Basically, I want older jurors rather than younger. Young people don't know the Troubles as well as older people. They don't understand the loss, the suffering, the fear, and the anger of this period. I think those who lived through the Troubles will be more sympathetic to Gráinne. Since this is a circumstantial trial, we want as much as possible to favor people who will have an open mind, individuals who may be less willing to automatically believe the theory of the prosecution and the police. We only need to establish doubt in one or two jurors' minds to get a favorable verdict. I don't think male or female is a significant selection factor in this case."

One hundred potential jurors form the pool. Twenty-five of the hundred numbers are drawn randomly and presented to counsel in the order drawn. The selection process moves quickly. Two potential jurors are excused because of scheduling conflicts. The prosecution challenges one "standby" candidate. Pascal uses only four challenges to get a mix of jurors he is comfortable with.

Eight women and four men are selected. Five of the jurors were ten years or older when the Troubles began in 1968. All but one of the remaining jurors should remember later significant events, including the Fountain Street bombing. One male and one female are selected as juror alternates.

The first juror selected, a retired schoolteacher, automatically becomes the jury forewoman. Pascal is happy with this. Anne Simpson is in her sixties. She has been familiar with the Troubles since their inception. She also should have the leadership and communication skills necessary to guide the panel through the deliberation process.

Counsel advises Judge Sinclair the trial will last approximately two weeks. He turns to the twelve selected jurors. "Is there anyone who cannot attend court for the next two weeks?" Two jurors indicate they have personal appointments that make them unavailable at certain times. Sinclair notes the information. "We'll recess early on those days to allow you to keep your appointments. Now, have any of you read or heard anything about this case which will make you unable to form a verdict based solely on the information presented to you in court during the trial?"

Gráinne wonders how any of them could not have heard about the case. However, there's no response, and the judge asks the clerk to swear in the jury and the jury keepers. He then addresses the jury. "You are now seated as a jury in the case of *Regina versus O'Connor*. At all times, while in court, you will be under the care of two jury keepers. They are responsible for ensuring that nobody tries to contact you during the trial. If you wish to communicate with others, including myself, you should do so through the jury keepers. When you are outside the court, do not discuss the case with anyone. We'll now adjourn for lunch until 1:30 p.m., at which time the prosecution will make its opening statement."

As the jury files out, Gráinne studies them carefully. She realizes her fate ultimately will be in their hands. She's troubled so many of the jurors are women. She feels women tend to judge other women more harshly.

At lunch, Pascal explains that her concern about female jurors may be valid in certain types of trials, such as rape. However, he believes that in a murder trial and particularly in this case, with Gráinne's personal suffering, women jurors should be beneficial. He points out their age. It's likely they too have experienced or know of loss during the Troubles. Gráinne feels more reassured.

At 1:30 p.m. sharp, the clerk calls the court to order. Martin Mulligan QC begins the case for the prosecution.

"If My Lord pleases, before I get to the charges and the facts of the case, I propose to give the jury a brief summary of how the trial will proceed.

"Members of the jury, first, I will outline the case for the prosecution. This is an opening statement. It sets the scene and, while it's not evidence, the prosecution will back up what it says in the statement with the evidence of witnesses. You will hear from about twelve witnesses. They'll be seated straight across the court from you and they'll be cross-examined by the defense. Once you hear all the witnesses, this will conclude the prosecution case.

"You'll then hear the defense case. They may call their own witnesses and I, or my associate, David Ingram, will cross-examine, as appropriate. At the end of the evidence, there'll be a speech from the prosecution, what we call closing arguments. The defense, also, will make closing arguments. Then His Lordship will address you. That, of course, is down the road. After His Lordship's address, you will retire to your room to consider your verdict in this case.

"Now, some of you may have served on juries before and some of you may not. There are pencils and paper in front of you. If you're like me, I hear something on a Monday and by Friday I may have forgotten it. Therefore, if you wish to make notes about the evidence you hear, you are free to do so.

"What you'll hear in this criminal trial are two things: the law and the facts. In his final speech, before you adjourn to make a verdict, His Lordship will explain the law. As to the facts, the twelve of you decide the facts of the case from the evidence presented to you. Your duty is to take the law from His Lordship and apply it to the facts to give a true verdict in accordance with the evidence.

"From time to time, you may stay in your room because legal matters are being discussed. Since you don't have to decide the law, there's no need for you to listen to legal arguments. You concentrate on determining the facts of the case. His Lordship will keep you right on the law. We'll do our best not to inconvenience you. We'll try to deal with legal issues at the start of the day, in which case you come in a little later, or in the afternoon, when you may get to leave early."

Mulligan pauses and smiles at the jury. "However, with the best will in the world, that doesn't always happen. Sometimes juries are in and out of the room like a jack-in-the-box. We'll try our best to minimize this. Use this time to focus on the facts of the case."

Gráinne notices that almost all of the jurors smile at Mulligan's reference to a jack-in-the-box. She thinks that he's carefully crafting a strong relationship with them from the start.

"Now, let me turn to the first document you were handed. This is known as the indictment. The indictment contains the charges against the accused. There are two charges. The first is the murder of Eamon Sullivan. The second is the murder of Kevin O'Neill.

"Your Lordship will explain to you, in his final instructions, that the accused is innocent unless and until the prosecution proves guilt. The accused doesn't have to prove her innocence. It's for us, the prosecution, through the evidence we present in this case, to prove to you that the accused did what we allege in the indictment.

"This is a high burden. To convict the accused, you must be convinced of guilt beyond a reasonable doubt. If you aren't firmly convinced, then you're not satisfied beyond a reasonable doubt, and your duty, in accordance with the oath you took this morning, would be to find the accused not guilty."

Gráinne thinks it's odd the prosecution is talking about what makes the accused "not guilty." She wonders if it's a ploy to enhance the credibility of the prosecution's arguments.

"Members of the jury, in relation to the indictment, I don't propose to go into detail at this time. Our position is quite simply that the accused murdered Eamon Sullivan and the accused murdered Kevin O'Neill.

"I want you to understand what murder is. I'll cover this slowly and as clearly as I can. Murder is a form of unlawful killing with malice aforethought. Malice aforethought is the intention to kill or to cause serious bodily injury. The person doesn't need physically to carry out the killing.

"For example, someone who's sitting in a car waiting to drive another person away from the scene of a crime could be equally guilty of murder if he knew what was going to happen beforehand. It's important you understand this example because the defendant isn't accused of physically killing Sullivan and O'Neill. Rather, the accused is charged with hiring a third party, whom you will hear referred to as Hugh Barr, to kill both Sullivan and O'Neill. This will make more sense as the evidence unfolds."

Gráinne notices most of the jury members don't put pen to paper until Mulligan starts to define murder. She writes down "malice aforethought" and notes the example given by the prosecutor.

Mulligan moves to the table and picks up his notes. "Members of the jury, the murder of Eamon Sullivan took place on Friday, March 1st, 2002. The murder of Kevin O'Neill took place on Sunday, March 2nd, 2003. However, the events we're concerned with in this case took place over an extended period before and beyond these two dates. In fact, the events started as early as the year 2001 and continued through early 2004.

"The prosecution will show that the defendant planned the first murder as early as the year 2001 and planned other murders as late as December 2003. Fortunately, the later planned murders didn't take place."

The information about other planned murders is news to almost everyone in the court. There's an audible murmur. The clerk calls for order. Herschel Solomon immediately rises to his feet.

"M'lord, the reference to 'later planned murders' isn't relevant to this case. The defense moves that all references to 'later planned murders' be struck from the record and the prosecution be directed not to introduce evidence related to the so-called other planned murders as the trial proceeds."

Sinclair asks Mulligan for a response.

"My Lord, the evidence on 'other planned murders' is relevant to this case as it not only shows the murderous intent of the accused, but it helps explain the defendant's motive for the murders. We respectfully ask that Your Lordship overrule the defense motion."

Solomon rises again. "M'lord, not only is the evidence related to 'other planned murders' irrelevant to the case before the court, but the evidence is based on hearsay and shouldn't be admitted. The defense strongly objects to the introduction of this matter."

The judge turns to the jury. "Members of the jury, this is a good example of what Mr. Mulligan told you earlier when he mentioned there may be legal issues that must be dealt with in your absence. Whether or not certain evidence is admissible under law is a legal issue. This is an important ruling and may take some time. I will hear arguments from counsel tomorrow morning at 9:30 a.m. so you needn't attend court until 1:30 p.m. tomorrow afternoon."

He faces Martin Mulligan. "Mr. Mulligan, please continue with your opening statement. Do not reference issues we will discuss tomorrow morning."

"Yes, My Lord."

Mulligan addresses the jury. "Members of the jury, I believe you've been given an information package. This includes a number of maps and photographs and other documents. These items are provided to help you identify the specific locations we'll reference in this trial. They also will help you follow and understand the evidence you'll hear.

"Now, I ask you to go to the map referenced PM1. This is a map of Belfast. North is to the top of the map, south to the bottom. There are two large red triangles on the map. The first, which has the number one on it, is located near the center of the map on a street highlighted in yellow. The yellow identifies Montgomery Street, while the red triangle indicates the location where Eamon Sullivan was murdered on March 1st, 2002.

"Remember, you may make notes on your copy of the map if you wish to. The second red triangle is a little to the north of the map. It has the number two. It is located on a street also highlighted in yellow. This is the Limestone Road, and red triangle number two indicates the location of Kevin O'Neill's murder on March 2nd, 2003.

"Now, I ask you to turn to the map referenced PM2. You will see this is a blowup of the City Centre. The City Hall is located in the lower left of the map. If you look to the right of the City Hall, you'll note the first street is highlighted in yellow and is labeled Donegal Square East. You will notice the number one in a blue circle. This marks the Ulster Bank.

"You'll hear a lot in evidence about the Ulster Bank because the prosecution will show that the defendant deposited certain sums of money into Hugh Barr's account there, and Hugh Barr withdrew these sums of money shortly after they were deposited. Remember that the prosecution will identify Hugh Barr as the person who physically killed Sullivan and O'Neill at the request of the defendant. Significantly, the withdrawals are right after the murders."

Mulligan had planned to identify other locations on the map but, in view of Judge Sinclair's admonition, he decides not to risk getting on his wrong side. "For now, I will just point out one other symbol. You'll notice a number of black triangles on the maps. These represent closed-circuit television cameras. We live in a city monitored by CCTV cameras. Some are placed by Belfast City Council to detect crime. Some are placed by business owners to protect their premises. There are thousands of cameras all over the city, and these cameras detect certain things. For the police, they're like extra eyes. Their significance will become clear in due course.

"By way of example, on Montgomery Street, you will notice a black triangle on the corner of Montgomery Street and Chichester Street. This camera is located at the Garrick Bar. Now, if you move south along Montgomery Street, you will notice a black triangle just before the intersection of Montgomery Street and May Street. This marks a CCTV camera located at Ross's Auctioneers.

"If you move back with me on the map to the Ulster Bank on Donegal Square East, you'll see two black triangles at the bank. There are CCTV cameras both outside and inside the bank. You will hear about and see footage from CCTV cameras, evidence that will prove beyond a reasonable doubt that the defendant and Hugh Barr knew each other and were directly responsible for the deaths of Eamon Sullivan and Kevin O'Neill.

"I'm not going to deal with map PM3 now other than to point out that what you have is a detailed map of the area surrounding the O'Neill crime scene. Now that we've gone over the maps, let me briefly review what's in the package of photographs and other documents that have been given to you.

"The photographs marked PP1 to PP10 are from the two crime scenes. Photographs PP11 through PP25 are stills taken from CCTV footage and include shots of Hugh Barr and the defendant at various times and places.

"Finally, there's a series of documents numbered with the letter R. These include copies of various bank account statements and transactions, copies of medical examiner reports, forensic evidence, and a copy of a note left to his wife by Hugh Barr shortly before he committed suicide. We won't discuss these today. They'll be referenced later as each document is brought into evidence.

"Now, let me tell you what you'll hear in testimony. You'll hear the results of the postmortems on Eamon Sullivan and Kevin O'Neill and other forensic evidence that establishes when and how they were murdered. This will not answer the question 'why?'

"However, you'll hear the accused is a victim herself, the victim of a terrible bombing that took away the lives of her husband and son. Although this happened twelve years ago, the tragedy of February 27th, 1993, is central to this case.

"You'll hear testimony that the Peace Agreement of 1998 reawakened deep anger within the accused, particularly the provisions that the people convicted of the bombing would be released in 2000 without completing their sentences. You'll hear testimony the accused set out to get revenge for the tragic loss she suffered. You'll hear arguments from the defense that the accused was motivated by her search for justice, not by the desire for revenge. The result is the same: the murder of Eamon Sullivan and the murder of Kevin O'Neill.

"As I mentioned earlier, you'll be presented with evidence that the accused entered into an agreement with a third party, Hugh Barr, to murder Eamon Sullivan and Kevin O'Neill. The evidence will show the accused paid Hugh Barr to commit the murders. I wish Hugh Barr could testify directly to you. You would have no doubts about the 'murder for hire' contract. Unfortunately, Hugh Barr is no longer with us. Realizing the enormity of his crimes, he took his own life early in 2004.

"You'll hear that the accused also realized the enormity of her crimes and in July 2004 confessed them to a third party."

Solomon quickly jumps to his feet. "M'lord, I realize Mr. Mulligan is making an opening statement in which he's outlining the prosecution case. However, I ask M'lord that tomorrow, when we discuss legal issues, the defense be allowed to challenge the admissibility of the accused's so-called confession."

"On what grounds, Mr. Solomon?"

"M'lord, I'm not sure at this precise moment. The challenge will depend on whom the prosecution presents as a witness to the so-called confession. If Sean Lynch and Brigid Maguire testify, the reason for my challenge will be that the evidence is 'hearsay.' On the other hand, if Brendan McArdle testifies, the basis of my challenge will be that the so-called confession was obtained under duress, by the most obscene of deceits. How can any of these three people, who murdered the defendant's only son and husband, have credibility before the court? How can they be allowed to testify against the defendant?"

Judge Sinclair responds. "Mr. Solomon and Mr. Mulligan, we'll hear legal arguments tomorrow. Members of the jury, given we now have two important legal issues to address tomorrow, it's unlikely there'll be time to also hear testimony in the trial. It's important to get these issues resolved early in the process. I ask for your understanding. Accordingly, there's no need for you to report to court tomorrow. You should report for jury duty again on Wednesday morning at 9:30 a.m.

"Mr. Mulligan, how much longer do you require for your opening statement? I'm trying to decide if we need to adjourn the opening statement until Wednesday morning or are we in a position to complete this today?"

"My Lord, I'm almost finished."

"Very well, Mr. Mulligan, continue."

"Members of the jury, when you've heard all the evidence in this case, you'll have absolutely no doubt that the accused is guilty of the murders of Eamon Sullivan and Kevin O'Neill.

"Before I close, I want to say that you must be objective. When you decide the facts of this case, you don't decide them based on sympathy. You objectively consider and look at the evidence, that is, the information you hear during this trial. You apply common sense and your experience of life to decide where the truth lies, whom you believe, and whom you don't believe. This concludes my opening remarks. Members of the jury, thank you for your attention."

Judge Sinclair addresses the jury. "This is the first day of many days. I remind you that you don't need to be in court until 9:30 a.m. on Wednesday morning. I also remind you, and will remind you every evening before you go home for the day, that you shouldn't discuss the case outside the court, not even with family members or friends.

"I also caution you, when you hear a witness, not to form an immediate view about that witness until you've heard all the evidence. One witness may persuade you one way, and then later in the case a different witness may persuade you a different way. I ask you to listen, pay attention, make notes if you wish, and carefully consider all the evidence. I will see you on Wednesday."

The clerk asks all to stand while Judge Sinclair leaves Court 12. Martin Mulligan, David Ingram, and Graham McIlhenny join the parents of Eamon Sullivan and the wife of Kevin O'Neill in a small conference room adjacent to the court.

Marie O'Neill and the Sullivans provide a distinct contrast in personalities and perspective. Marie O'Neill is tough. She has the face of a warrior. Although she dislikes and mistrusts the Department of Public Prosecutions, she expects Ingram and Mulligan to win this case on her behalf. This is her right.

Eamon Sullivan's parents sit quietly, holding hands. They, too, want justice, but they're not demonstrative. They understand this is a circumstantial case that may be difficult to win. Although they believe their son was convicted unjustly as a Fountain Street bomber and they grieve his murder, they harbor a greater resentment against the IRA than against Gráinne O'Connor. They understand her anger. They often discuss how, paradoxically, they and O'Connor are both victims of the same bombing.

"What are all these legal issues about?" Mrs. O'Neill asks right away. "How do they affect our case?"

McIlhenny explains the first issue is whether the prosecution can identify that the accused intended to kill all the Fountain Street bombers, not just Eamon and Kevin. This would help the prosecution tie in all the payments made by Gráinne O'Connor to Hugh Barr. "It's not a critical factor," he assures both families.

"The second issue is much more crucial. If the judge decides testimony by Sean Lynch and Brigid Maguire about O'Connor's confession is hearsay, then the only way to bring in O'Connor's confession is for Brendan McArdle to testify. However, McArdle hasn't indicated his willingness to do so.

"We should be able to get a conviction without the confession," McIlhenny says. "It'll just be more difficult. We'll have to rely on the jury accepting the CCTV footage and the trail of cash payments as evidence linking O'Connor to Hugh Barr."

In another conference room, on the other side of the Laganside complex, Gráinne meets with Pascal Bourke, Herschel Solomon, and William Litton. Pascal asks Gráinne how she feels.

"I'm tired. It's been a long day. How do you think it went?"

"Good," Pascal says. "We're happy with the jury. There were no surprises in the prosecution's opening statement. Today, you heard only one side. We'll have our chance to challenge the evidence and to convince the jury the facts are not as stated by the prosecution.

"We'll begin tomorrow by challenging the evidence the prosecution wants to introduce. We're optimistic our challenges will be successful. The nature of a trial is that we win some motions and lose some. What's important is, when all the evidence is complete, the jury has sufficient doubts so they render a 'not guilty' verdict."

Gráinne forces a smile. "It's like a game," she says.

"It is a game," Litton admits.

7

September 13, 2005

COURTROOM 12 ISN'T AS PACKED AS yesterday. There are empty seats in both the press and public galleries, and the jury is absent. Gráinne understands that legal arguments aren't what people want to hear. She's not sure she wants to hear them herself.

The court is called to order right at 9:30 a.m. Judge Sinclair is noted for punctuality and for resolving important issues with minimum delay. He's respected for his expertise in handling complex legal issues.

"Okay, Mr. Solomon, let's begin arguments on the first of the two motions we'll hear today. You've asked the court to suppress any evidence that relates to the defendant's intent to commit other murders subsequent to the murders for which she's charged."

"Yes, M'lord, that's correct. There are two reasons why any reference to later planned murders is inappropriate in this case. First, the defendant's charged specifically with the murders of Eamon Sullivan and Kevin O'Neill. The defendant isn't charged with the intent to commit other murders. Therefore, even if evidence related to later planned murders was otherwise admissible, the evidence should be excluded as irrelevant to the case and charges at hand.

"Secondly, M'lord, the evidence shouldn't be admissible, under any circumstances, because it's based on hearsay. Your Lordship, this hearsay is extremely prejudicial to the defendant.

"The information is contained in a verbal statement made to police by Mr. Sean Lynch. However, according to Mr. Lynch's statement, he obtained the alleged information secondhand, as the result of a phone call from his friend, Brendan McArdle. M'lord, this Mr. Lynch is the same person who was convicted in March 1995 of murdering the defendant's fourteen-year-old son and her husband.

"How can the hearsay evidence of a murderer be admissible against the mother and wife of the very people he ruthlessly slaughtered? The statement about later planned murders is prejudicial against the defendant and is likely to far outweigh its probative value. The defense respectfully asks Your Lordship to rule the evidence as inadmissible."

Judge Sinclair addresses prosecution counsel. "Mr. Mulligan, I assume you wish to respond."

"Yes, My Lord. The evidence on other planned murders is relevant to this case as it clearly shows the murderous intent of the accused. The killings of Eamon Sullivan and Kevin O'Neill were revenge killings for the murders of the defendant's husband and son. The defendant not only transferred cash to Mr. Barr for the murders of Sullivan and O'Neill, but she transferred a down payment to him to kill Sean Lynch and Brigid Maguire, two of the other bombers.

"This action shows the defendant was engaged in a premeditated plan to kill all the bombers. Including this evidence lets the jury understand that Mr. Barr's account at the Ulster Bank was totally funded by the defendant and had only one purpose, paying Mr. Barr to kill people identified by the defendant.

"In other words, it ties together all the deposits to and withdrawals from the account. How can this be prejudicial to the defendant when the purpose of the final payment, for the murders of Sean Lynch and Brigid Maguire, was identical in nature to the earlier payments? We respectfully ask Your Lordship to overrule the defense motion."

"Mr. Solomon, do you have any other comments on this issue?"

"Not at this time, M'lord."

"I'll consider the arguments and the law overnight and rule on this matter in the morning."

Judge Sinclair addresses Herschel Solomon. "Now, Mr. Solomon, let's hear your arguments on the second motion. You've asked the court to suppress the alleged confession made by the defendant, Gráinne O'Connor, to Brendan McArdle and subsequently communicated by

McArdle to Sean Lynch and Brigid Maguire, and then by them to the police. Is that correct, Mr. Solomon?"

"Yes, M'lord, you've summarized the motion precisely."

"Very well, go ahead."

Solomon rises from his chair and walks slowly toward the judge's bench, adjusting the lapels of his gown before speaking. "M'lord, our argument for dismissal of the alleged confession isn't dissimilar to our argument in the prior motion. The prosecution alleges the defendant confessed to the murders of Sullivan and O'Neill in a conversation with Brendan McArdle in July 2004.

"The prosecution further contends McArdle subsequently relayed the gist of this conversation to Sean Lynch and Brigid Maguire, who then relayed what they remembered of the conversation to the police.

"What we have here is a verbal statement to police that's third hand. Your Lordship knows hearsay evidence isn't acceptable for the good reason that messages get distorted as they pass from one mouth to the next. We've all participated in classroom exercises that show the unreliability of information passed from one person to another.

"Secondly, M'lord, the proposed witnesses, Sean Lynch and Brendan McArdle, have no credibility. I don't want to go into unnecessary detail. Let me just say, M'lord, that you'll recall the Fountain Street bombing killed the defendant's only son and her husband. Four people were charged and convicted of that bombing: Eamon Sullivan, Kevin O'Neill, Sean Lynch, and Brigid Maguire. Brendan McArdle, the fifth bomber, provided the bomb material but hasn't been apprehended and charged.

"Sullivan and O'Neill are dead, and the defendant is charged with their murders. Ironically, the only evidence that the defendant was involved in the murders is this alleged confession to one of the bombers, Brendan McArdle. Is it logical the defendant would make a confession to Brendan McArdle, the very person who caused her son and husband to meet such a horrible, tragic, and untimely death?

"I don't think so. It's unbelievable. Both the bombers, Brendan McArdle and Sean Lynch, are unreliable and biased witnesses, and the prejudicial effect of their testimony on the defendant greatly outweighs its probative value. M'lord, we respectfully ask the court to suppress any reference to the alleged confession."

Judge Sinclair looks at the prosecution table. "Mr. Mulligan, your response."

"My Lord, this is a very complicated issue, but I've every confidence that your expertise in the law will allow the prosecution to present its evidence as planned. It's true that, in the normal course of events and given the Fountain Street bombing, it's unlikely the defendant would talk to Brendan McArdle, never mind make a confession to him.

"However, in a strange turn of events, the defendant actually thought she was talking to a Catholic priest. In a bizarre twist of fate, the defendant actually made her confession to Brendan McArdle, while he was dressed as a priest. That's why she made her confession.

"Now, the defense is arguing the confession is hearsay because there's no recording of the confession and McArdle hasn't made a written statement or agreed to testify in court. However, the police have the statement of Sean Lynch. Why is this important? It's important to this case because, as Your Lordship knows, the courts have allowed the admission of hearsay evidence, provided the evidence is communicated as soon as could be expected.

"So let's look at the timeline. The confession was relayed by phone to Sean Lynch within hours, if not minutes, of McArdle's meeting with the defendant. Lynch relayed it to the police less than twenty-four hours after the defendant's confession to McArdle. In this case, there was no lapse of time. In other words, Lynch informed the police as soon as could be expected after he heard about the confession. Therefore, it's admissible.

"My Lord, as I intimated, Brendan McArdle has refused, to date, to sign a written statement documenting the confession of Gráinne O'Connor. He likely will refuse to testify to this court in person due to his fear of prosecution. He also resides outside Northern Ireland.

"We're confident we'll obtain McArdle's written testimony. We're continuing to work with his lawyers. However, failing this, we believe the statement made to the police by Sean Lynch, immediately after his conversation with Brendan McArdle, is admissible under law.

"The defense's argument that the confession is prejudicial to the defendant and that it outweighs any probative value simply isn't valid. Given the premature death of Mr. Barr, who could have substantiated all the evidence against the defendant, the confession has substantial probative value. However, this is a matter for Your Lordship to decide."

When Martin Mulligan sits down, Judge Sinclair makes some notes on his legal pad. He addresses both counsels. "Thank you for presenting the arguments for and against admissibility of evidence. As in the first matter, I'll consider the arguments and the law this evening, and communicate my decision in the morning. The court's adjourned for today."

The parents of Eamon Sullivan sit impassively through the arguments. Whether Brendan McArdle or Sean Lynch testifies won't bring Eamon back. But Marie O'Neill quickly realizes the significance of the arguments and the importance of Judge Sinclair's decision on the prosecution's likelihood of convicting Gráinne O'Connor. She attends the daily briefing by the prosecution team.

"How do you think the judge will rule?" she says.

McIlhenny responds. "We'll know tomorrow morning. I think this is one of those issues that could go either way."

Gráinne is somber as she waits for Pascal. She finds the legal arguments complex and, like Marie O'Neill, understands there's a lot at stake in the judge's ruling. Pascal and junior counsel, William Litton, join her. "What do you think?" she asks.

"I believe Herschel made a strong case to have the confession suppressed," Pascal says. "All we can do is to wait for the judge's ruling. How are you holding up?"

"I'm tired. I think I'll stay with my parents tonight. It helps not to be alone."

8

September 14, 2005

JUDGE SINCLAIR ADVISES THE jury keepers not to seat the jury until he has communicated to counsel his decision on the two legal issues. All eyes are focused on him when he enters the court.

"I've considered the matters you presented to me yesterday and reviewed applicable law. Let me say that it seems to me the two motions are interrelated. A ruling in one may affect the ruling in the other. Accordingly, I'll address the issues in this order. I'll rule first on whether the alleged confession of the defendant, purportedly made to an imposter, should be admitted into evidence. If my ruling is to allow the confession to be presented as evidence, then I'll rule on whether the part of the confession that addresses the defendant's intent to commit other murders should be admitted into evidence.

"There are no witnesses to the murders of Eamon Sullivan and Kevin O'Neill. The evidence is circumstantial. Therefore, it seems to me the testimony of Brendan McArdle is critical for the jury to hear. I agree with the prosecution that the confession has substantial probative value. Accordingly, my decision is to allow the defendant's alleged confession to Brendan McArdle to be admitted as evidence.

"However, I'm cognizant of the concerns expressed by defense counsel. While I disagree with the argument that the confession is so prejudicial to the defendant it outweighs the probative value of the confession, I believe the confession should be allowed only if defense counsel has the opportunity to cross-examine Mr. McArdle.

"The prosecution has indicated that it is unlikely Mr. McArdle will appear in court due to his fear of arrest if he enters Northern Ireland.

Mr. Mulligan, if you want the defendant's confession admitted into evidence, you need to work with the Director of Public Prosecutions to allay Mr. McArdle's fears. The confession will be admissible as evidence only if Mr. McArdle is present in court and defense counsel has the opportunity to exercise their right to cross-examine him.

"Further, if you're unable to get Mr. McArdle to testify, I will not permit Mr. Lynch, or the police, to provide testimony of Mr. McArdle's conversation with Mr. Lynch. To do so would deny the defense their right to cross-examine the original source of the alleged confession. Is that understood?"

Martin Mulligan's delighted with the ruling to allow O'Connor's confession into evidence. It's a major victory. "Yes, My Lord." He pauses for a moment before continuing. "Your Lordship, given your ruling, the prosecution respectfully requests the trial be adjourned to allow the prosecution time to make arrangements for Mr. McArdle to appear in court."

Solomon immediately objects. "M'lord, your ruling has no bearing on making arrangements for Mr. McArdle to attend court. With all due respect, the prosecution has had a year to make these arrangements. The jury's impaneled and, in accordance with your instruction, is waiting to continue the case."

"Mr. Solomon, I share your frustration. Arrangements for Mr. McArdle to testify should be complete by now. However, you'll understand from my ruling the importance I place on the jury hearing the alleged confession. Mr. Mulligan, I'm prepared to adjourn the trial until next Monday, September 19th, 2005. There'll be no further adjournments related to Mr. McArdle's appearance in court. Is that clear?"

"Yes, Your Lordship."

Judge Sinclair resumes his rulings on the remaining defense motion. "Before we adjourn, let me address the second issue as to whether the part of the defendant's confession that purportedly indicates the defendant's intent to commit other murders should be admitted into evidence. Obviously, if Mr. McArdle testifies in person, there's no issue of the evidence being hearsay.

"So the issue is whether discussion of other murders is relevant to the case before the court. Since the prosecution intends to introduce evidence of apparent payments by the defendant to the alleged gunman, Mr. Barr, my decision is that the reference to later planned murders is admissible. Mr. Mulligan, let me repeat, this will only happen if Mr. McArdle appears in court thereby giving defense counsel the opportunity to cross-examine him. The court stands adjourned until Monday, September 19th."

The prosecution briefing session with the Sullivan and O'Neill families is upbeat. The trial's going as planned. Eamon Sullivan's parents wonder whether Mulligan will be successful in getting McArdle to testify, but they remain silent during the briefing. Marie O'Neill also remains silent. She has plans of her own. She'll leave for Dundalk as soon as the briefing is over.

Pascal isn't surprised to find Gráinne pallid when he enters the conference room. He can't imagine what it'll be like for Gráinne to see Brendan McArdle face-to-face in court.

"Gráinne, I'm sorry about the ruling. I'm sorry you'll have to face Brendan McArdle in court. Maybe he won't show up," he says with a smile.

"You mean Father Casey."

Pascal, Herschel, and William smile at their client's response. Litton recognizes the courage in her humor.

"Touché," he responds, "We can be certain Father Casey will be a no-show."

9

September 15, 2005

I T ' S   A   B I T T E R ,   F R O S T - F I L L E D   autumn morning, one of those mornings where the crispness of the air makes everything crackle. Brendan's breath is a constant reminder of the cold. Hoping for warmth, he taps tobacco into his pipe and lights it.

Although it's 6 a.m., he's already walking Roscoe across fields etched in white. Roscoe seems oblivious to the cold. He runs wildly, nose to the ground, in a vain search for a rabbit's scent. It's not the chill that kept Brendan awake last night, but a series of phone calls that disturbed the solitariness of a quiet fall evening.

The first was from the Chief of Staff of the Provisional IRA. He made it clear the IRA expects Brendan to cooperate in getting justice for their fallen comrades, Eamon Sullivan and Kevin O'Neill. They expect him to testify against Gráinne O'Connor.

"Why do I have to testify?" he asked. "I can sign a written statement. That's all I've been asked to do."

"Not any longer. Today, the judge ruled the bitch's confession isn't admissible unless you appear in court, in person. Need I remind you about the long and heroic service Kevin gave to the cause? I'm telling you to honor Kevin's sacrifice and respect his wife, Marie, by testifying against O'Connor."

"And what if I don't?"

"Let's not go there. You know what'll happen." The Chief of Staff hung up without further comment. McArdle is sure the threat is real.

He thinks about the second call. It was even more surprising than the first. The call was from the Office of the Director of Public Prosecutions for Northern Ireland. It was short and to the point. The caller assured Brendan that, in return for his testimony against O'Connor, the Crown wouldn't prosecute him for crimes committed prior to the signing of the Peace Agreement. In fact, he would be free to return to Northern Ireland to live. The Department would take care of transportation and accommodation, but it is imperative Brendan travels to Belfast today.

The third call was less of a surprise. Marie O'Neill explained she was on her way to Dundalk. She needed Brendan's help and would like to stay the night at the farm. From the earlier calls, he didn't have to ask a lot of questions. He understood exactly what she wanted. Unlike the first two callers, she wasn't demanding. He was happy to wait up to see her, and in spite of her fatigue, they talked long into the early morning hours.

"Thank you for having me on such short notice. You know I wouldn't ask you to testify in a British court if it weren't the last resort. Your testimony is critical to convicting Gráinne O'Connor. The judge is emphatic he'll not allow her confession to be introduced as evidence unless you're present. I know you don't want to do this, but think of what Kevin sacrificed and suffered for the cause.

"The Maze was a brutal six years. Kevin was in constant conflict with the guards, especially a guard called Kennaway. He could always get under Kevin's skin. I remember once he tried to make Kevin a laughing stock by making him wear shoes and clothes that were too large for him. He insisted on Kevin calling him 'Sir.' There was no way that was going to happen.

"Kevin spent a lot of time in solitary, no reading or writing, no recreation, and at times, no chair, no table, and no bed. Kennaway told him he would break him. I think he came close. I know there were times after the beatings that Kevin felt like killing himself, but that would've let the screws win. Please, do this for Kevin, or if not Kevin, then do it for me."

"When do you want me to go?"

"Maybe we could leave around noon. That would give me a few hours to sleep. You'll need as much time as possible to prepare for your testimony. I'll call Mulligan as soon as I wake."

Shortly before ten, Marie calls Mulligan to advise him that Brendan has agreed to testify against O'Connor and will travel to Belfast with her later in the afternoon. Mulligan isn't available, so Marie speaks with David Ingram.

"Brendan wants the immunity agreement sorted out first. He has asked my personal solicitor to represent him."

"That's great news, Mrs. O'Neill. I'll talk with the Director. I'm sure we can meet late this afternoon in my office, say at 5:30 p.m. Once we finalize the immunity agreement, we'd like to brief Mr. McArdle on the charges against Mrs. O'Connor and have him file a written statement. We can make arrangements for his appearance in court. Thank you again, Mrs. O'Neill, for your help."

Gráinne's happy to have a few days out of court, but only in rare moments does she stop thinking about the chaos in her life. Judge Sinclair's ruling against defense counsel's motions has filled her with a melancholy reminiscent of the months following the death of Martin and Peter. Then, it swirled around her head like a heavy fog. Like a shadow, it moved with her everywhere she went. She sought relief by staying in bed. Her parents, friends, and Father D'Arcy tried to engage her but, unable to focus, she preferred to be alone. She stopped going to Mass. Father D'Arcy persuaded her to see a therapist, and gradually she tackled the things she had to do: filing for probate and a claim for compensation.

Life had been so good until the bombing. She had a loving husband and a son she idolized. She was working on her first novel. Then, on that Saturday around five o'clock, the phone rang. A neighbor asked her if she'd heard about the bombing in Fountain Street. Her first thought was Martin and Peter. They were in town shopping, spending time together. She switched on the television and listened to the breaking news.

". . . The bombing took place around three-thirty this afternoon. Eyewitnesses describe two men running from a white Vauxhall van before the explosion. Initial reports describe scenes of devastation, charred bodies, victims without limbs, and the stench of scorched flesh. No official count of the dead and injured is available at this time. . . ."

The television cameras panned from pavements littered with shattered glass to the shell of the van. She had phoned her parents to tell them about the bombing and that Peter and Martin were in town.

"I'm sure they're all right," her mother said. "They're probably on their way home. Do you want us to come over?"

"No. You're right. It must be chaotic getting out of town. I'm sure it's hard to get a phone line. If I hear anything, I'll call you."

She'd gone back to the television, switching from channel to channel. The pips sounded for the six o'clock news.

". . . Three deaths have been confirmed in this afternoon's bombing in Belfast. Scores of people have been injured from the force of the blast and by flying glass and debris. . . ."

She called her parents and asked them what she should do. They came over right away and phoned the police to find out if they had any information. They didn't, but the officer asked for a phone number, address, the names of her husband and son, and a brief description of what they were wearing.

Shortly after eight o'clock, BBC News confirmed that five people died in the bombing and over a hundred people were injured. A hospital spokesperson pleaded for all available surgeons to report to work. Gráinne phoned the hospitals, but by ten o'clock she had heard nothing. She feared the worst. Martin would have found some way to let her know if he and Peter were alive.

Just before midnight, she answered a knock at the front door. The sight of two uniformed police officers made her light-headed. She leaned against the doorjamb. Her father took her arm. The officers removed their caps and remained standing. "Mrs. O'Connor, you called about your husband and son. Have you heard from them?"

"No, sir," she replied.

"I don't want to alarm you, but it has been eight hours since the bombing and there are many unidentified people in hospitals. However, there are two unidentified bodies at the morgue. From the information we were given, there's a possibility they may be the bodies of your husband and son. I'm sorry to have to confront you with this possibility."

At the morgue, the attendant took them to a side room. Gráinne examined the blood-soaked, cream-colored sweater, running her fingers across the cable pattern. She lifted the child's sneaker and looked at the brand. "Oh, God, no," she screamed. "Why? Why? How can this be?" She studied the sneaker again and raised it to her breast. Her mother put her arms around her. Her father excused himself and called Father D'Arcy.

When they got home, her parents drew the blinds, covered the furniture with white sheets, and stopped the clocks. For two years her life stopped. The sentencing of the bombers brought a sense of justice and closure. Sean Lynch was sentenced to life imprisonment, Kevin O'Neill to twenty-five years, Brigid Maguire to fourteen years, and Eamon Sullivan to ten. Before he left the dock, Lynch raised his arm in a clenched-fist salute and shouted in Irish, "*Tiacfaidh ár La.*" Our day will come. Although he was referring to an Ireland free of British rule, in a way his day did come. The Peace Agreement allowed all of the bombers to leave prison early. It was a watershed moment in her life.

Her thoughts turn to Brendan McArdle. She wonders where he is and whether he will testify. She tries to picture him in court without his priestly garments, but she can only see him as Father Casey. She speculates about what he'll say on the stand and whether he'll look at her. She can't believe this is happening. She has no idea he's already on his way to Belfast.

Alone in her home, Anne Simpson is frustrated by the constant adjournments of the trial. What she thought might last two weeks is likely to continue much longer. She now understands why court cases take years to complete. She doubts it needs to be so complicated.

But she's happy with Judge Sinclair. Through the clerk, he keeps the jury informed about what's happening. The clerk has assured them the trial will really get going next week. She hopes so, not just for herself, but also for the other eleven jurors.

She never expected to receive so much documentation at the beginning of the trial. The adjournment gives her time to review the material. She appreciates the prosecution putting it together in such a comprehensive and cohesive manner, and she likes how Mulligan made time to explain what was in the documentation. The material will reduce the amount of note-taking. She'll only have to jot down information elicited from witness testimony.

10

September 19, 2005

THE TWO JURY KEEPERS ESCORT the jurors to their seats. Six sit in the front row, the other six file in behind them. Judge Sinclair speaks. "Members of the jury, first let me apologize for the delay you've encountered in this trial. These adjournments were authorized by me to allow for the proper resolution of legal issues and to facilitate the attendance of key witnesses at this trial. It is my understanding the prosecution is ready to call their first witness. The trial should proceed without significant additional interruptions. Are there any questions?"

One of the jury keepers approaches the bench and passes two notes to the judge.

"Juror number eight reminds me she has an appointment on Thursday afternoon and will need to leave the court no later than 1 p.m. We'll adjourn early on Thursday to facilitate this appointment. Jurors number two and eleven are asking if the recent adjournments will extend the trial beyond the original estimate of two weeks. Counsel, what's your opinion?"

Mulligan responds. "My Lord, as we're already into week two, there's a strong possibility the trial will continue into a third week. However, we'll do everything in our power not to inconvenience the jury and the court."

Sinclair continues. "Will this present a problem for any member of the jury?" To his relief, none of the jurors registers an objection.

"Members of the jury, thank you for your patience and understanding. I now call upon the prosecution to present their first witness."

The court is crammed. There are no empty seats. Marie O'Neill and

Eamon Sullivan's parents sit to the right and front of the public gallery. Gráinne O'Connor's parents and Father D'Arcy also sit toward the front, on the left. Father D'Arcy won't be able to attend most of the trial, but he feels it's important to be in court whenever possible to provide support for Gráinne and her family.

In the back row of the gallery, Sean Lynch and Brigid Maguire try to be as inconspicuous as possible. They're well aware this trial may refocus unwanted media attention on them. Like Father D'Arcy, Brigid only will be able to attend when her job permits.

Pascal has warned Gráinne that in comparison to the contentious issues that have dominated the trial so far, the next few days may be somewhat tedious. However, the evidence presented by the prosecution is vital for the jury and defense to hear. In effect, the prosecution will build its case, piece by piece. The jury may not understand why a particular witness has been called, or the significance of the questions they are asked. It will only be in summation, when all the pieces are pulled together, that the jury may understand the significance of each piece. However, defense counsel will listen carefully, for everything presented is a roadmap of where the prosecution is headed.

David Ingram takes the floor. He knows this highly visible case will be a test of his skills as a junior prosecutor, especially as he performs in front of his mentor, Martin Mulligan. He's grateful Mulligan's allowing him to play such a prominent and pivotal role. He sees this as a measure of the trust Mulligan has in him.

Gráinne notices that despite his clean-cut, baby-faced looks, Ingram has a tightly chiseled body, muscular, and compact as a pit bull. He has a winning smile and makes steady eye contact with the jury.

"Members of the jury, I, too, add my apologies for the unfortunate delays and thank you for your patience. As you know, this trial concerns the premeditated murders of two people, Eamon Sullivan and Kevin O'Neill, and it's the prosecution's contention the defendant, Mrs. Gráinne O'Connor, paid a third party, Hugh Barr, to do the killings. You'll now hear evidence from a number of witnesses beginning with Mrs. Stella Price, the first person to discover the body of Eamon Sullivan."

The court crier brings a cue card to the witness stand. He instructs Stella Price to put her hand on a Bible and to read the oath printed on the card. Ingram asks Price to state her name, address, and occupation.

"Now, Mrs. Price, would you tell the court what you were doing on the evening of March 1st, 2002?"

"I was cleaning offices in downtown Belfast."

"Did the offices you clean include the office of a young solicitor named Eamon Sullivan?"

Solomon notices Ingram is leading the witness, but decides there's no benefit objecting at this time.

"Yes, sir."

"How often did you clean Mr. Sullivan's office?"

"Every Friday evening."

"At what approximate time did you arrive at Mr. Sullivan's office on the night in question?"

"I would say it was around 10:30 p.m."

"Mrs. Price, can you describe for the jury what happened on the evening of March 1st when you went to Eamon Sullivan's office?"

"When I arrived, I was surprised to find the light on in the reception area. I have a key to the outer office, but I found the door unlocked. This was unusual. No one answered when I asked if anyone was there, so I went inside. I hung up my coat and began to dust. It was then I noticed the light was on in Mr. Sullivan's private office and the door was slightly ajar. So I looked in."

Stella's face grows pensive and her voice quiet. Ingram tries to provide support.

"I know this is difficult for you, Mrs. Price. Take your time and tell the jury what you found when you looked into Eamon Sullivan's office."

Her voice quivers as she speaks. "I found Mr. Sullivan slumped across his desk. There was blood matted on his head. I felt sick. I ran to the phone and dialed 999."

Ingram approaches the jury. "You're now going to hear a recording of the 999 call made by Mrs. Price."

The clerk is instructed to play the call.

"This is 999. What's your emergency?"

"A man's been shot. Please help."

"Where are you located?"

"Montgomery Street. I'm not sure what the number is. It's the law office of Eamon Sullivan. Please hurry."

"You say a man's been shot. Is he alive, is he breathing?"

"I don't know. Can you hurry?"

"The police and an ambulance are on their way. What's your name?"

"My name is Stella Price."

"Stella, the police will be with you shortly. I want you to stay on the phone until they arrive."

"Okay. I think I hear sirens."

Ingram resumes questioning the witness. "About what time did the police and ambulance personnel arrive on the scene?"

"I would say it was close to eleven o'clock."

"Do you know if Mr. Sullivan was dead?"

Solomon objects. "M'lord, the witness isn't qualified to answer such a question."

Ingram quickly withdraws the question. He thanks Stella Price for her testimony and indicates he has no further questions.

Judge Sinclair asks defense counsel if they wish to question Mrs. Price.

Solomon responds. "M'lord, I have just a few questions for the witness. Mrs. Price, when you arrived at the Montgomery Street offices of Eamon Sullivan, did you notice anyone leaving the building or see anyone in the building other than the victim?"

"No, sir. I didn't see anyone until the police arrived."

"Now, you testified that you started to clean the outer reception area before you noticed that the door to Mr. Sullivan's office was open?"

"Yes, sir."

"Did you clean or tidy the receptionist's desk that evening?"

"I was just starting to polish it when I noticed the light in Mr. Sullivan's office."

"Did you notice an appointment book on the receptionist's desk?"

"I think there may have been one. I can't remember."

"So you didn't touch it, write in it, or read anything in it?"

"No, sir."

"Thank you, Mrs. Price. M'lord, I have no other questions for the witness at this time."

"In that case Mr. Ingram, you may call your next witness."

The prosecution calls the first police officer to arrive at the Montgomery Street crime scene. He's sworn in and gives his name, rank, and station identification.

"Sir," Ingram says, "is it correct that you were the first officer to arrive at Eamon Sullivan's office on the night of March 1st, 2002?"

"That's correct."

"Explain to the jury what you found when you arrived."

"Mrs. Price, the cleaning lady, was in the outer reception office. She was distraught. She told me Mr. Sullivan was in his office and appeared to be dead. I checked on Sullivan but couldn't find a pulse. I radioed for backup. The ambulance personnel confirmed they could do nothing for Sullivan. I took a statement from Mrs. Price."

"My Lord, I have no further questions for this witness."

Judge Sinclair asks defense counsel if they wish to question the witness.

Solomon indicates he would like to do so.

"When you examined the crime scene, did you find a weapon?"

"My initial responsibility was to secure the site. I noticed shell casings on the floor in front of the victim's desk and adjacent to the desk. I didn't notice a weapon."

"Did you find any evidence of a break-in?"

"Mrs. Price told me she found the outer door unlocked. I found no evidence of forced entry in my examination."

"Did you notice an appointment book at any time during your initial inspection?"

"I think I may have seen one on Mr. Sullivan's desk, but to be honest, I'm not sure."

"My Lord, I've no further questions."

Ingram speaks to the jury. "You've heard how the body of Eamon

Sullivan was discovered. We're now going to establish how the body of Kevin O'Neill was found."

The prosecution calls Dominic Cassidy to the stand. He's sworn in and gives his name and address. He advises the court he's unemployed.

"Mr. Cassidy," Ingram continues, "is it correct that you are the person who found Kevin O'Neill's body on the night of March 2nd, 2003?"

"That's correct."

"Please explain to the court how you came to find Mr. O'Neill's body on that evening."

"I was walking my greyhounds. They'd raced the previous evening at Dunmore Park. I like to give them a good stretch the next day."

"About what time did you come across Mr. O'Neill's body?"

"It was around 8:30 p.m., maybe a little later."

"Where did you find the body?"

"It was lying on the pavement outside the wee mission hall."

"And where is the 'wee' mission hall?" Ingram asks, mimicking Cassidy's last answer. A ripple of laughter emanates from the public gallery.

"It's at the bottom of the Limestone Road, you know, near North Queen Street."

"And what did you do when you found the body?"

"I didn't do anything, for I heard sirens and, almost immediately, a police car arrived. The policeman took my name and address and told me he would be in touch if he needed me."

"Thank you, Mr. Cassidy. My Lord, I have no further questions."

Judge Sinclair again asks the defense if they wish to question the witness.

Solomon approaches the witness stand. "Mr. Cassidy, apart from the victim, did you see anyone else that night when you were walking your greyhounds?"

"No, sir. It was bucketing down hard. I didn't see a soul, but I did hear the screech of tires just before I saw the body."

"Did you see what caused the screech of tires?"

"I saw rear lights of a car further up the Limestone Road, but I don't know if the screech was caused by that car or not."

"Did you recognize the make or color of the car?"

"Not really, sir. It was dark and the car was too far away. I think it may have been a taxi."

"Thank you, Mr. Cassidy. M'lord, we have no further questions at this time."

The prosecution next calls the police officer who spoke with Dominic Cassidy at the O'Neill crime scene. He's sworn in and gives his name, rank, and station identification.

"Sir," Ingram says, "is it correct that you were the first officer to arrive at the O'Neill crime scene on the night of March 2nd, 2003?"

"That's correct."

"Please explain to the court how you found Mr. O'Neill's body."

"We received a request in response to a 999 call to go to the Jesus Saves Mission Hall."

"Do you know who made the call?"

"I was told it came from a dispatcher at the Sure Cabs Taxi Company."

"About what time was that?"

"It was around 8:30 p.m."

"And what did you find when you arrived at the Jesus Saves Mission Hall?"

"I first saw Mr. Cassidy walking his greyhounds. I then noticed what appeared to be a body."

"Where was the body?"

"It was lying on the pavement outside the Mission Hall."

"What happened next?"

"I went over to the body to see if the person needed help."

"What did you observe at that time?"

"The victim was dead. He'd been shot in the head."

"What did you do next?"

"I reported what I'd found and requested backup. I questioned Mr. Cassidy and helped secure the area."

"Were you alone when you responded to the call?"

"Yes, sir."

"And did other officers respond to the call?"

"Yes. Two other patrol cars and an ambulance arrived shortly after I called for assistance."

"My Lord, I've no further questions."

Defense counsel passes on cross-examination, since there is nothing the defense can gain by challenging or questioning this witness.

After questioning the other patrol officers, the prosecution calls the taxi dispatcher to the stand. Ambrose Devlin confirms that Kevin O'Neill was an employee of Sure Cabs. O'Neill made a number of trips after reporting to work at 2 p.m. and responded to the call for a disabled-friendly taxi around 8 p.m. Devlin indicates that when he lost radio contact with O'Neill, he dialed 999.

The clerk is asked to play the 999 call.

"This is 999. What is your emergency?"

"My name is Ambrose Devlin. I'm a radio dispatcher at Sure Cabs. I've been unable to maintain contact with one of my drivers for the last fifteen minutes and I'm concerned."

"What is the name of the taxi driver?"

"His name is Kevin O'Neill."

"And where was Mr. O'Neill headed to?"

"He was to pick up a fare outside the Jesus Saves Mission Hall on the Limestone Road."

"Do you know if he picked up the fare?"

"He radioed that he had arrived. That's when I lost contact. That's why I'm concerned."

"I have police on the way. Please stay on the phone."

Ingram indicates he has no further questions.

Solomon takes the opportunity to cross-examine the witness. "Mr. Devlin, you say the call for a disabled-friendly taxi came in around 8 p.m. Can you tell the court the name of the person who made that call?"

"I can't. Kevin took the call. As best I remember, he didn't obtain the information."

"Do you know if it was from a man or a woman?"

Ingram objects. "If Mr. Devlin didn't take the call, he's in no position to answer the question."

"I'll let the witness determine that," Judge Sinclair says. "Go ahead and answer the question."

"It was from a man. I know that because I heard Kevin say, 'Yes, sir.'"

"So you're sure it wasn't from a woman?"

"Yes, sir!" Devlin's raised voice elicits a few chuckles.

Solomon waits for quiet then walks deliberately toward the dock. When he's close enough, he points to Gráinne O'Connor and says to Devlin, "So we know the phone call that led to Kevin O'Neill's unfortunate death definitely didn't come from Mrs. O'Connor. Am I correct?"

Ingram considers objecting, but holds his tongue.

"I believe so," Devlin responds.

"M'lord, the defense has no further questions for this witness."

"In that case let's adjourn for lunch. We'll resume at 1:30 p.m."

At lunch, Pascal explains to Gráinne that the witnesses called so far were simply called to establish a timeline around the murders and to identify the location of the crimes. In the afternoon, the prosecution will put medical, forensic, and police representatives on the stand to add layers of detail such as the exact time of death, the cause of death, and the results of the police investigation. Some testimony will be brief. Some, like the police evidence, may be lengthy. Normally, the lead investigator is the key witness as he lays out the results of the investigation. But Pascal knows this case will be different. The key witness for the prosecution is likely to be Brendan McArdle.

The jurors normally eat together, although Anne Simpson already notices some regular groupings have begun to form. As a rule, the men, Paul Ingram, Philip Brady, Samuel Brown, and Mark Campbell, sit beside or across from each other. Frequently, their discussion centers on whichever sports event is in the headlines. The females have formed three small groups, more or less defined by age. Marta Sheehan and Agnes Thompson sit beside each other. It's usual for Marcella White, Helen Cunningham, and Valerie Wilson to form a group. The two youngest, Tricia Fitzgerald and Imogene Healy, are always with each other.

Simpson uses lunch to get better acquainted with each juror. She feels this will pay dividends when they start their deliberations. She's surprised at what emerges in the more casual conversations.

Marta Sheehan has confided in her that she lost her niece in a 1973 bombing. Simpson wonders how she can be objective in this case but, until they deliberate, it's too soon to worry about this. She feels she doesn't have to advise Judge Sinclair unless it becomes clear Sheehan isn't considering the facts as presented in evidence. For now, she deserves the benefit of the doubt.

Paul Ingram is one of two jurors who make Simpson nervous. He's very confident and frequently talks about his work as an aerospace engineer at Bombardier's facility at Queen's Island. He's proud Bombardier built planes for the Wright brothers and designed the first all-metal aircraft, the first vertical take-off and landing research aircraft, and the world's first all-computer designed business jet. He's articulate and, Simpson is sure, an excellent analyst. But he tends to be somewhat domineering, or as Tricia Fitzgerald puts it, "a bit of a wiseass."

The other is Agnes Thompson. It's not her quiet personality that concerns Simpson but her tendency to be late. Given Judge Sinclair's paranoia with punctuality, Simpson has taken it upon herself to call Thompson each morning there's court.

Ingram is the first to speak when the trial resumes. "My Lord, the prosecution plans to call representatives of the medical examiner's office to the stand, but before doing so, I would like the jury to refer to certain documents in their package so they may follow along more easily.

"The medical examiner's reports on the deaths of Eamon Sullivan and Kevin O'Neill are referenced R001 and R002, respectively."

Bradley Jordan from the medical examiner's department takes the stand. After some preliminary questions establishing his credentials, Ingram focuses on Jordan's report. "Mr. Jordan, please summarize for the court what you found when you examined the body of Eamon Sullivan."

"We found Mr. Sullivan had been shot twice in the head and died as a result of these bullet wounds. We estimate the time of death to be around 6 p.m. on March 1st, 2002."

"Thank you, Mr. Jordan. My Lord, the prosecution has no further questions for this witness."

Judge Sinclair asks Herschel Solomon whether he wants to question the witness.

"Yes, M'lord, I have a few questions. Mr. Jordan, you say the shooting of Eamon Sullivan occurred around 6 p.m. But isn't it true that estimating the time of death is as much art as science?"

"No, sir. I don't believe that to be the case."

"Well, let me quote Dr. Francis Camp, the renowned pathologist. Wasn't it Camp who said, 'The only way to tell the time of death is to be there when it happens?' In other words, there's no way in a lab to determine the precise time of death. The best you can do is to give a range, and that range may be one, two, or three hours or more depending on the circumstances. Isn't that true?"

Jordan's face flushes. "There're many variables that impact the calculation of the time of death, but in this case we're not talking about a body that was subjected to the elements. We're not talking about decomposition. The temperatures of the corpse, taken over a period of time, tell us death occurred around 6 p.m."

"That's to say it could have occurred anywhere between, say, 5 p.m. and 7 p.m. on that day? Is that a fair statement?"

Jordan hesitates, then smiles. "I guess that's a fair statement."

"Thank you, Mr. Jordan. M'lord, I've no further questions for this witness."

The prosecution calls another medical examiner to describe the autopsy findings on Kevin O'Neill. Like Sullivan, he died from two bullet wounds to the head. He estimates the time of death to be somewhere around 8:30 p.m. on March 2nd, 2003. Because Dominic Cassidy and Ambrose Devlin already have corroborated the time estimate, Solomon elects not to cross-examine the witness.

Ingram advises the jury that documents R004 and R005 are the forensic reports on the bullets and casings found at the Sullivan and O'Neill crime scenes. He then calls a ballistics expert, Richard Peebles, to the stand.

"Mr. Peebles, I believe you examined the bullets and casings found at both the Sullivan and O'Neill crime scenes. Is that correct?"

"That's correct."

"Were you able to identify what types of weapons were used to murder Sullivan and O'Neill?"

"Yes. The land and groove markings on the slugs indicate both victims were shot with a Browning 9-millimeter automatic, and the markings tell us that both were shot with the same gun."

"So it's reasonable to assume the same person may have killed both Sullivan and O'Neill?"

Before Peebles can respond, Solomon objects. "M'lord, that statement should be stricken from the record. Because the same gun was used in both murders in no way means it was used by the same person."

"Agreed." Judge Sinclair tells the court stenographer to expunge the statement from the record.

Ingram continues. "To the best of your knowledge, was anyone else killed with the gun used to kill Sullivan and O'Neill?"

"Yes, sir. The gun was used by Hugh Barr when he committed suicide in 2004."

"So from a forensics perspective, we know the gun used by Hugh Barr to commit suicide in 2004 is the same gun used to kill Eamon Sullivan in 2002 and Kevin O'Neill in 2003. Is that correct?"

"That's correct."

When Ingram indicates he has no further questions, Solomon rises to cross-examine Richard Peebles. "Mr. Peebles, isn't it also true the gun in question is tied to at least two other murders, one in 1989 and the other in 1992? In fact, isn't it true this particular gun has been used in numerous crimes in East Belfast over the past thirty years?"

"That's my understanding."

"Now, East Belfast is a stronghold of the UVF, and the UVF claimed responsibility for both the 1989 and 1992 murders. Therefore, any number of Loyalist gunmen may have used the gun, and there's no ballistic evidence that conclusively ties Hugh Barr to the killings of Sullivan and O'Neill. Isn't that so?"

"From a forensics perspective, we can say conclusively that Hugh Barr used that gun to kill himself. We also can state conclusively that the same gun killed Sullivan and O'Neill."

"But you cannot state conclusively that Hugh Barr used the gun to kill Sullivan and O'Neill?"

"That's correct."

"And there's no evidence the defendant, Gráinne O'Connor, used the gun to kill Sullivan and O'Neill?"

"There's no forensic evidence Gráinne O'Connor used the gun to kill Sullivan and O'Neill."

Solomon thanks Richard Peebles and advises Judge Sinclair he has no further questions. Sinclair addresses David Ingram. "Mr. Ingram, I understand your next witness will be Detective Inspector Higgins."

"That's correct, My Lord."

"How long do you think Inspector Higgins may be on the stand?"

"My Lord, I think it's reasonable to expect the Detective Inspector to be on the stand for most of a day."

"In that case, I believe it's appropriate to adjourn for today. Before we do so, I remind the jury you shouldn't discuss this case outside the court, not even with family members or friends. The court stands adjourned until tomorrow at 9:30 a.m."

Gráinne's glad to get the first day of witness testimony behind her. During the testimony, she periodically looked at the jurors to see their reaction. For the most part, they seem content to listen, but she notices four of the female jurors and one of the male jurors regularly takes notes. She feels Herschel did an effective job establishing that there's no forensic evidence that ties Hugh Barr to the murders. In fact, the documented history of the weapon's extensive UVF use suggests the murders of Sullivan and O'Neill were UVF-sanctioned sectarian killings.

Anne Simpson, too, is glad court's over for the day, but her thoughts rarely stray from the trial. Each day, she watches the trial news on television and reads most of the newspaper reports. From the coverage, she's aware this trial has galvanized public curiosity. It's the lead in almost every news edition. The concise, factual nature of the reporting impresses her.

Her husband hasn't asked any questions. She's grateful for that. Despite the judge's caution, she knows she's forming opinions about what she has heard. She isn't worried about this. She feels this is human nature. She understands the need to hear everything before she develops a conclusion. From what she has observed today, that point is a long way off.

Marie O'Neill invites the Sullivans, Brendan, Sean, and Brigid to join her for a drink at the Garrick bar. The Sullivans decline because of their animosity toward IRA members. Brigid would like to go with Sean but she knows her parents will be angry if they find out she's socializing with Brendan, an active IRA dissident. Rebuilding their trust has been difficult since her release from prison.

"It's good to see you again, Sean," Brendan remarks as he settles on the booth seat. He orders Guinness for everyone. When the drinks arrive, he raises his glass and says, "Tiacfaidh ár La."

Sean wishes he'd gone with Brigid. He feels intimidated by Brendan and Marie. Lost for words, he asks Brendan how he feels about having to testify.

"There's no 'having,'" Brendan responds icily. "I'm glad to do anything I can to honor Kevin. If there were more people like him we would have our united Ireland. Sooner or later, you and your comrades will realize the Peace Agreement is just another British ploy to delay the unification. We needed the Easter Rebellion to set up a free Republic, and history teaches us the only way the Brits will leave Northern Ireland is at the point of a gun."

"I'm not so sure," Sean says. "Thirty years of armed struggle and we're no closer to a united Ireland than we were in 1969. There has to be another way. We need to give the political process a chance." He smiles at Marie and says, "You know the old saying, Marie, 'A nation that keeps one eye on the past is wise. A nation that keeps two eyes on the past is blind.'"

"Where did you learn that?" she asks.

"You mean to tell me you've been coming here all these years and never read the wall outside?"

Marie isn't sure if Sean is serious. "Believe it or not, I come here to drink and enjoy the craic. I don't read walls."

Nevertheless, when she leaves the Garrick a little later, she studies the gable wall and blushes.

11

September 20, 2005

LONG LINES FORM OUTSIDE THE Laganside Courthouse early on Tuesday morning. Security allows the public to enter Court 12 shortly after 9 a.m. When the trial resumes, David Ingram calls Detective Inspector Rory Higgins to the stand. After taking the oath, Rory removes a small notebook from his jacket pocket and rests it on his knee.

"Inspector Higgins," Ingram begins, "how long have you been a member of the RUC?"

"I've been a member for twenty-eight years."

"How long have you been involved with criminal investigations?"

"About twenty-five years."

"You're the lead investigator in the murders of Eamon Sullivan and Kevin O'Neill?"

"Yes, sir."

Ingram walks toward the jury and addresses them. "Detective Inspector Higgins will describe the investigation of the murders of Eamon Sullivan and Kevin O'Neill. From time to time, he may refer to specific documents, all of which you possess. As My Lord indicated previously, you may make notes on the documents if you feel this will help you with your deliberations."

He returns to the witness stand. "Inspector Higgins, please outline for the jury the results of your investigation into the death of Eamon Sullivan."

"Eamon Sullivan was found shot on Friday evening, March 1st, 2002, at his offices on Montgomery Street. His body was found by an office cleaner around 10:30 p.m. Sullivan was dead at the scene. There were no witnesses to the shooting. The medical examiner estimates time of death to be around 6 p.m.

"On the day of his death, his appointment book had a pencil entry for 6 p.m. It simply said 'NC,' but we don't know what, or whom, 'NC' stands for. We believe he had a 6 p.m. appointment, even though his secretary didn't make the appointment, and it was unusual for him to stay that late on a Friday afternoon."

Ingram stops Rory. "So, if I understand you correctly, Inspector Higgins, the killing of Eamon Sullivan was not a random killing. It was a planned, premeditated act."

Herschel Solomon stops Rory from responding. "I object, M'lord. The fact Sullivan had an appointment, and was killed around the time of the appointment, doesn't prove premeditation. Many killings are the result of spur-of-the-moment decisions. If 'NC' killed Sullivan, they may have had an argument which led to the murder."

"I withdraw my remark," Ingram concedes. "Inspector Higgins, has the investigation identified Eamon Sullivan's killer?"

"We reviewed footage from CCTV cameras located on Montgomery Street that show the movement of people around the time of the crime. An individual male is seen entering Sullivan's building just before 6:00 p.m. The same individual leaves the building at 6:12 p.m. From a comparison of the footage to surveillance photographs taken by the police in the course of our investigation and to photographs provided by his family, we believe the person in the footage is a Mr. Hugh Barr."

"And who is Hugh Barr, Inspector Higgins?"

"Hugh Barr was a member of the East Belfast UVF. He committed suicide in 2004."

"Thank you, Inspector. Now let's turn to the investigation of the murder of Kevin O'Neill."

Rory leafs through his notebook. "Kevin O'Neill was found shot on Sunday, March 2nd, 2003, outside the Jesus Saves Mission Hall on the Limestone Road. The body was found around 8:30 p.m. by police responding to a call from the dispatcher of the taxi company that employed O'Neill.

"O'Neill was dead when police arrived. There were no witnesses to the shooting. We reviewed footage from CCTV cameras located at the junction of the Limestone Road and North Queen Street. An individual male is seen in a wheelchair outside the Jesus Saves Mission Hall at the time O'Neill's taxi arrives. This individual subsequently shoots Mr. O'Neill. We compared the Limestone Road footage with the footage from Montgomery Street. We believe the person in the wheelchair also is Hugh Barr."

Ingram stops Rory. "So this is the same Hugh Barr you believe killed Eamon Sullivan?"

"That's correct."

Ingram approaches the jury. "Members of the jury, I direct your attention to the screen located behind and slightly to the left of Judge Sinclair. The clerk now will show you the footage from the CCTV cameras on Montgomery Street and the Limestone Road.

"The first video is taken by the CCTV camera at Ross's Auction. If you look at the map referenced PM1, you'll note the camera, the black triangle with the number two, is located close to the junction of Montgomery Street and May Street. The camera is pointed toward Chichester Street. When you watch the video, you will see an individual walk toward the camera, that is, he's coming from the Chichester Street direction toward May Street. You will see him turn right into Sullivan's building. Notice the time stamp on the video is 5:53 p.m. Please run the video."

When the video finishes, Ingram introduces the second video. "Now, you will see the same individual leave Sullivan's building and go back toward Chichester Street. Again, he's facing the camera because a CCTV camera located at the Garrick Bar recorded this video. If you look at the map referenced PM1, you'll note the camera is marked by the black triangle with the number one. Please note the time on the video is 6:12 p.m. Please run the video."

At the conclusion of the video, Ingram speaks again to the jurors. "Members of the jury, we're now going to play the CCTV footage from the Limestone Road killing. You can see the location of the cameras on map PM3. However, I want to warn the jury and family members who may be present in court that the video is graphic. It shows the killing of Kevin O'Neill. You'll see his body fall to the pavement. You'll see the killer shoot the victim a second time in cold blood. The stamp on the video says 8:26 p.m. Please run the video."

"One moment," Judge Sinclair says. "I want to reiterate what Mr. Ingram has conveyed. This is a very graphic video. I'll not tolerate any outbursts in the courtroom. So, if you don't think you can keep your emotions in check, now is the time to leave."

Nobody leaves. Except for the steady whirring of the video player, there's complete stillness in the court. The video shows a taxi pulling up to the curb. The driver gets out and approaches an individual in a wheelchair. He appears to talk to the person, then goes to the back of the taxi and pulls out the ramps. He attaches them to the taxi floor and wheels the passenger into the taxi. He bends down and is lost from sight of those viewing the video. The footage then depicts a body being shoved out of the taxi by a foot. When it settles on the pavement, someone leaves the back seat of the taxi carrying a gun. He goes over to the body and fires a solitary shot into the head of the victim.

Despite the judge's warning, Marie O'Neill screams when the killer shoots her husband in the head. Gráinne feels her stomach turn. She has never witnessed a cold-blooded killing before. She empathizes with Marie O'Neill's distress. When the video ends, Judge Sinclair orders a twenty-minute recess.

"I'm sorry you had to see that," Pascal says to Gráinne. "Did you recognize Hugh Barr?"

"I'm not sure. I couldn't really see his face. The film is quite dark, and everything happened so quickly."

When the trial resumes, Ingram addresses Rory Higgins. "Inspector, please summarize for the court the key evidence that points to Hugh Barr as the murderer of Eamon Sullivan and Kevin O'Neill."

"The forensics indicates the same gun killed Sullivan, O'Neill, and Barr, and we know without a doubt Barr used the gun to kill himself. The gun was located under his body at the site of his death. The gun was a UVF gun, and Mr. Barr was quartermaster of the East Belfast UVF.

"The CCTV evidence related to both murders provides a picture of the killer. We are satisfied from our surveillance of Barr subsequent to the O'Neill murder that the person shown on the CCTV footage from both Montgomery Street and the Limestone Road is in fact Hugh Barr. His UVF commander also believes the person in the videos is Hugh Barr.

"We also have a statement from a witness, Brendan McArdle, that the defendant confessed to him that she paid Hugh Barr to harm Eamon Sullivan and Kevin O'Neill and also that she paid Hugh Barr an advance to harm two of the other Fountain Street bombers, Brigid Maguire and Sean Lynch."

In the public gallery, Sean Lynch slides down in his seat. He's glad Brigid isn't present.

"Thank you, Inspector Higgins. Now I want to turn to the reason we're in court today. In the course of your investigations, what evidence did you find to link Hugh Barr to the defendant and to link the defendant to the murders of Eamon Sullivan and Kevin O'Neill?"

"We discovered a large sum of cash at Mr. Barr's home, approximately £30,000. Subsequent research identified that he had an account at the Ulster Bank. The investigation established a pattern of payments into the account around the time of the murders, and withdrawals by Mr. Barr soon after the murders. CCTV cameras at the bank link the defendant to the deposits and Mr. Barr to the withdrawals.

"The sworn statement of Brendan McArdle says the defendant not only admitted making the deposits but confessed to hiring Hugh Barr to harm Sullivan and O'Neill."

"Now, Inspector, Mr. Sullivan was a solicitor and Mr. O'Neill was a taxi driver. These are two very different occupations. From your investigation, what links the two victims, and what motive would the defendant have to kill them?"

"Both Mr. Sullivan and Mr. O'Neill were convicted of membership of the IRA and both were sentenced to prison for their part in a bombing which killed the defendant's husband and son. Both were released early from prison under the terms of the 1998 Peace Agreement. Our investigation established that the early release of the IRA bombers angered the defendant, and she hired Hugh Barr to harm them. We believe Hugh Barr murdered Sullivan and O'Neill as a result of this contract between him and the defendant."

Ingram pauses to let the weight of Rory's testimony fertilize the minds of the jurors. He then speaks directly to them. "Members of the jury, over the next few days you will hear direct testimony from the key witnesses referenced by Detective Inspector Higgins. Specifically, you'll hear from Hugh Barr's wife, Queenie Barr; from William Preston, a Loyalist UVF commander and Hugh Barr's boss; from officials of the Ulster Bank; and from Brendan McArdle. Your Lordship, I've no further questions for Inspector Higgins at this time."

When Ingram sits down, Judge Sinclair asks defense counsel if they have any questions for Detective Inspector Higgins.

"Yes, M'lord."

Herschel Solomon consults his notes. "Inspector Higgins, I think most of my questions related to your theory of the murders will be answered best by the witnesses who will testify shortly. However, I want to clarify a few things for the jury. In your testimony, you indicated that Sullivan had a scheduled six o'clock appointment with someone identified as 'NC' yet, according to your theory, Hugh Barr killed Eamon Sullivan. You've no witness to support this, and you don't explain how 'NC' metamorphosed into 'HB.'"

A brief ripple of laughter relieves the tension. Solomon continues. "It seems to me, in the absence of a witness, it's just as reasonable to conclude someone known as 'NC' killed Sullivan, and 'NC' is still at large. Isn't that logical?"

Rory takes his time before responding. He wishes he hadn't mentioned the 'NC' notation. "I think, in the absence of other evidence, your conclusion might be reasonable. But given the totality of the evidence—the history of the gun, the forensics, the CCTV evidence, Mr. Barr's suicide note, and the transfers of money to Barr's Ulster Bank account—I think it's amply clear Hugh Barr killed both Sullivan and O'Neill."

"Then why did Sullivan make an appointment with NC?"

Ingram objects. "My Lord, only whoever made the entry on the appointment book knows the answer to that. For all we know, NC means 'new client' or it represents some fictitious name Barr gave Sullivan when he set up the appointment. I don't think Barr called Sullivan and said, 'My name is Hugh Barr and I'm coming to kill you. Can you put me down for six o'clock?'"

Laughter erupts across the gallery. Solomon grins, and Judge Sinclair indicates it's a good time to adjourn for lunch.

Anne Simpson joins Tricia Fitzgerald and Imogene Healy at the lunch table. She's ready for the break.

"Your Lordship's in a good mood today," Tricia says. "I saw him smile when Ingram joked about Barr calling Sullivan to tell him what time he was coming to kill him. That was a good one."

"I thought it was funny," Imogene says, "but I didn't like the video that showed O'Neill being killed. That was gruesome. Why did they have to show it?"

Anne explains. "They want us to see all the evidence that led police to charge Gráinne O'Connor. Every day, they're providing additional pieces of information, hoping we'll be able to see the big picture and determine what really happened."

When court resumes, Herschel Solomon continues his cross-examination of Detective Inspector Higgins. "Now Inspector, your testimony suggests you investigated the murders of Eamon Sullivan and Kevin O'Neill and all the pieces fell nicely into place. You identified Hugh Barr as the triggerman, you established he had received money from the defendant and so concluded that the defendant hired Hugh Barr to commit the murders. But isn't it true that for almost all of your two-year investigation the defendant was not a suspect?"

"That's correct."

"But Hugh Barr was a suspect from early in the investigation, even though you had no indication that he knew the defendant. In other words, you believed he had the motive and the means to murder Sullivan and O'Neill and this had nothing to do with Gráinne O'Connor."

"Our preliminary investigation identified Mr. Barr as a suspect."

"And why was that?"

"Eamon Sullivan was murdered in March 2002. We quickly established he was killed with a UVF gun, and we suspected this may have been a UVF-sanctioned killing. In May 2002, a prison guard who also was an intelligence officer in the UVF was murdered. We established he was shot with a known IRA gun. Initially, it looked as if this might be a retaliatory killing. So, when Kevin O'Neill was murdered in March 2003, the three murders presented a real possibility of a return to the tit-for-tat killings we experienced during the Troubles."

"And isn't it true that, because the RUC believed these three killings were related, you were given oversight of all three murder investigations?"

"I headed a task force that looked at possible connections between the murders."

"And isn't it true that Mr. Barr was detained and interrogated about the Sullivan and O'Neill murders long before the defendant's name came into the picture?"

"That's correct."

"Now, Detective, when you arrested Mrs. O'Connor, did you get a search warrant for her home?"

"Yes, we did."

"Did you remove her computer and a journal notebook?"

"We did."

"What did you find in the computer that indicates a plan to commit the crimes the defendant is charged with?"

"We didn't find any evidence."

"You didn't find she had searched for information on the UVF?"

"No, sir."

"Did you find any reference to Hugh Barr, his phone number, or address?"

"No, sir."

"So there was nothing on her computer that relates to this case."

"No, sir."

"Now, let's turn to her journal. From your examination of the journal, did it appear Mrs. O'Connor made entries on a daily basis?"

"She appeared to write something on most days."

"And you examined what she wrote in her journal?"

"Yes."

"And what did she write in 2001 about going to a UVF funeral?"

"We didn't find any reference to her attending a UVF funeral."

"What about meeting Mr. Barr?"

"No, sir."

"And in 2002 and 2003, what did she record about making deposits to Hugh Barr's account?"

"We didn't find anything."

"So what I hear you telling this court is that although you have testified that Mrs. O'Connor entered into a contract with Hugh Barr to kill Eamon Sullivan and Kevin O'Neill, there isn't one word on her computer or in her journal about planning to do so, about meeting Hugh Barr, or about money transfers. You found absolutely nothing to connect her to the crimes."

"Yes, sir."

Solomon faces Judge Sinclair. "M'lord, I've no further questions for this witness at this time."

Judge Sinclair grants Ingram's request for a redirect.

"Detective Inspector, did you find anything on the computer or in Mrs. O'Connor's journal about her visit to Maghaberry Prison in July 2000?"

"Yes, she had searched on the computer for directions to the prison. There were also searches relating to the release of IRA prisoners."

"Did she record anything in her journal about her visit?"

"Yes, she referenced her visit. She wrote and underlined the words 'Justice is blind.'"

"And what did you take this to mean?"

Solomon objects. "My Lord, this calls for speculation."

"I agree."

Ingram continues. "When you read Mrs. O'Connor's entries related to the release of the bombers, could you tell how she was feeling from what she wrote?"

Solomon again objects.

Judge Sinclair overrules him. "I'll allow it."

"I believe she was very angry at the prisoner release."

"Your Lordship, I've no more questions for this witness."

"Detective Inspector Higgins, you may step down. Mr. Ingram, are you ready to call your next witness?"

The prosecution calls Mrs. Queenie Barr. David Ingram approaches the witness stand. "Mrs. Barr, you are the widow of Hugh Barr who, I believe, was known to his family as Shooie."

"That's correct."

"Mrs. Barr, we know testifying here today isn't easy for you. I think you're representative of the many innocent victims that have resulted from the Troubles. Let me say, first, we're sorry for your loss. Mrs. Barr, how long were you and Shooie married?"

"For almost thirty-five years."

"And Mr. Barr worked in the shipyard until he became unemployed in 1985?"

"Yes, sir."

"The Troubles were well under way by then. To the best of your knowledge, was your husband involved with the UVF before he became unemployed?"

"No, sir."

"When would you say his association with the UVF began?"

"I'm not sure. I think it was a gradual thing. He didn't talk about it, but I think I first suspected it in the early '90s."

"Mrs. Barr, let's move forward in time. Please tell the jury what happened on the afternoon of January 5th, 2004."

"I came back from shopping. I think it was about 2:30 p.m. I saw a large parcel and a note sitting on the kitchen table."

Ingram stops Mrs. Barr and hands her a piece of paper. "Mrs. Barr, is this the note you found? Members of the jury, this is exhibit R008 in your package."

Queenie reads the note:

Dear Queenie,

I know this will be a shock to you and I'm sorry for any pain you feel. I'm not good at this. I haven't written a letter in a long time and I'm sorry to write you this one. I hope you know I love you.

This has nothing to do with you. I wish I could explain everything to you, but I can't. I made a terrible mistake, one that I regret and must pay for.

The parcel on the table is for you. You should hide it in a drawer and not tell anyone. I think you should destroy the letter as soon as you read it. I hope this final gift tells you how much I appreciate all you have done for me.

Love,
Shooie

Queenie sobs quietly. Ingram gives her time to compose herself.

"Mrs. Barr, is that the note you found on the afternoon of January 5th, 2004?"

"Yes, sir."

"Mrs. Barr, can you tell us what was in the package on the table?"

"It was money. I believe there was £30,000."

"All in bank notes?"

"Yes, sir."

"Do you know where this money came from?"

"Shooie's note said he was leaving it for me."

"So you believe the money came from your late husband, Hugh Barr. Is that so?"

"Yes, sir."

"Your Lordship, the prosecution has no further questions for this witness."

Sinclair asks Solomon and Litton if either wish to question the witness. Litton indicates he does.

"Mrs. Barr, I too am sorry for your loss . . . Let me take you back for a moment to your first interview with police after Mr. Barr disappeared. I believe that was on January 6th, 2004. When the police asked you to explain where the money came from, what did you tell them?"

"I'm not sure. I can't remember."

"Just think a while. There's no hurry."

Litton waits quietly. He knows the silence will get to the witness.

"I think I told them it was probably UVF money."

"In other words, money he'd received from the UVF for his work on their behalf?"

"I don't know."

"Why did you think it might be money belonging to the UVF or paid by the UVF to Shooie for his work on their behalf?"

Ingram objects. "My Lord, the witness is being asked to speculate about something she has said she does not know."

"I'm going to overrule the objection. The witness has admitted she told police the money was probably UVF money."

"Thank you, My Lord." Litton speaks to the witness. "Mrs. Barr, why did you originally assume the money on the table might be connected to the UVF?"

Mrs. Barr cringes and blushes. "Well, Shooie had no job so someone must have given it to him. I thought it might be the UVF. Around May 2003, Shooie took me to the pictures one night to see *Veronica Guerin*. It's about a real-life news reporter who exposed drug trafficking in Dublin and was murdered for doing so. Shooie wasn't much into movies, but he liked thrillers and this movie was intense. He said it was the best movie he had ever seen.

"Shooie was never one to talk about the UVF, but during the movie he pointed out parallels to the UVF operations in East Belfast: the trafficking in drugs to finance operations and build personal wealth, the ruthlessness of the new rich and their determination to cling to power at all costs, the people who had moved from the ranks of the unemployed to become 'big men' in the community, with their drivers and bodyguards.

"That probably was the first time I realized he might be a lot more involved with the UVF than I'd thought. Anyway, that's the night that Shooie began to change."

Mrs. Barr removes a handkerchief from her purse and wipes away a tear. Litton waits patiently. There's no need to intervene.

"As we left the theater, a man in dark glasses and a black leather jacket approached Shooie. I didn't recognize him, but I sensed he and Shooie knew each other. Shooie immediately excused himself. He told me he would just be a second. When he finally came out from the cinema, he told me 'to go along home.'"

Mrs. Barr dabs her eyes, and Litton takes the opportunity to ask a question.

"Mrs. Barr, you say that was the night Shooie began to change. Can you explain that for the jury?"

"When he came out into the street he was tense. I think he was embarrassed, but more than that, I think he was afraid. When I got up the next morning, I realized he hadn't been to bed. I know he came home, for the cigarette tray was on the kitchen table and it was overflowing with butts and ash. His car was gone. I was mad. I wanted to ask him how he could've dismissed me so summarily after such a nice evening.

"He finally came home about two or three o'clock in the afternoon. He looked haggard and upset. He apologized, and I asked him who that man was and what was so important he couldn't walk me home from the pictures. He didn't go into a lot of detail, but he told me the man was a UVF commander and he had an urgent assignment."

As she takes a breath, Litton asks, "Did he tell you what this commander wanted him to do?"

"No, sir."

"Did Shooie tell you the commander's name?"

"Yes, sir. He didn't give me his real name, but said the man was known as 'Defender.'"

"Did you ever see Defender again?"

"No, I didn't."

"So, on that evening in May 2003, you saw that Shooie was afraid of

Defender, and I believe you indicated that evening was a turning point in Shooie's life?"

"That's correct. He had trouble sleeping and started to drink heavily."

"To the best of your knowledge, would you say your husband was an alcoholic?"

"I don't think so. He always liked his evening pint with the boys, but he was never drunk, at least not until after that night at the pictures. After that evening, he spent more time away from home. He would leave in the mornings and return late at night. I could see he was drinking more. I asked him what was wrong, but he told me not to worry. He had a few problems, but he was taking care of them."

"Did you notice that he had more money?"

"No. I never saw any extra money until I found the package on the kitchen table."

"And given Shooie's meeting with Defender, and knowing Defender was a UVF commander, and observing the deterioration in Shooie's health, and having read his letter, your initial instinct was that the money must somehow be related to UVF activity. Isn't that so?"

Ingram wants to object but knows the judge has already overruled his earlier objection.

"Yes, I thought it must be UVF money."

"Thank you, Mrs. Barr. Your Lordship, I have no further questions."

Ingram is granted a redirect by the judge. "Mrs. Barr, when you said, 'I thought it must be UVF money,' that was just a momentary thought. You had no actual evidence the money belonged to the UVF. Shooie could have gotten it from gambling, he could have robbed a bank, or he could have been given it by the defendant, Mrs. Gráinne O'Connor. Isn't that so?"

"Objection, My Lord," Litton says. "This requires the witness to speculate on the source."

Ingram withdraws the question. "Let me rephrase my question, Mrs. Barr. Was there anything that identified the £30,000 as belonging to the UVF?"

"No, sir."

"Thank you, Mrs. Barr. I've no more questions, My Lord."

"Let's take twenty, after which we'll hear the next witness."

After the recess, Ingram walks to the jury box. "Members of the jury, you're now going to hear from Mr. William Preston, known also by the name 'Defender.' A copy of the statement he made to police is referenced R007 in your package."

"Mr. Preston, you are or were a member of the Shankill Road UVF?"

"I was a member of the Shankill Road UVF."

"Is it true you were the commander of the Shankill Road UVF and, as such, had knowledge of UVF Belfast operations?"

"Yes, I was commander of the Shankill Road UVF. I had knowledge of all West Belfast operations and some knowledge of operations in East and North Belfast due to intelligence sharing."

"Let me show you two photographs. Members of the jury, these are exhibit numbers PP24 and PP25 in your package. These are still photographs from the CCTV videos you watched this morning.

"Mr. Preston, do you recognize the individual in the photographs?"

The photographs have been blown up from the surveillance video, spreading out the pixels and making the image grainy. However, Defender's response is immediate and assured.

"Yes, sir. That's Hugh Barr or Shooie, as I called him."

"Members of the jury, for your information, exhibit PP24 and PP25 are images of Hugh Barr on Montgomery Street on the evening Eamon Sullivan was murdered." Ingram turns to face Defender. "Mr. Preston, how did you know Hugh Barr?"

"He was a member of the East Belfast UVF."

"What was his role?"

"He was mainly a driver, but he also had responsibility for the storage of weapons."

"Mr. Preston, in your statement to police, exhibit R007, you deny the UVF had anything to do with the murders of Eamon Sullivan and Kevin O'Neill, and such matters would have been authorized by you. Is that a true statement?"

"Yes, sir."

"Why would you have been the one to authorize the murders if they were UVF murders?"

"Both Sullivan and O'Neill lived in areas under the jurisdiction of the Shankill Road UVF. They wouldn't have been carried out by East Belfast UVF without my approval."

"You further state, and here I quote, 'If Shooie had anything to do with the murders, then he did it on his own,' end quote. Mr. Preston, when you used the term 'murders,' were you specifically referring to the murders of Eamon Sullivan and Kevin O'Neill?"

"Yes, sir."

Ingram addresses Judge Sinclair. "Your Lordship, I've no further questions for this witness."

"Mr. Litton, do you have any questions for the witness?"

"Yes, Your Lordship, I do.

"Mr. Preston, how do you know the murders of Eamon Sullivan and Kevin O'Neill weren't carried out by the UVF or, for that matter, by another Loyalist paramilitary group?"

"I know they weren't carried out by the UVF, for I would have authorized—"

Litton stops Preston's response. "Now, now, Mr. Preston, isn't it true when you met with Detective Inspector Higgins for the first time, you had absolutely no idea Sullivan and O'Neill were killed with a UVF gun?"

"Yes, but—"

Litton again interrupts. "What you're saying, Mr. Preston, is you don't and didn't have complete knowledge of UVF Belfast operations. How could you? How could anyone? You also had next to no knowledge of rival Loyalist operations. So am I correct in saying you don't really know if Mr. Barr acted alone or at the behest of a Loyalist organization?"

"I guess so."

"Now, let's go back to the evening you went to the Strand Theater to meet with Mr. Barr. I believe that was back in May. What was the purpose of meeting with him?"

"I can't remember."

"Well, let me try to refresh your memory. It was the evening Mr. and Mrs. Barr went to see a movie called *Veronica Guerin*. Now, in the grand scheme of things, I wouldn't expect you to remember everything that happened in May 2003, but whatever you needed Mr. Barr to do was so important that you had him send Mrs. Barr home. It was so urgent you couldn't let them enjoy their evening together. I'm pretty sure you remember the purpose of the meeting."

"Yes, I remember now. Detective Inspector Higgins had met with me a few days previously and questioned me about the murders of Eamon Sullivan and Kevin O'Neill because they were on my patch. He told me both murders were committed with a known UVF gun from East Belfast. He implied the UVF was behind the killings. I told him that wasn't true. Mr. Barr was responsible for UVF East Belfast weapons storage, so I met with Shooie to get his help in investigating who might have used the gun in the murders. This was important because the UVF had endorsed the Peace Agreement. Although we hadn't decommissioned our weapons, there was a tacit understanding the war with the IRA was over."

"So, you were convinced after meeting with Detective Inspector Higgins that in some way, with or without your knowledge, the UVF was involved in the murders?"

"I believed Inspector Higgins when he told me a UVF gun was involved and that concerned me."

"Your Lordship, I've no further questions for this witness."

"Then let's adjourn for today. Again, I remind the jury you shouldn't discuss this case outside the court."

12

September 21, 2005

WHEN COURT RESUMES, INGRAM addresses the jury. "Members of the jury, you're now going to hear and view testimony that's at the heart of this case. Much of the testimony, to date, has related to Hugh Barr and his role in the murders of Eamon Sullivan and Kevin O'Neill.

"However, the case before you isn't about Hugh Barr. It's about the defendant, Gráinne O'Connor. In the copy of the indictment, which you received at the beginning of the trial, it is the contention of the prosecution that the defendant paid Mr. Barr to commit the murders. That's why the defendant, Gráinne O'Connor, is charged with murder.

"The evidence you're about to hear concerns a bank account at the Ulster Bank in Donegal Square East. For reference purposes, you may wish to look at exhibits R009 through R017. These include certified copies of a savings account in Mr. Barr's name and certified copies of all the account transactions during the relatively short period the account was active.

"I want you to pay close attention to the dates of these transactions in relation to the dates of the murders of Mr. Sullivan and Mr. O'Neill. Let me remind you, Eamon Sullivan was murdered on March 1st, 2002. Kevin O'Neill was murdered on March 2nd, 2003."

Ingram moves to a large chart strategically located in view of the jury, the witness, and Judge Sinclair. He flips the cover to show the key dates of the murders and bank account transactions.

"Mr. Dale, I believe you're representing the Ulster Bank."

"That's correct."

"For the record, what is your position with the bank?"

"I'm the manager of the branch of the Ulster Bank located in Donegal Square East."

"Is that the branch where Mr. Barr had a savings account?"

"Yes, sir."

"When was that account opened?"

"The account was opened on February 18th, 2002. Mr. Barr made a £50 deposit."

"Members of the jury, that's exhibit R009. I assume Mr. Barr opened the account himself. Is that correct?"

"Yes, sir. The date and time on the deposit information correspond with the date and time of CCTV footage which shows Mr. Barr at the teller station."

"Members of the jury, I draw your attention to the video screen."

The clerk runs a video showing Hugh Barr at the teller station. Ingram then turns to the jury. "Members of the jury, Hugh Barr opened a savings account on February 18th, 2002. Eamon Sullivan was murdered on March 1st, 2002. Mr. Dale, please tell the jury what happened on February 25th and March 8th, 2002."

"A deposit of £10,000 was made to Hugh Barr's account on February 25th. The money was withdrawn on March 8th."

"Who made the deposit, Mr. Dale?"

"The date and timing on the deposit, and CCTV footage of the teller station on that date and at that time, shows the deposit was made by a lady."

"Mr. Dale, can you identify the lady in court today?"

"The lady is the defendant."

A loud murmur breaks out among people seated in the public gallery.

"Quiet, please," the clerk orders.

"Members of the jury, I draw your attention again to the video screen."

The clerk runs a video that shows Gráinne O'Connor at the teller station on February 25th.

Ingram continues. "Who made the withdrawal on March 8th, Mr. Dale?"

"Mr. Barr."

The clerk runs the video that shows Hugh Barr at the teller station.

"And the date and time on both the withdrawal slip and the CCTV footage match?"

"Yes, sir."

Ingram patiently and meticulously leads the jury through the evidence of the remaining account transactions up until the time the account was closed. "Members of the jury, what you've observed this afternoon is clear evidence of the relationship between the defendant, Gráinne O'Connor, and Hugh Barr. Gráinne O'Connor paid Hugh Barr to kill Eamon Sullivan and Kevin O'Neill. Your Lordship, I've no further questions for the witness."

"Mr. Solomon, do you or Mr. Litton wish to cross-examine the witness?"

William Litton indicates he does. "Mr. Dale, this afternoon you testified in a manner that suggests to the jury that the synchronization of the date and time of deposits and withdrawals with the date stamp on CCTV footage is evidence of who made the deposit or withdrawal. Is that so?"

"I guess. I would think so."

"Mr. Dale, we're dealing with facts. Thinking isn't good enough. Is there synchronization or not?"

"No, there's no synchronization."

"Thank you. Now, how many teller stations are there at your branch?"

Dale thinks for a moment. "I believe there are six cashier stations and two reserved for travel transactions, such as currency exchange."

"And there's a video camera for each of the teller stations?"

"That's correct."

"And there could be more than one customer at each teller station at the same time?"

"Yes, sir."

"In fact, Mr. Dale, given the location of your branch in busy downtown Belfast, one could say with certainty that, at any given time of the day, there are multiple teller stations in use?"

"I guess so."

"In other words, what I hear you telling the jury is there's no way on God's good earth that anyone, not even the branch manager, could say with certainty that Gráinne O'Connor made any deposits to Hugh Barr's account. All we know is she was in the bank. Am I not correct?"

"She was in the bank at the time deposits were made to Hugh Barr's account."

"No, Mr. Dale. Let me ask the question again so the jury can understand your answer. There's no way on God's good earth that anyone, not even the branch manager, can say with certainty that Gráinne O'Connor made any deposi-ts to Hugh Barr's account. Am I not correct?"

"Yes, sir."

"Thank you, Mr. Dale. I've no further questions."

Litton faces the jury. "Members of the jury, it's clear the prosecution hasn't established a relationship between Mr. Barr and the defendant, certainly not a relationship that goes beyond reasonable doubt."

When Litton sits down, Judge Sinclair adjourns the trial until after lunch.

"Well, Gráinne, what do you think?" Pascal asks.

"I'm concerned. All the evidence seems to favor the prosecution."

"That's because, at the moment, the prosecution is at bat. In a day or so, we'll be able to present defense arguments. Remember, there are no witnesses to the murders, and no one who can say for sure that Hugh Barr committed the murders.

"Similarly, there's no direct evidence you knew Hugh Barr. There's no CCTV footage of you and Barr together. There are no recordings you ever had a conversation with him. The prosecution's evidence is purely circumstantial, so what we've done, yesterday and today, is cast doubt on that evidence.

"For example, Herschel got the forensics expert to admit there's no conclusive evidence Hugh Barr used the gun to kill Sullivan and O'Neill. William Litton got William Preston to state he doesn't know if Barr acted alone or at the behest of a Loyalist organization. Queenie

Barr admitted she first told Detective Inspector Higgins the cash belonged to the UVF.

"Despite all the copies of bank deposits and CCTV footage, the branch manager admits no one can say for certain you made deposits to Hugh Barr's account. So even before we present our arguments, we've cast doubt on the prosecution's case."

"I hope so," Gráinne says. She sighs and adds, "I'm not looking forward to this afternoon."

"I understand. It'll not be easy for you to look at Brendan McArdle. But I believe you can do it. Remember, he's responsible for the death of Martin and Peter. He's the face of evil. For the first time, you, through your counsel, will be able to unveil this evil visage. He may have immunity from prosecution, but he'll not leave Laganside Courthouse unscathed. We'll show the world, especially the jury, that you're the true victim."

"Thank you, Pascal. I'll try not to let you down."

Gráinne enters the dock ten minutes before the scheduled afternoon start time. The barristers and solicitors already have taken their seats, and Gráinne notices additional security officers at the back of the court.

She checks that her parents are in their usual place and notices that Father D'Arcy is sitting beside them. Sean Lynch and Brigid Maguire have moved forward to sit with the O'Neill family members. The court crier orders all to stand as Judge Sinclair enters the courtroom. There's a hum of expectation as the jury take their seats.

After arranging his notes, Judge Sinclair speaks to the jurors. "Good afternoon, members of the jury. I hope you had a good lunch. This afternoon you're going to hear from the final prosecution witness, Mr. Brendan McArdle. I want you to know that one of the issues I've dealt with is whether I should permit this witness to testify.

"I believe it's important for you to hear what this witness has to say. However, I want you to know Mr. McArdle has an involved history with the defendant and has only agreed to testify after being given immunity from prosecution for any part he may have had in the Fountain Street bombing."

This creates a stir in the public gallery. The clerk asks for silence.

"That bombing, in February 1993, as you have heard throughout this trial, resulted in the death of the defendant's husband and son. To the best of my knowledge, Mr. McArdle hasn't admitted he had a role in the bombing.

"You'll also hear Mr. McArdle met the defendant under unusual circumstances. Mr. McArdle dressed up as a priest to entice the defendant to talk to him, and it's alleged that during their conversation, she confessed that she was responsible for the deaths of Eamon Sullivan and Kevin O'Neill."

Again, a loud murmuring requires the clerk to intervene.

"I also remind you that both Mr. Sullivan and Mr. O'Neill were sentenced to jail for their part in the Fountain Street bombing. I'm giving you this background so you've knowledge of the history between the defendant, the witness, and the two victims. It'll be up to you to determine the facts. With this, I ask the court crier to administer the oath to Mr. McArdle, after which the prosecution may proceed."

Gráinne's eyes follow Brendan all the way to the stand. She looks directly at him but he keeps his head bowed. He appears more haggard than she remembers him, but this may be due to the shadow of stubble on his chin and the absence of his priestly garments.

Martin Mulligan leads the presentation of evidence. He has a tall, narrow body and long claw-like fingers. He paces constantly, like a falcon ready to pounce, his eyes alert and piercing.

"Mr. McArdle, I'll move quickly to the core of your evidence, but before I do, I want to clarify one thing. Did you dress up as a priest on July 28th, 2004, and go to the Church of Mary of the Assumption in Newcastle, County Down?"

Brendan raises his head and looks at Mulligan. "I did."

"What was the purpose of dressing up as a priest?"

"I wanted to talk with the defendant, and I thought it might be possible to accomplish this if she believed I was a priest."

For the first time, Brendan glances at Gráinne. She keeps her eyes riveted on his face.

"Why did you want to talk with the defendant?" Mulligan says.

"When Kevin O'Neill was murdered about a year after the killing of Eamon Sullivan, I felt that the murders might be more than a coincidence. I thought maybe the UVF was targeting former IRA members.

"The thing that kept coming to my mind was that both Eamon and Kevin had spent time in the Maze Prison for their part in the Fountain Street bombing. I wondered if, maybe, some of the victims or their families might be trying to get revenge for the injuries or deaths that occurred from the bombing. If this was the case, then Sean Lynch and Brigid Maguire, who had also been jailed for their part in the bombing, might be next."

Martin Mulligan interrupts Brendan. "I understand your concern, but the bombing was in 1993. The murders of Sullivan and O'Neill didn't take place until 2002 and 2003. Doesn't the time lapse make it unlikely there was a relationship between the Fountain Street bombing and these two murders?"

"That's what Sean and Brigid thought, but you have to remember that Eamon and Kevin were incarcerated from 1994 to the middle of 2000 in what was regarded as the most secure prison in all of Europe. I'm not saying that killing them in prison was impossible, but highly unlikely without the collusion of prison personnel. The killings were relatively soon after their release from prison, and it struck me that the early release of the prisoners might have angered the families of the victims. I had seen television coverage of the victims protesting the early release provisions of the Peace Agreement. But it was only a hunch."

"So how did you come to focus on the defendant out of all the victims of the bombing?"

"Well, I was lucky, you might say. Sometime after Kevin was murdered, and this blows my mind, the defendant called Brigid Maguire's father to ask if she could meet with Brigid."

Herschel Solomon quickly objects. "M'lord, this is hearsay and has no relevance to these proceedings."

Martin Mulligan responds. "Your Lordship, the witness is explaining why he focused on the defendant. If necessary, I can call Mr. Maguire to the stand to verify Mr. McArdle's account."

"Okay. For now, the objection is overruled. Mr. McArdle, please continue."

"The defendant gave some cock-and-bull story to Mr. Maguire. She said she was an author, and she felt talking to Brigid would somehow give her inspiration."

This generates a ripple of laughter in the public gallery. The clerk asks for quiet.

Mulligan takes the opportunity to clarify the significance of the testimony. "If I understand you correctly, Mr. McArdle, in using the words 'cock-and-bull story,' you're really saying you don't believe writing a novel was the motive behind the defendant's request to talk to Brigid."

Solomon decides against complaining that Mulligan's leading the witness.

"Hell, yes. Immediately after the defendant spoke to Mr. Maguire, Brigid and Sean called me in a panic. They were certain Brigid's time had come. They asked me what they should do. I told them to get the hell out of Northern Ireland, but Brigid said she couldn't leave her family. Since the defendant had never seen me, I offered to do some investigation. I came up to Belfast and followed the defendant for a few weeks. Every Wednesday she would take the bus to Newcastle. She always went to the Church of Mary of the Assumption, so I knew she was Catholic. Well, from her name I knew she was Catholic, but now I knew she was a practicing Catholic. That's when I got the idea to dress as a priest."

Brendan smiles and steals another glance at Gráinne. She's unsure how to react. She hopes the jury can see his arrogant pride. She notices all the jurors and the gallery are engrossed by Brendan's testimony.

"So tell us what happened on July 28th, 2004," Mulligan says.

"I waited in the shadows of the bus station. The defendant got off the bus from Belfast about 1:30 p.m. and walked up Main Street. I followed at a distance. Across from the Donard Hotel, she turned left onto Savoy Lane and walked a couple of hundred yards to the church. She went down the concrete steps and opened one of the two large wooden doors that access the church. I waited until I was sure she would be settled and followed her inside."

"And what happened inside?"

"It's one of those modern churches, circular in shape. Twelve rows of bench seats are divided into three sections, each separated by an aisle on either side of the middle segment. They form a semicircle around the raised marble altar in the center of the church. The afternoon sun was slanting through the stained glass windows, but I saw Gráinne, I mean, the defendant, kneeling in the sixth row to the left side. I walked slowly down the right side aisle and turned into a pew two rows in front of her, toward the center. I knew I was clearly in her sight.

"I knelt down and pretended to pray." Brendan smiles, and Gráinne senses he's enjoying himself. "I had to fight the urge to turn around. After all, a priest must talk to God for at least a little while. I tried to relax, but I wasn't used to kneeling, and to tell you the truth, the Roman collar was killing me."

Brendan runs his fingers under his collar. This evokes loud laughter. His performance annoys Solomon, but he senses the laughter is a release of tension. The clerk calls for order.

"So I looked up at the crucified Christ and counted to twenty. Enough is enough. I made the sign of the cross and walked in as dignified a manner as possible to the left aisle. This brought me back past the defendant. She was no longer kneeling but sitting quietly. Our eyes met so I said, 'Good afternoon, sister. How are you?'

"She said she was fine and asked how I was. I explained I'd some business in Newcastle and thought I'd visit Saint Mary's. I told her it was a beautiful church and asked her if she was from Newcastle. She told me she was visiting from Belfast. She liked to come to the church for quiet. It gave her time to think.

"I was thinking feverously. I had to find a way to establish trust. The role of a priest proved a godsend. I told her we all need time to think and reflect. Life's so hectic it's good to talk to God and listen to what He has to say to us. We find peace in prayer and confession.

"She blushed when I mentioned confession. She didn't say anything, so I seized the opportunity to move the conversation to a personal level. I asked her if she found peace in confession. I felt bad for her. Her cheeks just burned. I realized I'd put her on the spot so I apologized for doing so. I told her I'd made an assumption that, maybe, I shouldn't have.

"She told me it was okay. I think she felt she'd embarrassed me. She explained she went to Mass every Sunday, but hadn't been to confession in a long time. I sat down beside her and said, 'I'm Father Casey, from Dundalk.' She told me she was Gráinne O'Connor. I told her not to worry about confession, for it's not for everyone these days. I was dying to get some fresh air, so I asked her if she'd like to walk along the beach and take in the beauty of the Mourne Mountains. She said that would be nice.

"We walked along the shore. The tide was out, the sand firm, and the sea breeze refreshing. I knew somehow I had to get her to talk. But I took my time, making small talk about the weather and how erosion was changing the character of the shoreline. When I felt the time was right, I said, 'Is there anything you would like to talk to me about, Gráinne?'

"She turned, walked toward the rocks, and sat down. She looked out at the sea. I could see tears in her eyes. I knew I'd touched a chord. I couldn't believe it. She just looked me in the eye and said, 'Father, I've sinned. I have this terrible secret. I think I killed two people.'"

Almost every head in the court turns to look at Gráinne. She feels her face warming, so she looks down. She's glad when McArdle continues.

"I asked her if she wanted to tell me about it, and she just told me everything."

"What do you mean by 'everything,' Mr. McArdle?"

"Like a breached dike, her words tumbled out one upon the other, finding their own path with no regard for consequences. I think she just wanted to get it all out. She said, 'In 1993, I lost my husband and son in a bombing in Belfast. The people responsible were caught and sentenced to long terms in prison. They got what they deserved, so although it didn't bring Martin and Peter back, I felt it was justice.'

"'But then, there was the Peace Agreement. At first, I was happy, like everybody else. All the shootings, bombings, and killing would stop. What I didn't appreciate was the price of peace. Martin and Peter's killers were set free . . . after only six years. They were supposed to serve ten years to life. At first, I didn't believe it. I thought there must be some mistake, but my solicitor said no. I asked him what we could do about it. He said we could do nothing, for referendums in both Northern Ireland and the Republic of Ireland had ratified the Agreement. How's that for justice?'

"I could see the growing, visible anguish on her face but I didn't want to interrupt her. She talked about a day in July 2000. I think it was the day when all the prisoners got out of the Maze. She said, 'I was there. I'd never been to the Maze before, although I'd read plenty about the H-shaped concrete cellblocks, the hunger strikes, the brutality.' Anyway, she said that when she got off the bus, she wasn't sure where to go. She saw a man in a green Avenger. He was smoking. He looked like a nice man so she asked him where she should go. He directed her to the main gate.

"She said she saw a cluster of people near the gate. Some were holding placards, so she went over to investigate. She told me one read, 'In memory of Siobhan. Gone but not forgotten,' and she wished she'd made one in memory of Martin and Peter. She looked at pictures of prisoners the protesters had inserted in the wire mesh fence under a sign, 'The Face of Evil.' She said she didn't recognize anyone.

"She was going into great detail. At times, I actually thought she was reliving things. Eventually, in the afternoon the IRA prisoners were released. She couldn't believe the celebrations: the popping of champagne corks, and the loud cheering of relatives and friends. It was such a contrast to the stark silence of her victims' group.

"The first batch included Eamon Sullivan. She commented that he'd aged little from his five years in prison. The last batch included Sean Lynch and Kevin O'Neill. Their faces had lived with her every day during their trial. She blamed them most for Martin and Peter's deaths, for O'Neill built the bomb and Lynch abandoned the van with the bomb inside. Lynch exited the turnstiles and embraced a couple she assumed were his parents. She felt numb as she remembered his clenched-fist salute. O'Neill was one of the last to exit. She thought he'd aged beyond his sixty-four years, but then she never expected him to see the light of that day."

Judge Sinclair interrupts the testimony. "I can see that Mr. McArdle's testimony is going to take some time. As I've noted, this testimony is material to understanding the facts of this case. I don't want to rush anyone. I feel it's appropriate to adjourn for the day."

"My, I'm exhausted," Agnes Thompson says when Marta Sheehan joins her and Anne Simpson in the jury room.

Marta ignores the comment and says, "Quite the actor, I would say."

"You mean the witness?" asks Agnes.

"Yes. I've never seen such an arrogant, self-serving performance. He thinks he's Mr. Wonderful. He thinks he's a comedian. I think he's nothing but a cold, calculating murderer who should be in the dock and not the witness stand. I'm glad the judge told us about him."

"He is funny, you have to admit," Agnes says.

"Funny, my ass. I didn't see Gráinne O'Connor laugh. Do you think he should be allowed to testify against the wife and mother of the people he killed? How can we believe one thing he tells us?"

Anne Simpson says, "That's why the defense will be able to cross-examine him. Then we can determine what fact is, and what fiction is. Remember, His Lordship cautioned us against forming opinions before we've heard everything."

"'His Lordship?' I don't understand 'M'lord' this and 'M'lord' that. It's so sniveling. I wish they'd talk like normal human beings."

This causes Agnes to laugh. "Well, I'm sure Mr. Solomon will give McArdle what for when he gets the chance!"

At her parents' home, Gráinne eats little at teatime. She excuses herself and goes upstairs to the guest bedroom. She changes into her pajamas and takes down a scrapbook from the bookcase adjacent to her bed.

She flicks quickly through the pages of photographs of her childhood until she comes to photographs of her and Martin. The images bring back memories of happier times: a photograph of Martin and her at a school dance in her junior year, a photograph on her wedding day taken under the stained glass rose window as she entered the front door of the Church of the Little Flower with her father. The early prints of Peter as a baby and later shots of holidays at the caravan in Newcastle—Peter fishing along the Shimna River, Peter climbing the Mourne Mountains, Peter eating breakfast, his plate stuffed with potato farls, soda bread, eggs, and bacon. She smiles. She had forgotten how he liked his bacon crisp.

Her parents have built the album by date. The photographs from Newcastle must have been the summer before the bombing, for when she turns the page there are pictures of Peter's last Christmas and a single photograph of the headstone on Martin and Peter's grave. She thinks about the funeral and shivers as she recalls standing at the cemetery on that cold gray winter afternoon. The coffins had been closed when they arrived at her home from the morgue. Even in death, she had been denied her right to say a meaningful goodbye. Tears stream down her cheeks. She closes the scrapbook and buries herself under the bedclothes, trying to soften the sound of her deep sobs.

13

September 22, 2005

MULLIGAN SPEAKS FIRST WHEN the trial resumes. "Mr. McArdle, you told us what the defendant said about visiting the Maze Prison on the day Sullivan and O'Neill were released. Can you describe her demeanor when she talked to you?"

"I'd say she was angry . . . especially when she talked about Sean Lynch and Kevin O'Neill."

"What else did she tell you on the beach that day?"

"She told me she was demoralized and all she thought about was how to get justice now that the killers of her husband and child were free. I believe she went to Scotland over New Year's, in January 2001. She made a resolution to do what she could to get justice for Martin and Peter. She said she had no idea how to do it, but knew she wouldn't get it through the courts.

"Then one day, watching television footage of a Loyalist paramilitary funeral, she got the idea someone in a Loyalist paramilitary group might help her. After all, they were enemies of the IRA. She waited weeks for the right opportunity. A member of the UVF was killed in an altercation between rival Loyalist paramilitary groups. She decided if she was going to do anything, this was the moment. She went to the funeral.

"She said, 'It was a rainy day, a real downpour. There were a lot of mourners and reporters outside the house. I was nervous. I'd never been in a hard-line Loyalist area before, and I wasn't sure who to approach or what to say. But it turned out to be easier than I expected. Most of the UVF volunteers were young, in their teens or twenties. They all wore black leather jackets and dark glasses. I couldn't talk to them. They wouldn't understand my loss. They were too young. I looked for someone older. And amazingly, I saw the man I had spoken to at the Maze Prison, the one who directed me to the main gates.'

"'He was standing at the rear of the column. He had on all his UVF gear, but I still recognized him. He was in an outside rank, beside the pavement. That made it easier. I just got the strength. I edged through the crowd, slowly, and went up to him. I asked him if I could talk with him after the funeral. I'm not sure that he recognized me. He looked at me like I was mad. He was probably embarrassed, but he said we could meet. So I met him at the Stormont Hotel. He no longer wore his uniform. He bought me a drink.'

"'I told him about the bombing. I made sure he knew it was an IRA bombing. I told him about Martin and Peter and my frustration at the early prisoner release. I asked him if he knew anyone who could help me get justice.'"

"And who was the person, the UVF volunteer that the defendant was talking about?" Mulligan asks.

"She told me his name was Hugh Barr, although his family called him Shooie."

"How did Mr. Barr respond when the defendant asked him if he knew anyone who could help her get justice?"

"He told her it depended on what she meant by justice. She said she wasn't sure. She didn't want the bombers to live in peace, as if they hadn't committed a crime. He asked her if she was willing to pay to get justice. She told him she hadn't thought about that, but she agreed that she could. She would use money she received from the victims' compensation fund. Because her husband was relatively young and had a good job with strong potential earnings, she'd received a large settlement from the government for loss of future earnings. She told me it was blood money.

"Hugh Barr told her he would have to think about it. She asked him to place a specific ad in the legal notice section of Wednesday's *Belfast Telegraph* if he agreed to help her. If he did, they would meet on Thursday at the Renoir Café on Queen Street. I think the wording she gave him was something like, 'We remember the dead with justice.' She said when she read the ad in the paper, it said, 'Justice is for the living, not the dead,' but she knew he'd placed the ad. She understood what he meant and why he had changed the words.

"They met upstairs at the Renoir, and he told her he would help. But he warned her that if his handlers knew what he was doing, he'd be six feet under. No one else must know. He asked her for ten thousand quid. I think she suggested five, but he told her he was risking his life to get involved with the IRA. If she wanted his help, she needed to get serious. She said he didn't have much of a sense of humor."

Brendan pauses and grins. "Then, I nearly blew it. Too much knowledge is a dangerous thing. I'd always wondered why Eamon Sullivan was the first to be killed, so I asked her why. She looked at me funny and said she didn't really know. I realized I'd made a mistake, for she hadn't told me Eamon was first. I backtracked and pretended not to know about the murders. I asked her what Barr did for the £10,000. She seemed to accept this, for she just said, 'He killed Eamon Sullivan.'

"I said something like, 'My God, that's terrible. Did you ask Barr to kill him?' She said, 'I don't think so, Father. I asked him to get me justice. Why would I want Sullivan killed? I wanted him to experience my living hell.' I felt she was trying to mitigate her responsibility.

"I reminded her she'd said she might be responsible for the deaths of two people. She said, 'Yes. Hugh Barr also killed Kevin O'Neill. About a year after Sullivan's murder, he called me and threatened me that, if I didn't pay him another £10,000, he would leak my involvement in Sullivan's murder to the IRA. I was terrified, so I made the payment. I didn't think he'd kill again, but then he murdered Kevin O'Neill.' She started to sob deeply. I tried to comfort her. I told her it was okay. She asked me if God would forgive her. I really had no idea. I tried to remember what I'd heard when I went to Mass as a teenager. I told her, 'Yes, Jesus teaches us if we confess our sins, He will forgive. You have confessed to the Lord's servant and, in the name of the Father, I forgive you.'

"She said, 'What penance must I do?' I wondered where the conversation was going. Then I had another word of knowledge. I told her, 'You must regularly confess your sins. Remember, you find forgiveness through the sacraments. You will experience God's healing power of love.'"

Brendan smiles again. "I couldn't believe how easily my words were flowing. For a moment, I wondered if I'd missed my calling. I asked her if she would do that for me. She said, 'I will, Father. I talked to Hugh Barr in December. We met in town. I was surprised how he'd aged. I hadn't seen him in a year. His hands trembled. He looked ill. His face was ashen, etched with stubble and worry. When I told him he looked pale, he said he'd been partying in preparation for the holidays. I think he had a drinking problem, but I minded my own business. He promised me there would be no more killing if I made one final payment of £10,000.' She said she felt it was worth it, if this would bring the killing to an end.

"I immediately thought about Sean Lynch and Brigid Maguire. I told the defendant she must stop making these payments, for, as long as she made them, Barr would keep on killing and come back for more.

"She said, 'I don't think you have to worry about that, Father. I can assure you there will be no more payments.'

"I asked her what she meant. She said, 'Hugh Barr's obituary was in the paper last Monday evening. He's being buried this afternoon.'

"I asked her what happened to him. She said she didn't know. The obituary was kind of strange. It didn't say when or how he died. Then she looked at her watch and told me she needed to catch her bus. She was grateful for the chance to talk with me and was sorry for taking up so much of my time. I walked her back to the station."

"Then what did you do?"

"I called Sean Lynch and suggested he should go to the police."

Mulligan's examination of Brendan takes most of the morning. He wants him to share every detail. When he feels all the facts have been laid out for the jury, he looks directly at the witness. "Mr. McArdle, is it your sworn testimony that the defendant, Gráinne O'Connor, said to you, 'I think I killed two people'?"

"That's correct."

"Why should the jury believe you?"

"I've admitted I dressed up as a priest to deceive the defendant. I'm a reluctant witness. I've no desire to be here in this court of British injustice. I've nothing to gain from lying."

Mulligan faces Judge Sinclair. "Your Lordship, the prosecution has no further questions for this witness."

"Okay. Juror number eight has another appointment this afternoon so we will adjourn until tomorrow at 9:30 a.m., when the defense may cross-examine the witness. I remind the jury you shouldn't discuss the case outside the court, not with family members or friends. I also remind you not to form a view about what each witness says until you've heard all of the evidence. I ask you to continue to listen, pay attention, make notes if you wish, and carefully consider all the evidence. I'll see you tomorrow."

Mulligan meets with Eamon's parents and Marie O'Neill. Although not formally invited, Brendan tags along with Marie.

"How'd I do?" he asks right away.

"You did great," Marie says before Mulligan can answer.

"I agree," Mulligan adds. "You did an excellent job describing the confession, how you got her to make it, and her reason for making the contract with Barr. Most important, you came across as believable. Given your history with the defendant, this is a major accomplishment. It's just what we needed."

"I told you he would come through," Marie says.

"Just be aware tomorrow will be more difficult. The defense will try to destroy your credibility. Be prepared for them to attack your statement that Gráinne said, 'I think I killed two people.' Are you sure those were her words?"

"Of course he is," Marie states.

Gráinne meets with Pascal, Herschel, and William.

"How do you think he did?" she asks Herschel.

"He did what the prosecution wanted. There were no surprises. Tomorrow we'll show that he's a self-serving liar, and a cold, callous killer. I think you'll see him sweat much more than he did today."

After Gráinne leaves, Solomon talks with his team. "Tomorrow is critical. Gráinne's guilt or innocence is likely to be decided based on who the jury members believe. We must destroy any credibility McArdle established today."

14

September 23, 2005

HERSCHEL SOLOMON WALKS BACK and forth between his table and the witness stand. Brendan moves uneasily in his seat. He's impatient for the questioning to start. The sooner it commences, the earlier it will end. But Solomon's in no hurry. He expects to keep McArdle on the stand for most of the day.

Gráinne, too, wishes Solomon would begin. She fidgets with her fingers and feels a bead of sweat trickle down her brow. She knows this is the most important stage of the trial. The cross-examination of McArdle is likely to determine her guilt or innocence in the minds of the jury.

"Mr. McArdle, are you an actor?" Solomon begins.

The question takes Brendan and the court by surprise. There's some laughter, but the clerk lets it go. Brendan thinks with pride about the role he played as a priest. It had been unbelievably effective.

"I guess I am," he responds with a smile.

"Would you say you're a good actor, Mr. McArdle?"

"I guess so."

"What, in your opinion, makes a good actor?"

Mulligan objects. "Your Lordship, really, what does this have to do with the matter at hand?"

Judge Sinclair turns to Solomon. "I'll allow you some latitude, Mr. Solomon, but let's get to the point."

"I will, M'lord. Mr. McArdle, I asked you what makes a good actor?"

"I guess the ability to play a part and to make it believable."

"Play a part . . . Make it believable . . . Would you say the ability to deceive is another way to put it?"

"I guess so."

"Mr. McArdle, your life as an IRA operative has long been one of deceit. Just to survive, you have to pretend to be something or someone that you're not. Isn't that so?"

Brendan shrugs his shoulders. "I guess so."

"So how do we know when you're telling the truth or outright lying or just exaggerating? You've been an actor for over thirty years. Acting is so much a part of your persona that you're not always sure what's true and what's not. Isn't that so?"

"I don't know what you mean."

"Let me clarify. You told the defendant you were Father Casey. Isn't that so?"

"Yes."

"So you told her a lie?"

"I was trying to win her confidence."

"But you told her an outright lie?"

"Yes."

"And when you told the court the defendant said, 'I think I killed two people,' you lied?"

"No. That's the truth."

"Is it? Let me refresh your memory. Sean Lynch, in his statement to police . . .'"

Solomon pauses and leafs through the documents in his well-ordered binder. "Members of the jury, I'm referring to exhibit R008. This is a statement Mr. Lynch made to police describing what the witness told him about the defendant's so-called confession. Let me quote. 'She said, Father, I've sinned. I'm responsible for the death of two people.' End of quote. There's a huge difference between killing people and being responsible for their deaths. A person who deliberately runs down two people with a car is guilty of murder. A person who accidentally goes through a red light may feel responsible for their deaths, even though they had no intent to kill. Remember, Mr. McArdle, you are under oath. Isn't it true that Mrs. O'Connor only told you she felt responsible for the deaths of two people?"

"My understanding was that she killed them."

"I don't think so. Later, Lynch, relaying what you told him, states, and again, I quote, 'She told me she wanted Barr to help her get justice, and when I asked her what she meant by that, she said she wanted the bombers to suffer as she had suffered.' End of quote. Isn't it true, Mr. McArdle, the defendant never confessed to murdering Sullivan and O'Neill? What she told you was that she felt responsible for the deaths of Mr. Sullivan and Mr. O'Neill because she'd asked Hugh Barr to make them suffer?"

Brendan looks down. "I don't remember the exact words, but I knew what she meant. I told her she must stop all this killing."

"But she never confessed to killing anyone. She only admitted being responsible for the deaths of two people. You're interpreting her words. You're putting your spin on them. Isn't that true, Mr. McArdle?"

Martin Mulligan rises from his seat. "Your Lordship, counsel is playing semantics. Murder is murder."

Judge Sinclair adjusts his half-moon spectacles and smiles as he responds. "Believe it or not, Mr. Mulligan, I understand what murder is. The issue is what did the defendant say? I believe the jury can discern the facts. So, Mr. McArdle, answer Mr. Solomon's question and then let's move on."

Brendan isn't quite sure what he's answering. "Can you repeat the question?" he asks Solomon.

"My question is, did the defendant confess to killing Eamon Sullivan and Kevin O'Neill, or did she simply say she was responsible for their deaths?"

"I believed she was confessing to murder."

"I'm not asking you what you believe. I'm asking you a specific question and expect you to answer yes or no. Didn't the defendant only tell you she was responsible for two deaths?"

"I can't remember her exact words. Like I said, I took it she was confessing to murder."

Judge Sinclair intervenes. "I think we have the point, Mr. Solomon. I think the jury can determine what the defendant said or didn't say. Let's move on."

Solomon consults his notes. "Mr. McArdle, you testified earlier you followed the defendant because you'd been given information the defendant might have killed Sullivan and O'Neill and might be planning to kill Brigid Maguire and Sean Lynch."

"Yes."

"Who gave you that information?"

Mulligan immediately objects. "Your Lordship, I don't think this information is relevant or necessary."

"Mr. Mulligan, we'll let the jury determine relevance. The witness opened the door when he disclosed the information voluntarily. Mr. McArdle, answer the question."

"Sean Lynch and Brigid Maguire advised me they were concerned the defendant may have been involved in the murders and that they might be in danger themselves. This was right after the defendant had asked Brigid's father if she could meet with Brigid."

"Who are Sean Lynch and Brigid Maguire?"

"They participated in the Fountain Street bombing."

"They participated along with Sullivan, O'Neill, and you?"

"No, they participated along with Sullivan and O'Neill."

"And what's your relationship to Lynch and Maguire?"

McArdle hesitates. He looks to Judge Sinclair for relief, but gets none.

"We are . . . were members of the IRA."

"And you provided the material that was used in the Fountain Street bombing?"

"I'm not required to answer that."

Judge Sinclair reminds McArdle that he has been given immunity from prosecution.

"I don't recognize the British court system," Brendan says. "I reserve my right not to answer questions unless they deal with the confession of the defendant."

Solomon looks at the jury. He waits until he establishes eye contact and walks toward them. "We'll take that as a yes. Mr. McArdle provided the material that was used in the bomb that killed the defendant's husband and only son."

He walks back to the witness stand. "In fact, Mr. McArdle, given you murdered the defendant's husband and fourteen-year-old son in the Fountain Street bombing, isn't it ironic you're the only person to testify that the defendant confessed to killing two of your murderous accomplices?"

Solomon knows he won't receive a response. He paces slowly in front of the witness box. "Let me ask you a question, Mr. McArdle. Are the lives of Sullivan and O'Neill, two convicted murderers, more important than the lives of Martin O'Connor, a teacher, and his only son Peter, aged fourteen? Two innocent family members spending quality time together on a Saturday afternoon, only to be killed by an IRA bomb planted by an active service unit under your command."

The silence in court is absolute. Solomon lets it linger for as long as he can. Gráinne sobs quietly, but noticeably. When there's no response from the witness, Solomon engages the jury. "I guess we'll take that as a no."

Brendan sweats profusely. He wonders why he agreed to testify. He looks at Marie O'Neill, but she looks away.

Solomon takes his time. He consults his notes regularly and walks slowly between his table and the witness stand. "Mr. McArdle, yesterday you said you've nothing to gain from lying. Even that statement isn't true. By testifying here today, you've been granted immunity from prosecution for your role in the murders of the defendant's husband and son. Isn't that true?"

Martin Mulligan objects. "My Lord, counsel is badgering the witness. The court already is aware the witness has received immunity from prosecution. There's no justification for this line of questioning."

"Mr. Solomon, what is it you're trying to establish?" the judge says.

"M'lord, I'm simply highlighting areas of the witness's testimony which make it hard for the jury to believe him. By his own admission he lied to the defendant when he told her he was a priest. According to what Sean Lynch told police, the defendant never told Mr. McArdle she murdered anyone. Mr. McArdle knows full well he has everything to gain from being a witness here today, and he's lying when he denies involvement in the Fountain Street bombing. What we're seeing here is a pattern of pathological lying. It's important the jury understands the character of this witness."

"Mr. Solomon, I believe the jury understands the point you're making. I also think it's time for a break."

"How do you feel today, Gráinne?" Pascal asks when they counsel.

"I feel better. I'm glad Herschel is setting the record clear. I can't believe McArdle lied on the stand. I hope the jury sees he's not a credible witness."

"I believe they will, and we're not finished yet."

In the prosecutor's chambers, Mr. and Mrs. Sullivan sit quietly, listening as Marie O'Neill mutters to herself. She clenches and unclenches her fist. When Mulligan arrives, she immediately confronts him.

"How could you let them treat Brendan like that? I persuaded him to testify. He must feel humiliated. They made him look like shit."

Mulligan is shocked. He looks at the Sullivans and shakes his head. "Marie, please calm down. This trial isn't about Brendan. He's fortunate. He's the one with the amnesty. Whether you like it or not, the cross-questioning of a witness is at the heart of our judicial process, and that's a right of the defense as well as the prosecution. You need to trust we know what we're doing. We wouldn't have brought Mrs. O'Connor to trial if we didn't believe we could get a conviction."

"I'm sorry," she says, but when she leaves the room her cold goodbye signals that her anger still burns.

When court resumes, William Litton takes over for the defense. He starts on the attack. "Mr. McArdle, you said you believed the defendant was confessing to murder, but isn't it true when you asked her if she wanted Hugh Barr to kill Eamon Sullivan, she said to you, 'Why would I want him killed? I wanted him to experience my living hell'?"

"I don't remember."

"Let's see if your memory is totally blank. Isn't it true the defendant told you that Barr blackmailed her, that if she didn't pay him more money, he would leak her involvement in Sullivan's death to the IRA?"

"I don't remember."

"Then, why did you tell her that as long as she continued to make payments, Barr would keep on killing and coming back for more?"

"I don't remember that."

"But according to the statement made by Sean Lynch to the police, that is what you told him when you called him immediately after meeting with the defendant. How can you not remember? Mr. McArdle, I believe this is a case of selective memory. Maybe the Director of Public Prosecutions won't remember he gave you amnesty."

The remark infuriates Mulligan. "Your Lordship, counsel's statement is inappropriate. If the witness doesn't remember, he doesn't remember."

Judge Sinclair agrees. "Mr. Litton, please confine your comments to the case at hand."

Litton paces back and forth between his files and the witness stand, taking time to form his next question. He clears his throat.

"Well then, Mr. McArdle, since your memory is so poor, let me ask you a different question. Earlier, my colleague, Mr. Solomon, broached the subject of the importance of one life versus another. I understand how difficult that is to answer, for all lives are important. Maybe we should evaluate loss from another perspective. Let's look at it in terms of the victims' families."

Brendan feels a knot in his stomach.

"The trouble I'm having, Mr. McArdle, is to understand who the victim is or who the victims are. Your testimony says the victims are Mr. Sullivan and Mr. O'Neill. I think we can all agree Mr. Sullivan and Mr. O'Neill didn't deserve to die the way they did. We understand the grief and loss of the Sullivan and O'Neill families.

"What about Gráinne O'Connor? Mr. McArdle, look at the defendant. The Fountain Street bombing happened over twelve years ago. Did you see her tears when the deaths of her son and husband were discussed? Do you think her grief is any less with the passage of time?"

William Litton waits for an answer, knowing there will be none. He plays with the tuft of hair under his lip and debates asking Judge Sinclair to force McArdle to answer his questions. After letting him twist for a moment, Litton changes tack. "Mr. McArdle, there's perhaps another way to look at this. How much time have you spent in prison for the murders of Martin and Peter O'Connor?"

David Ingram jumps to his feet.

"Your Lordship, Mr. McArdle isn't on trial here and, in fact, hasn't been charged with any crime related to the Fountain Street bombing."

"I agree. The jury should disregard that last question."

"Let me try to rephrase the question," Litton says. "Mr. McArdle, you've been given immunity from prosecution for all crimes related to the Troubles. To the best of my knowledge, you've not lost family as the result of the violence, and yet we have Mrs. O'Connor, who lost both her son and husband in the violence, and who hasn't been offered immunity related to two deaths you tie to the Troubles. Is that fair?"

Ingram again objects to the question.

"I've no further questions for the witness," Litton says.

Judge Sinclair checks the time. "Let's adjourn for lunch. When we resume, the defense will have the opportunity to call witnesses."

The defense has spent many hours debating whether to put Gráinne on the stand. Pascal, who knows Gráinne best, is opposed to doing so. His concern has nothing to do with his confidence in Gráinne. His general philosophy, as a solicitor, is not to put a defendant on the witness stand unless there's absolutely no alternative. He feels there's usually more downside risk than upside opportunity.

Herschel Solomon and William Litton both argue that, on balance, it will be helpful to the defense case to let Gráinne testify. Litton's position isn't as firm as that of Solomon. He feels caught in the middle.

Solomon is senior counsel, but Litton has known Pascal a long time and grown to respect his advice.

"As we expected, the prosecution has made the most of presenting evidence through documentation, CCTV footage, and witnesses," Solomon observes.

"The testimony of Dale, the bank manager, and Brendan McArdle are the strongest evidence for the prosecution. While I believe that we established there's no way anyone can verify Gráinne made deposits to Hugh Barr's bank account, and while I think we've blown away McArdle's objectivity, I'm concerned if we present no witnesses, the testimony of Dale and McArdle is what the jurors will remember."

"The prosecution has presented at least fourteen witnesses. I don't think we can present no witnesses, and Gráinne is our only material witness. Gráinne alone can testify with assurance what she actually asked Hugh Barr to do and what she subsequently told Brendan McArdle."

"I understand," Pascal counters. "You're making valid points, but once Gráinne takes the stand, she'll be asked if she hired Hugh Barr to kill Eamon Sullivan and Kevin O'Neill. How will she answer under the strain of testifying? How will she respond to the question of whether she made deposits to Hugh Barr's account? We cannot control Gráinne's answers. It'll be like throwing her to the wolves."

William Litton shares his thoughts. "I think, Pascal, you're underestimating the strength of someone who's battle-hardened, who's spent the best part of a year waiting for this encounter, waiting for the opportunity to clear her name.

"There's one other aspect of this case we've not discussed. This is a case about justice. How do victims get justice, victims like Gráinne? I believe putting her on the stand will help the jury see her as a victim as well as a defendant.

"While I've noted her inner strength, this isn't the side of Gráinne we need the jury to see. We want them to see a middle-aged, lonely, vulnerable victim who, after twelve long years of suffering, is still trying to get justice. That's the picture we'll paint."

Pascal smiles at his associates. "I guess I've known your leaning for some time. I'm just trying to give it one last shot. I believe you'll do a good job. How does Gráinne feel?"

"I think she's fine," Solomon responds. "I've explained to her the pros and cons of putting a defendant on the stand. I believe she knows what to expect."

There's a brief murmur across the court when Herschel Solomon confirms he'll call Gráinne O'Connor as a witness. The murmur is more pleasure than surprise. Like tennis spectators longing for a fifth set, the public wants to see every point played. They have a morbid fascination with the grim details, and only Gráinne knows them.

As soon as Gráinne is sworn in, Solomon rises and approaches the witness stand. "Good afternoon, Mrs. O'Connor. I dare say today is a day you've been anticipating with mixed emotions. It gives you the opportunity you want to set the record straight, to tell exactly what happened. And yet, it is a daunting experience to testify in front of so many people. Except for the trial of the Fountain Street bombers, am I correct you've never been in a courtroom before?"

"That's correct."

"And you've never been charged with a crime before."

"No, sir."

"You've not even had a speeding ticket."

"That's correct."

"So to be charged with murder must be somewhat of a shock?"

"Yes, sir."

"I want to make sure you understand why you're here. It's not because you physically murdered anyone. Rather, it's the Crown's contention someone else committed murders but you are somehow responsible. Is that your understanding?"

"Yes, sir."

"Now, the person reputed to have committed the murders, a UVF gunman called Hugh Barr, unfortunately is no longer with us. This means, Mrs. O'Connor, the only people who can establish the facts for the jury are you and Brendan McArdle. Since Brendan McArdle can only tell the jury what you told him, common sense says the most important testimony for the jury to hear is your testimony. So that's why you've taken the stand, to give the jury the truth."

"Yes, sir."

"So let's try to establish the facts. Not 'he said, she said,' but the facts as only you know them. Let's clarify an important aspect of this case: your relationship or lack of relationship with Hugh Barr. Were you a friend of Hugh Barr?"

"No, sir."

"Did you know Hugh Barr?"

"Yes, I met him."

"When did you meet him?"

"It's a long story."

"I understand, but this is a story the jury needs to hear from you, for it will clarify everything about your relationship with Hugh Barr. Take your time."

"I first met Hugh Barr at a funeral."

"And when was this?"

"I can't remember the exact date but I know it was in 2001, maybe March or April. There was a UVF funeral in East Belfast and I went to it."

"Did you always go to UVF funerals?" Solomon asks with a broad smile.

A small wave of laughter breaks across the court.

"No, sir," she says and blushes.

"But you did on that day in March or April 2001?"

"Yes, sir."

"And why was that?"

"This is where it may get long."

"That's okay."

"As the court has heard during this trial, I lost my husband, Martin, and my only son, Peter, in a bombing in Fountain Street on February 27th, 1993."

"How long were you married, Mrs. O'Connor?"

"Almost sixteen years." Gráinne takes a handkerchief from her dress pocket.

"And what age was Peter?"

"Peter was fourteen." Gráinne dabs her eyes and apologizes.

Mulligan considers objecting to the line of questioning but decides against it. Solomon waits a few moments before continuing.

"That must have been hard for you?"

"Yes. I thought my life was over."

"But you somehow found the strength to continue?"

"Not immediately, but I had support from my parents and my parish priest, Father D'Arcy. He promised me there would be justice. I also saw a psychologist for three years."

"How did that help?"

"She helped me understand what I was feeling . . . the pain, the anger, the depression. She helped me understand that I could do nothing about the past and that I needed to focus on my life as it was."

"Were you able to do that?"

"It took a while, but yes. I started to work at my writing again."

"What were you writing?"

Mulligan again resists the temptation to intervene. He realizes the defense is building sympathy for their client, but he's afraid his intervention may be counterproductive if it creates conflict with the jurors.

"I was working on a novel. It was published in 2000."

"And you mentioned that Father D'Arcy said you would get justice. Was he right?" Solomon asks with a smile, thinking about the conviction of the bombers.

But Gráinne doesn't return the smile. She takes her time before responding. "No. But it wasn't his fault."

"What do you mean?"

"At first, I got what I thought was justice. The bombers were tried and sentenced to long terms in prison. But then there was the Peace Agreement. Initially, I thought it was good. There would be no more killing. I didn't realize all the bombers would be set free. I couldn't believe it. I felt betrayed. The slate was wiped clean. It was as if the bombing never happened. It was as if Martin and Peter didn't matter. I fell apart again."

"And it was because of this . . . betrayal . . . you met eventually with Hugh Barr?"

"Yes. I wanted justice. Nobody seemed to care. All that mattered was peace. I asked my solicitor what I could do. He told me there was nothing I could do, for the people had approved the Peace Agreement in a referendum. Every time I thought about the bombers getting out of prison, I felt sick. I felt there was no justice. Then, one day it came to me. If I couldn't get justice through the justice system, maybe the UVF could help me. The bombers belonged to the IRA, and the UVF were the sworn enemies of the IRA. One day, I heard about a UVF funeral. I decided to go to it and that's how I met Hugh Barr."

"You didn't know him before going there."

"Well, I'd actually met him at the Maze Prison when all the prisoners were released, but I don't think he remembered me. At the prison, I only asked him for directions."

"Now, Mr. McArdle testified you hired Mr. Barr as a hit man, to murder the people who killed your husband and son. Is that true?"

"No, sir. I asked him if he knew anyone who would help me get justice."

"But didn't he think initially you meant killing the five people responsible for the bombing?"

"Yes, sir, but I explained I wasn't asking anyone to commit murder. I wanted justice. I wanted the bombers to suffer as I have suffered. I felt they weren't suffering, walking the streets of Belfast. In fact, two of the bombers are here in court today. How can that be?"

All around the court, heads turn as people wonder who the bombers are and where they're sitting. Gráinne resists the temptation to identify Sean and Brigid.

"Now, Mr. McArdle also testified you told him you paid Mr. Barr money to get justice. In fact, he testified you paid money to Hugh Barr to murder Sean Lynch and Brigid Maguire. Did you pay money to Hugh Barr?"

"Yes. He said he wouldn't help me get justice unless I paid him. There were too many risks. He was paranoid about the IRA."

"So Mr. Barr asked you for money?"

"Yes, sir."

"So the facts are you asked Mr. Barr to help you get justice by making the bombers suffer. To do so, Mr. Barr asked you for money and you agreed to pay him?"

"Yes, sir."

"How much did you pay him?"

"I paid him £10,000 in February 2002."

"Was that before or after the murder of Eamon Sullivan?"

"It was before the murder. I didn't know he was going to kill Mr. Sullivan."

"How did you feel when you heard Mr. Sullivan had been murdered?"

"I was concerned, but I didn't know Hugh Barr was responsible."

"Did you make any other payments?"

"Yes. About a year after the murder of Mr. Sullivan, Hugh Barr called me and threatened he would tell the IRA I was responsible for Sullivan's death if I didn't pay him another £10,000. I was afraid, so I put another £10,000 into his account."

"So Mr. Barr started blackmailing you?"

"Yes."

"Did Mr. Barr tell you he planned to kill Kevin O'Neill?"

"No, sir."

"How did you feel when you heard Mr. O'Neill had been murdered?"

"I felt sick. I wondered if Hugh Barr was responsible. I tried to shut it out of my mind. Mr. O'Neill had built the bomb that killed Martin and Peter. I didn't want him dead, but in a way I felt he got what he deserved."

"Was that the last payment?"

"No. Hugh Barr called me again in December 2003. He promised me this would be the last payment. I never heard from him again."

"How much did you pay this time?"

"I paid another £10,000."

"Now, you made the payment although you knew he killed Kevin O'Neill following the previous payment."

"Yes, sir. I didn't know what to do. I felt trapped but hoped this would be the end of it."

"In other words, Mrs. O'Connor, Mr. Barr was nothing but a low-life criminal who took the opportunity to make money at your expense?"

Mulligan objects. "My Lord, this calls for speculation. Only Hugh Barr knows the motives for his actions."

"I agree. The jury will ignore counsel's last remarks."

Herschel Solomon goes back to his table and leafs through his notes. He takes a deep breath and paces in front of the witness box.

"Mrs. O'Connor, let's go back to your decision to work with Mr. Barr. What did you hope he would do if he didn't kill the bombers?"

"I hadn't a clear idea. I knew the paramilitary groups had their own justice system. They punished people by tarring and feathering them, by kneecapping, by threatening them. I just left it up to Mr. Barr."

"Now, Mrs. O'Connor, let's clarify another aspect of this case and that is how you feel about the Peace Agreement."

Martin Mulligan immediately objects. "Your Lordship, you already ruled that the Peace Agreement doesn't have any bearing on this case."

Judge Sinclair turns to his notes and, after a few moments, responds to the objection. "Mr. Mulligan, I believe, if you read my ruling, I specifically indicated I wasn't rendering an opinion on whether the provisions of the Peace Agreement apply to this case or not. I also stated I wasn't making a decision on whether the charges against the defendant relate to the Troubles. I stated these issues would require further review, should they come into play.

"Now, we may be at that point, so I think this is an appropriate time to recess for thirty minutes. Members of the jury, when we resume, I'll meet with both counsels on the issue raised by Mr. Mulligan. I'll let you know, as soon as I can, whether we need a further adjournment to address the issue or whether both sides are prepared to continue with the case. So let's recess."

Martin Mulligan, David Ingram, and Graham McIlhenny meet on the issue. "I think His Lordship is sending us a message," Ingram says when they sit down. "He expects us to continue with the case. Why else would he raise that possibility rather than just assume an adjournment is necessary?"

"I agree," McIlhenny affirms. "We're on the horns of a dilemma. If we continue with our objection, we may alienate the jury. I think they're tired of delays. On the other hand, if we withdraw our objection, we give the defense what they want."

Mulligan stirs from deep thought. "This could be a pivotal moment. I think you're right. His Lordship doesn't want to rule on these issues. I also think the risk of alienating the jury isn't something we want to do. It's a largely symbolic victory for the defense if we withdraw our objection. We still have the opportunity to cross-examine the defendant."

Judge Sinclair reenters the court. He immediately addresses both sides. "I think you know the ramifications of this issue. It will take significant time for me to make a specific ruling on such a broad and untested area. In fact, the delay may last months.

"Any decision is likely to be appealed to a higher court. What I'm being asked to decide is whether the provisions of the Peace Agreement can have application to events occurring after the signing of the Peace Agreement. Given the present provisions of the Agreement related to victims, equality, and justice, I'm not sure I know the answer. I certainly won't know the answer this afternoon.

"There are two other aspects I have to consider. One is the right of the defendant to a speedy trial. The other is we have a seated jury. If this issue will take months to resolve, I believe we've no alternative but to dismiss the jury and order a retrial. I'll hear arguments."

Mulligan responds. "Your Lordship, thinking through these issues, my associates and I recognize the position you're in. Accordingly, we're agreeable to withdraw our objection."

"Thank you, Mr. Mulligan. I'll ask the jury keepers to bring in the jury."

When the jury is seated, Judge Sinclair addresses Martin Mulligan. "Mr. Mulligan, prior to the break, you objected to defense counsel asking the defendant questions related to the Peace Agreement. I understand you've had a change of heart."

"Your Lordship, the prosecution doesn't wish to place a burden on the jury by necessitating a further adjournment to deal with a complex legal issue. Accordingly, the prosecution withdraws its objection."

"Thank you, Mr. Mulligan. The defense may continue to question the witness."

Solomon approaches the witness stand. "Mrs. O'Connor, you'll recall I asked you about the Peace Agreement. This is not a general question. You understand the prosecution initially objected to my question. So I want you to confine your remarks to why you feel the Peace Agreement is relevant to this case."

"Yes, sir. The Peace Agreement resulted in a travesty of justice for the victims of the Troubles. We were not consulted about the terms for peace. I'm a victim of the Troubles. I lost my husband and son."

Gráinne pauses and then looks at the jury members. "I know people are tired of hearing this." She wipes away a tear before continuing her response.

"But the foundations of law and order are justice and equality. I need justice. The early release of Eamon Sullivan, Kevin O'Neill, Sean Lynch, and Brigid Maguire isn't justice. That's not what a court like this intended when it sentenced the bombers to long prison terms. So, my question is, have we given up on justice, just to silence the guns?"

Gráinne pauses again. There is not a sound. Every eye is focused on her. People listen to every word. She speaks slowly and softly, but clearly.

"I need equality. If Brendan McArdle is given amnesty from prosecution for the murders of my husband and son, if he cannot be sentenced to jail, why am I here? How can the Peace Agreement apply to someone who is not a victim of the Troubles by any definition, but not apply to me, someone who has lost everything in life that matters?"

The tension of the trial and the raw emotion of testifying can be heard across the court. Gráinne knows she can say no more. She's exhausted. She covers her head with her hands and weeps.

Solomon addresses Judge Sinclair. "M'lord, I've no further questions for this witness."

Judge Sinclair is cognizant of Gráinne's distress. "Let's recess for thirty minutes at which time the prosecution may cross-examine the defendant."

Herschel meets alone with Gráinne. "You did fantastic, Gráinne. No one could have done any better. I'm truly proud of you. I understand the strain you're under. You've just one hurdle to go, the cross-examination. I'm sure it will be difficult, but just keep the goal of justice in front of you and you'll do fine. Take your time. Don't let the prosecution bully you into quick responses. Try to answer with as few words as necessary and only address what is asked. I'll do my best to protect you from unfair questions."

In the jury room, there's a rare moment of silence. Philip Brady, who tends to speak off the top of his head, breaks the silence. "Quite an act," he remarks.

Mark Campbell feels awkward at the remark. He giggles nervously and bites his fingernails. Marta Sheehan looks directly at Brady. "You obviously haven't lost anyone in the Troubles. If you had, you'd know that was no act. That's what happens when you lose a loved one, when you lose your entire family, when you lose everything."

She walks away. Brady blushes, and silence returns.

Tricia Fitzgerald tries to ease the tension. "It sure was good of Mr.

Mulligan not to place a burden on us," she says with a laugh. The absence of a response tells her the time isn't right for humor.

"Mrs. O'Connor," David Ingram begins, "there are no words to describe what you've gone through as a victim of the Troubles. Only you know what you've suffered. I'm sorry . . . I wish I could take your pain away. However, I can't. Nothing can restore Martin and Peter to you. Not even the killing of Eamon Sullivan and Kevin O'Neill. Such actions only create more victims, more pain, more suffering—the very thing the Peace Agreement seeks to end.

"I don't want to be insensitive to your loss, Mrs. O'Connor, but I'm puzzled by a number of things. I understand you made a good recovery from your tragedy, good enough to write a successful novel. I'm not a writer, but I think you need focus and drive to complete a novel. Is that not so?"

"When Martin and Peter were murdered, I went into a deep depression. I couldn't work on my novel. I just gave up. But three years of therapy and the conviction of the bombers helped me work through my loss. I was able to resume writing and fortunate enough to get my novel published. It gave me a purpose in life."

"So you're capable of putting your loss behind you. You're capable of making a choice. Yet, at some point, you made a conscious choice to take the lives of Eamon Sullivan and Kevin O'Neill. Isn't that so?"

"No. When the Peace Agreement, to appease the killers of my family, undid the sentences passed by the court, I chose to resume my fight for justice."

"That's not what I asked you. Did you or did you not decide to take revenge on Eamon Sullivan and Kevin O'Neill? I just need a simple yes or no answer."

"I asked Hugh Barr to help me get justice."

"You hired Hugh Barr to murder Eamon Sullivan and Kevin O'Neill."

"With due respect, I asked him to help me get justice."

"Okay, Mrs. O'Connor. If getting justice wasn't killing Sullivan and O'Neill, explain to the court what exactly you mean by justice."

Pascal feels his stomach muscles tighten. This is the type of open-ended question he fears.

"Sir, I don't want to sound flippant, but I no longer know what justice is. I thought I did once. Did I get justice when the judge sentenced the bombers to prison? I think I did, but the Peace Agreement turned the sentences on their head. So what is justice? You've said there are no words to describe what I've suffered. So, in my case, what is justice?"

Judge Sinclair intervenes quickly. "Mrs. O'Connor, please refrain from asking questions of counsel. Just answer the question. Do you understand?"

"Yes, sir. I'm sorry."

"Thank you, Your Worship," Ingram says before turning back to Gráinne.

"Mrs. O'Connor, I respectfully submit the defense has tried to muddy the waters for the jury."

Solomon immediately objects, but Sinclair gives Ingram the benefit of the doubt.

"Overruled, Mr. Solomon. Be careful, Mr. Ingram, how you phrase your arguments."

"Mrs. O'Connor, let's try to simplify the facts for the jury. Again, a 'yes' or 'no' answer will suffice."

Solomon gets to his feet again. "I object, Your Worship. The witness should be able to answer questions as she sees fit."

"Mr. Solomon, counsel is only suggesting that a simple yes or no answer is often adequate and clearer for the jury. The witness may answer as she sees fit with one proviso, she must answer the question."

"Okay, Mrs. O'Connor. Let's try again. In March or April 2001, you initiated a meeting with a complete stranger, Hugh Barr?"

"Yes, sir."

"You suspected Hugh Barr might be willing to assist you because he was in the UVF and your targets were in the IRA."

"Yes, sir."

"Now, let's confirm your payments to Hugh Barr. You made a deposit of £10,000 into Hugh Barr's bank account on February 25th, 2002, just four days before the murder of Eamon Sullivan?"

"Yes."

"You made a deposit of £10,000 into Hugh Barr's bank account on February 17th, 2003, just before the murder of Kevin O'Neill?"

"Yes."

"You made a deposit of £10,000 into the bank account of Hugh Barr on December 29th, 2003?"

"Yes."

"And that was after you'd made efforts to set up a meeting with Brigid Maguire."

"I'm not sure what you mean. The deposit had nothing to do with Brigid Maguire."

"But isn't it true, Mrs. O'Connor, you continued to make payments to Hugh Barr even after you knew he murdered Eamon Sullivan and Kevin O'Neill? Didn't you make these payments to Hugh Barr to murder the rest of the IRA members responsible for killing your husband and son? Only Mr. Barr's suicide prevented further killing."

Herschel Solomon addresses Judge Sinclair. "I object, M'lord. The defendant categorically denies murdering anyone or hiring anyone to commit murder. She has testified under oath that she asked Hugh Barr to make the bombers suffer as she suffered, and she's very much alive."

"Overruled. It's up to the jury to determine the facts from the evidence that both counsels present. The witness should answer the question."

"I made an agreement to pay Mr. Barr £10,000 to get me justice. He said he wouldn't help me unless I paid him. I kept my word. I didn't know he would kill Eamon Sullivan. I didn't know he would blackmail me and keep on killing."

"Yet you kept on paying even after knowing Mr. Barr was willing to kill to fulfill his part of the contract. Your Lordship, I've no further questions for the witness."

Solomon asks the judge for a redirect.

"Mrs. O'Connor, did you ever ask Hugh Barr to murder Eamon Sullivan?"

"No, sir."

"Did you ever ask Hugh Barr to murder Kevin O'Neill?"

"No, sir."

"Did you ever pay money to Hugh Barr to murder or harm Brigid Maguire?"

"No, I did not."

"Thank you Mrs. O'Connor. M'lord, I've no further questions."

Judge Sinclair addresses the court. "I believe we've reached a suitable point to adjourn court for this week. I thank the jury for your attention and remind you not to discuss the case outside the court. We'll resume on Monday at 9:30 a.m., when we'll hear closing arguments. The court is adjourned."

15

September 26, 2005

THROUGHOUT THE WEEKEND, Gráinne feels numb. She rehashes her testimony and wonders if she should have answered the questions differently. She wishes the trial was over. The thought of twelve strangers determining her fate fills her with fear. She tries not to think about the ramifications of the potential verdict.

Anne Simpson's thoughts, too, are preoccupied by the trial and, in particular, by the emotional testimony of Gráinne O'Connor. Simpson frequently pictures O'Connor sobbing with exhaustion and grief. She tries hard not to form conclusions but to wait patiently for Monday's closing arguments. She hopes counsel will lay out the facts clearly and concisely so a fog of uncertainty won't cloud jury deliberations. She replays the sharp exchange between Marta Sheehan and Philip Brady and hopes the tension is not a sign of things to come.

On Monday morning, Martin Mulligan makes the closing arguments for the prosecution. He understands the jurors have heard a lot over the course of the trial. They've listened to the same point hammered home two or three times. It's all part of the game, trying to get attention, trying to leave a lasting impression. This morning his objective is to be concise, to leave jurors with facts presented in an orderly, believable, and memorable manner.

"Members of the jury, first of all let me thank you for your attention and patience throughout this trial. You've listened carefully to the key witnesses as they presented evidence on behalf of the prosecution, and you've heard these witnesses cross-examined by the defense.

"Shortly, you'll be asked to recess, to enter into deliberation on what you've heard. Your responsibility is to sort out the facts, to determine what's believable, what's not believable, and then decide the defendant's guilt or innocence.

"The prosecution contends the defendant, Gráinne O'Connor, is guilty of the murders of Eamon Sullivan and Kevin O'Neill. I remind you, to be guilty of murder, it's not necessary the defendant pulled the trigger of the gun that killed Sullivan and O'Neill. All that's required is that she participated in the crime with knowledge.

"In the case before you, the prosecution contends the defendant paid the killer, Hugh Barr, to murder the victims. This morning, I'll summarize the clear facts we've heard in testimony over the past few weeks. I ask you to listen carefully, one last time. Make notes if you wish. Then, determine the verdict.

"Detective Inspector Higgins presented evidence that both Sullivan and O'Neill were found murdered: Sullivan on March 1st, 2002, and O'Neill on March 2nd, 2003. Both were murdered while working: Sullivan in his solicitor's office, O'Neill in the taxi he used to earn a living.

"You heard the forensics expert testify that Sullivan and O'Neill were murdered with the same gun, and this gun was used by Hugh Barr to commit suicide in 2004. Why do we believe Hugh Barr murdered both Sullivan and O'Neill?

"First of all, what's the likelihood three people were killed with the same gun and in such a relatively short period of time, but not by the same person? How much does that likelihood increase if only one person had access to or owned the gun? You've heard William Preston testify that Hugh Barr was the UVF quartermaster and, as such, he controlled access to the gun.

"You've heard Mrs. Barr testify her husband left a note in which he stated, 'I made a terrible mistake, one that I regret and must pay for.' You've seen CCTV footage showing Hugh Barr at the site of Sullivan's office immediately before and immediately after the murder.

You've seen CCTV footage of Hugh Barr actually shooting Kevin O'Neill.

"I believe when you consider the forensic evidence, the CCTV footage, the note left to his wife by Hugh Barr, and the testimonies of both Brendan McArdle and Gráinne O'Connor, there's absolutely no doubt Hugh Barr killed Eamon Sullivan and Kevin O'Neill.

"Now, as far as this trial is concerned, the issue isn't whether Hugh Barr killed Sullivan and O'Neill but whether, as the prosecution contends, Gráinne O'Connor paid Hugh Barr to commit the murders. Let's review the evidence.

"You may or may not like Brendan McArdle. He has admitted being a member of the IRA. It's alleged he provided the material for the Fountain Street bombing. You've been advised that he received immunity to allow him to testify in this case. And yes, he deceived Gráinne O'Connor when he dressed up as a priest. However, it was this meeting with her that ultimately alerted and convinced the police that Hugh Barr didn't act alone.

"The defense portrays Brendan McArdle as a liar. However, the defendant admits she met Brendan McArdle at the Church of Mary of the Assumption on the day he dressed as a priest. She admits she told him she was responsible for the deaths of Sullivan and O'Neill. She confirms McArdle's testimony that she paid Hugh Barr.

"The defendant even explained why. She told us of the intense anger she felt when she found out Sullivan and O'Neill were to be set free under the terms of the Peace Agreement, how she no longer felt there was justice, and how she set about getting justice. Members of the jury, you can ignore Brendan McArdle if you like. Concentrate on the testimony you've heard from Gráinne O'Connor.

"She wanted justice, plain and simple. She says she didn't ask Barr to kill the bombers, but she gave him carte blanche to determine justice, and even after she knew he had killed Mr. Sullivan, she continued to pay him. The defendant says she was being blackmailed, but she didn't go to the police. She even paid Barr again, knowing he'd murdered Mr. O'Neill. Was that third payment because she was being blackmailed or was it the next installment in her plan to kill all the bombers? Was this the payment to kill Brigid Maguire? Is it just a coincidence that she tried to set up a meeting with Brigid Maguire? Members of the jury, you have to decide the true facts."

Mulligan pauses, causing all eyes in the jury box to focus on him. "Without a doubt, the defendant, Gráinne O'Connor, is guilty of the charge of murder in the case of Eamon Sullivan. Without a doubt, the defendant is guilty of the murder of Kevin O'Neill. I believe, if you consider the facts that have been offered into evidence, you'll find the defendant, Gráinne O'Connor, guilty of murder on both counts. Thank you for your attention. Your Lordship, the prosecution rests."

Judge Sinclair orders a twenty-minute recess.

During the break, Eamon Sullivan's parents and Marie O'Neill meet with the entire prosecution team. Mrs. Sullivan, who has spoken little during the trial, is the first to speak. "Thank you, Mr. Mulligan. That was an excellent summary. It was clear and concise. I think you and your team set out the arguments perfectly."

"I agree," her husband says. He puts his arms around her shoulders. Marie O'Neill is unusually silent.

"What do you think, Marie?" David Ingram asks.

"I agree. I hope the jury does."

As senior counsel, Herschel Solomon presents the defense's closing arguments. Although the evidence is circumstantial, he knows the prosecution has made a strong case. However, jurors are human. They frequently are swayed by their emotions. They're influenced by their empathy, or lack of it, for the defendant.

As with all defense arguments, it's important to plant seeds of reasonable doubt among the jury. This will be his last opportunity to do so. He doesn't have to get all twelve jurors to agree with him. If he can get one or two to vote "not guilty," he will be well on his way to getting a dismissal of the charges, or at least a hung jury. He doubts Gráinne wants a retrial, but a deadlocked jury creates all sorts of new possibilities for settling the case. He'll challenge the prosecution's evidence. Within reason, he'll remind jurors that Gráinne O'Connor is the true victim.

"Members of the jury, I, too, thank you sincerely for your attention during this trial. That attention is pivotal because the jury system gives you, as citizens, a truly important role in the administration of justice. You are here not only to ensure justice for the Sullivan and O'Neill families. You also must ensure justice for the defendant.

"Based on what you've heard in court, each of you has the responsibility of deciding whether the defendant is guilty or not guilty of the alleged offenses. What an awesome and difficult responsibility.

"I say difficult because the accused is innocent unless and until the prosecution proves guilt. You must be convinced of guilt beyond a reasonable doubt. If you have any doubts, then you must find the accused not guilty.

"It's my responsibility, in closing, to refresh your memory on the key facts of this case. I believe this will help each of you make the appropriate decision.

"Let me say, the prosecution has told you Hugh Barr killed Eamon Sullivan and Kevin O'Neill. The forensics expert testified the same gun killed Sullivan, O'Neill, and Hugh Barr. However, the expert also testified he couldn't conclusively state that Hugh Barr killed Sullivan and O'Neill.

"William Preston, a senior member of the UVF, has testified that although the gun in question was a UVF gun, and Hugh Barr was a member of the UVF, he doesn't know who killed Eamon Sullivan and Kevin O'Neill, because this gun has been used in so many UVF operations for years, by many volunteer members.

"There are simply no witnesses to these killings and no evidence to make such an assertion. Perhaps, most significantly, no one has been able to explain the letters 'NC' on Sullivan's appointment book. If Hugh Barr didn't kill Sullivan and O'Neill, then any relationship between the defendant and Hugh Barr is moot.

"Secondly, even if you conclude that Hugh Barr did kill Sullivan and O'Neill, did he do it because the defendant requested it? The defendant says she never asked Barr to kill anyone. Why then might he have done so? Every one of you understands the bitterness between Loyalists and Republicans. Logically, he may have done so because he was a UVF member who hated IRA volunteers.

"You also are aware not all members of the IRA support the Peace Agreement. That's why we still have dissident bombings and killings. The same is true on the Loyalist side. Not all members of the UVF agree with the Peace Agreement. Maybe Hugh Barr was continuing the struggle or, like many paramilitary volunteers, he just seized the opportunity to make a quick kill, both literally and financially.

"Is it possible that 'NC' murdered Eamon Sullivan for reasons we don't know, and Hugh Barr saw the opportunity to blackmail the defendant and to keep the blackmail going by killing Kevin O'Neill? Or maybe, it was easier and less risky to kill his victims than to continually harass them. These are all questions you must try to answer for yourselves and to do so beyond a reasonable doubt. If you have doubts, you must find Gráinne O'Connor not guilty.

"The defendant acknowledges she asked Hugh Barr to help her get justice, to make the bombers suffer as she has suffered. What did she mean? She was after a punishment that would remind the bombers about what they'd done, that would keep their crime before them for a long time, just as the courts originally decided. I think you will agree that killing them wouldn't achieve this objective.

"To get justice, sadly, the defendant had to go to Hugh Barr, an unlikely source. To paraphrase the defendant, she did this because the politicians had silenced the judiciary in order to silence the guns.

"What I'm saying to you is the defendant, Gráinne O'Connor, didn't mean for Sullivan and O'Neill to be murdered. You've heard the defendant state she no longer knows what justice is. I believe that was true also when she asked Hugh Barr to help her. If Hugh Barr did kill Sullivan and O'Neill, the decision to kill was a decision made by Hugh Barr and by Hugh Barr alone.

"Members of the jury, think carefully about this. The only reason Gráinne O'Connor is in court today is due to a phone call made by Brendan McArdle to Sean Lynch, another of the Fountain Street bombers. But what have we learned in court about Mr. McArdle?

"First of all, he's a self-confessed terrorist, a senior and long-standing member of the IRA. Secondly, he's a murderer, responsible for the deaths of the defendant's only child and husband. He's such a fanatic, so used to a life of killing, that he cannot accept the Peace Agreement. Thirdly, he's a liar. He admits lying to the defendant that he was a priest. On the stand, he has lied about what the defendant said to him. The defendant never confessed to killing Sullivan and O'Neill. She only confessed to being indirectly responsible for their deaths. She even admits Barr blackmailed her into making payments subsequent to Sullivan's death.

"Members of the jury, the question is: do you believe McArdle, or do you believe the defendant? You know McArdle is a practiced liar. But not one shred of evidence has been presented by the prosecution that would indicate that the defendant hasn't told the truth. How you evaluate the credibility of these two witnesses will determine the outcome of this trial. To find the defendant guilty, you must not have any doubts. Thank you for your attention. M'lord, this concludes the defense's closing arguments."

Sinclair checks his watch. "I believe this is an excellent time to adjourn for lunch. I'm sure everyone's hungry. We'll resume at 1:45."

Judge Sinclair begins the afternoon session by thanking the jury for their attention and patience. "Your attendance has been exemplary. Now you have the opportunity and responsibility to determine the guilt or innocence of the accused.

"At the outset of this trial, you were advised that a trial has two aspects: the law and the facts. Throughout these past few weeks, you've heard evidence from both the prosecution and the defense. This morning, both sides did an excellent job of summarizing their positions.

"It's now time for you to determine the facts. You must decide who to believe and who not to believe. That, in conjunction with the law, will establish the guilt or innocence of the defendant.

"Let me talk about the law. The defendant, Gráinne O'Connor, is charged with the murders of Eamon Sullivan and Kevin O'Neill. It's therefore appropriate I explain the charge of murder.

"Murder is unlawful killing with malice aforethought. That is, the intention is to kill. It's not an accident. It's not incidental to some other objective. There must be the intent to kill. To be charged with murder, a person doesn't have to be the one who commits the actual killing. However, they must have participated in the plan to kill. That is, they're involved and have knowledge of what is going to happen.

"Perhaps the clearest example I can give you is one you're familiar with. In most paramilitary bombings, someone builds the bomb, someone drives the vehicle with the bomb, and someone drives the getaway car. Now, if people are killed in the bombing, all are guilty of murder under the law: the bomb maker, the bomb driver, and whoever drives the getaway car.

"Now, under the law, there's a presumption of innocence. As far as you're concerned, when you first enter the jury box, the defendant is innocent. The defense doesn't have to prove the defendant is innocent. To convict the defendant, you must be convinced of her guilt only by the evidence you heard in court, and that guilt must be beyond a reasonable doubt. If you're not convinced beyond a reasonable doubt, you must acquit the defendant.

"What is reasonable doubt? It's the level of certainty a juror must have to find the defendant guilty. You base this doubt upon your reason and common sense, after careful consideration of the evidence. It doesn't mean absolute certainty.

"Now, let me touch on a few issues that arose in the course of this trial. The defense argued in your absence that under the Peace Agreement the defendant is a victim of the Troubles and shouldn't be charged for actions directly stemming from the Troubles. They've argued the defendant isn't being treated with the equality and justice foreseen by the signatories to the Peace Agreement.

"The defendant clearly is a victim of the Troubles. She lost both her husband and son in a terrible bombing. I've examined the arguments made by defense counsel and have ruled there's no basis to dismiss the charges against the defendant.

"There's no doubt the defendant has suffered much. As human beings, we may feel sympathy or empathy with the defendant. However, when you decide the facts of this case, you must not decide them based on sympathy. You consider the evidence you've heard here in court, and based on that evidence alone, you decide what the facts are.

"I want to remind you there are two charges against the defendant: the murder of Eamon Sullivan and the murder of Kevin O'Neill. These are separate charges, so although there may be similarities to the murders, you're being asked to consider the two charges independent of each other and to render a verdict in each.

"Now, you may well have questions you need answered during your deliberations. These questions may relate to the law or they may relate to a piece of evidence you are unsure about. Please be assured I will attempt to address your questions as expeditiously as possible. You should forward any questions to me through your jury keepers.

"Finally, you must reach, if you can, a unanimous verdict. I've every confidence that as you deliberate on the evidence you'll arrive at a just and appropriate result. I wish you well in your deliberations. The court is adjourned."

As a reader, you have heard all of the evidence presented to the jury. Additionally, you've had access to the legal arguments.

Before you read the jury deliberations, you have an opportunity to play the role of a juror. Consider the evidence as presented by the prosecution and the defense. Render your own verdict on Gráinne O'Connor's innocence or guilt. Document your reasoning.

In the matter of count number one,
the murder of Eamon Sullivan, what is your verdict?
    GUILTY or NOT GUILTY
    Your reasoning:

In the matter of count number two,
the murder of Kevin O'Neill, what is your verdict?
    GUILTY or NOT GUILTY
    Your reasoning:

To participate in the online vote, please visit
www.thepriceofpeace.net
and complete the survey

Then turn to Chapter 16 to read the jury
deliberations and their verdict.

PART II

*The goal of pursuit of justice must not
simply be that justice happens but
that reconciliation also happens.*

—MIROSLAV VOLF

*Justice does not come from the
outside. It comes from inner peace.*

—BARBARA HALL

16

September 27, 2005

ALL EYES IN THE JURY ROOM center on Anne Simpson, the jury forewoman. Now that they're at the deliberation stage, the other jurors, seven women and four men, look to her to take the lead. She asks one of the jury keepers to refresh their water supply, to provide additional flip charts, and to bring in loose-leaf notepaper.

They sit around a rectangular oak table. Five members, including Anne, sit on each of the two longer sides. The remaining two jurors occupy chairs at each end of the table.

Anne sits in one of the middle chairs with two female jurors each to her left and her right. The three remaining female jurors sit beside each other, directly opposite Anne. Two of the four male jurors occupy seats at the end of the table while the other two sit directly beside their male counterparts on the opposite side of the table from Anne.

Although known to the court only by numbers, the jurors address each other by first name. Anne had spent the weekend thinking about how best to start deliberations. She's aware of the pressure jury members are under, for they are being forced to make decisions whether they want to or not. Unfortunately, this is a complex case. But what they decide will have a lasting impact on the life of the defendant. She's curious where the members stand at the outset, so she suggests they have a secret ballot to communicate whether they think the defendant's guilty or not guilty on each charge.

"In the future," she explains, "we'll vote openly. However, to see whether we agree at the start, and to ensure each of us feels comfortable with the process, we'll do the initial ballot in secret. I'll hand out unmarked pieces of paper for each charge, and we'll simply write 'guilty,' 'not guilty,' or 'undecided' on the ballot."

To build confidence in the youngest juror, Simpson asks Imogene Healy to act as counter and communicate the tallied results to everyone. Healy's twenty-four and relieved to have an active part in the process.

The jurors are unanimous that this is a good way to begin. It'll break the ice and tell how hard they may have to work to obtain agreement. To no one's surprise, there's no consensus from the initial ballots. On the Sullivan murder charge, three say "guilty," four vote "not guilty," and five are undecided. On the O'Neill murder charge, five vote "guilty," two "not guilty," and five are undecided.

Imogene asks, "What happens if we never agree?"

"I'll clarify that with the judge, if it happens," Anne says. "But we all heard his closing remark. We must reach, if at all possible, a unanimous verdict."

Anne explains the next steps. "Let's destroy the ballots. Then, I would like us to list all the issues you feel we need to discuss. We won't worry about priority at this time. Let's just get the issues on the table. Then we can decide how to address them."

Samuel, who is nearest the flip chart, offers to write them down. Paul, an engineer and the youngest of the men, responds first. "I think there's a logical approach to our discussion. It pretty much follows the prosecution case. As the judge indicated, our job is to decide the facts. The prosecution has presented evidence it says establishes certain facts. The defense disputes some of these facts. Our job is to decide who is telling the truth."

"I wish it were as simple as that," Agnes says. "Both sides seem so convincing. How do we really know?"

Anne's pleased to hear Agnes speak for during the lunch breaks she has mostly remained silent. Her neutral-colored granny dresses remind Anne of a maiden aunt. It's Anne's observation that Agnes's personality mirrors her taste in wardrobe. She doesn't talk about herself and shows no passion about anything discussed by the group.

"We don't for sure," Anne explains. "That's why the judge said we don't have to be certain. We just have to be convinced beyond a reasonable doubt."

"I'm not sure I grasp what he means by reasonable doubt," Helen says.

Anne tries to reassure Helen and get the discussion back on track. "Helen, we'll get further clarification from the judge, if we need to, but for now let's list any issue you want us to discuss. Maybe, Paul, you could start," she says, hoping that throwing him a bone will stroke his ego.

"I'd be happy to," he answers. "Maybe we should begin with Hugh Barr. Do we agree he killed Eamon Sullivan and Kevin O'Neill? We might discuss why we think Sullivan and O'Neill were killed. Then we could move on to the key issues. What do we believe about Gráinne O'Connor and her relationship with Hugh Barr? Do we all believe she paid him money and, again, why did she do so? That may be enough to begin with. We can add to the list as issues emerge in our discussion. It should help explain why each of us voted as we did and where each of us stands."

Anne's delighted with the insight provided by Paul. She agrees a discussion of these questions will identify each juror's leaning. They agree to discuss whether Hugh Barr physically killed Sullivan and O'Neill.

Tricia, who at twenty-eight is the second youngest juror, begins the discussion. She does so without reference to notes. This doesn't surprise Anne; she's not sure Tricia made any notes throughout the trial. "I think it's pretty clear Hugh Barr killed the two victims. Look at all the evidence. I mean, the police say he did it. The forensics expert says he did it. The UVF commander says he did it. The defendant says he did it. Brendan McArdle says he did it. What more is there to say?"

Anne notices a few polite smiles among the other jurors. She resists smiling herself. When Philip, who also hasn't made many notes, concurs with Tricia, Paul takes control of the discussion. "I agree Hugh Barr killed the two bombers. Nevertheless, just for the record, I don't recall that the forensics expert and the UVF commander were able to prove Hugh Barr did it. Brendan McArdle only said Hugh Barr did it because that's what the defendant told him. It's the police CCTV footage and the defendant's own testimony that provide the compelling evidence."

Tricia blushes noticeably as Paul speaks. Anne feels sorry for her. She doubts Tricia attended college, but wonders if it's more her appearance that makes Paul so dismissive. She's a wispy strawberry blonde and given to wearing low-cut dresses and too much perfume. She loves to check herself in the mirror. Paul, a professional, is at an advantage in analyzing arguments and articulating them to others. When he finishes speaking, Anne says, "I think Tricia's right. The evidence, as I see it, says Hugh Barr committed the actual murders. Is there anyone who disagrees?"

Samuel Brown asks, "What about the defense argument that the person known as 'NC' may have committed the murders?"

Anne isn't surprised by the question, because Samuel was as diligent as anybody in taking notes during the trial.

"The entry in the appointment book is interesting," says Paul, "but no evidence was presented to explain what it means or who it refers to. We simply don't have any facts. I think the evidence we heard that Hugh Barr did the killing is compelling. Is there any disagreement?"

No one speaks. "Okay, we're all in agreement. Hugh Barr murdered Eamon Sullivan and Kevin O'Neill." Anne looks away from Paul as she speaks. "I think the next question is why we think he committed the murders. Would anyone like to begin?"

Valerie, who hasn't spoken so far in the deliberations, indicates she's willing to do so. She looks through her notes before responding. "I think he did it for the money. To me, that's clear. Like, he only got involved after the defendant approached him. There's no evidence he intended to kill Sullivan and O'Neill until she offered him money to do so. I know defense counsel spoke about whether he did it because he was in the UVF and hated the IRA, but nobody, as far as I know, proved that—not the police and not the UVF commander. Does anyone think otherwise?"

Again, there's no disagreement. Anne summarizes where they are in their deliberations. "So we agree Hugh Barr committed the murders and that he did so for money. Good. Now, I think this brings us to questions about Gráinne O'Connor. Do we agree she gave him the money and, if so, why did she hire Hugh Barr? What is it that she wanted him to do?"

"Aye, there's the rub," Paul quips.

"Who will begin?" Anne asks.

"Well, I think the answer to the first part of the question is clear," Imogene says. "I think Gráinne O'Connor admitted on the stand that she made deposits to Barr's account. The bigger issue is why. What did she want him to do when she hired him?"

"And what do you think?" Anne asks.

"That's what I'm unsure about. That's why I answered 'undecided' in the poll. She says she never asked Barr to kill anybody. Sometimes I believe her. Other times, I'm not sure."

"Why's that?"

"Well, she knew Barr had killed Sullivan yet she continued to make payments after the killing. She even made another payment after Barr murdered O'Neill. It's difficult to believe she didn't know what was likely to happen to O'Neill, given what happened to Sullivan."

"How do the rest of you feel?"

"How do you feel?" Paul says sharply. "You're good at asking what we think, but you never say what you think."

Anne tries to moderate her voice. "Fair enough, let me share what I believe. Like Imogene, I believe the defendant admitted making payments to Hugh Barr. Maybe she didn't know or care what happened to Sullivan. Maybe she thought Barr might blow up Sullivan's business, or kidnap him, or kneecap him, or something.

"But after Sullivan was murdered, she surely was in no doubt, when she deposited more money, of the risk that Hugh Barr would kill Kevin O'Neill or one of the other bombers. I believe Barr would've killed Sean Lynch and Brigid Maguire, too, had he not committed suicide. But, fortunately, we don't need to go there."

Paul immediately responds. "I agree with you. Is there anyone who doesn't accept that Gráinne O'Connor's guilty?" he asks, as if the answer is a certain "no."

Marta shifts in her seat. She looks Paul in the eye with disdain. "Yes, I don't think she's guilty."

"And why's that?" Paul says.

"I don't have to explain my answer to you," Marta replies softly. "I believe I'm able to weigh the evidence and form my own conclusions."

For the first time Anne senses a potentially serious rift among the jurors. She's not sure if the tension is based on principle or simply the perception that Paul is coming across as a know-it-all. She suggests they break for lunch. This will give her a chance to talk one-on-one with him.

Before the afternoon deliberations continue, Paul apologizes to Marta. "I'm sorry, Marta, if I gave the impression the answer is obvious, and no one should disagree with me. That wasn't my intent."

Marta doesn't acknowledge the apology. She remains silent. Anne realizes Marta is a lot more self-assured than her quiet demeanor implies. Anne reminds the jurors of their morning discussion.

"I believe we're all agreed Hugh Barr murdered Sullivan and O'Neill for money, and Gráinne O'Connor made payments to Hugh Barr. We started to discuss what the defendant had in mind when she entered into this verbal relationship with Barr. I've shared my viewpoint on this, and Paul has added his perspective. It would be good if everyone did so because I believe this is the crux of our deliberations."

Anne doesn't press for input. She knows silence will cause someone to fill the void. Philip does so. "I agree with Anne and Paul. I believe the defendant paid the money to Hugh Barr to have Sullivan and O'Neill killed. It's a simple case of revenge."

Tricia quickly follows. "Yes, I agree with Anne, Paul, and Philip. I think she's guilty."

Marta clears her throat. All heads turn to her. "'It's a simple case of revenge,'" she says, as she looks at Philip. "I don't think so. When the Fountain Street bombers killed her son and husband, did the defendant go out and try to kill them? No. When she sat in court during their trial, did she vent her anger that there's no death penalty? I don't think so. When the bombers were convicted and sent to jail, did the defendant get on with her life? I believe so. Even the prosecution acknowledges this. As far as we know, she was quite content that they were going to spend significant time in jail for their crime."

Marta consults her notes and continues. "Yes, she wrote a successful novel. She got her life together again. There's no indication of revenge. So what changed? Almost ten years after she lost her son and husband, did she just start to seek revenge? I don't think so. Something significant caused the defendant to change. I think it's just as she told us. Justice was undone. The prisoners were released before they'd served their time."

Marta again looks over her notes. "She said she wasn't asking anyone to commit murder. She just wanted the bombers to suffer as she'd suffered. In fact, when defense counsel asked how she felt when she learned that O'Neill had been murdered, she stated, 'I felt sick. I wondered if Hugh Barr was responsible. I tried to shut it out of my mind. Mr. O'Neill had built the bomb that killed Martin and Peter. I didn't want him dead, but in a way I felt he got what he deserved.' She actually testified that she didn't want him dead."

Marta's words are slow and deliberate. "I believe her. She wanted justice, not revenge. I can't convict her any more than I can convict Brendan McArdle. And I can't do that. It all boils down to who we believe, Gráinne O'Connor or Brendan McArdle. I know who I believe."

Silence cloaks the conference room. Anne isn't sure this silence will resolve itself. She's stunned, unsure where to go. Her mind's a blank.

Then Marta continues, reading from her notes. "She said, 'I need justice' . . . 'I need equality' . . . 'If Brendan McArdle is given amnesty from prosecution for the murders of my husband and son, if he can't be sentenced to jail, why am I here?' . . . 'How can the Peace Agreement apply to someone who is not a victim of the Troubles, but not apply to me, someone who has lost everything?'"

Marta closes her notebook. When no one speaks, Anne asks if anyone can recall what the judge said about the Peace Agreement. No one is sure. One by one, they search their notes, or pretend to rummage around.

She isn't surprised when Paul responds. "Judge Sinclair told us as human beings we may feel sympathy for the defendant. However, he said when we decide the case we're not to do so on the basis of sympathy."

He flips back a page and reads his notes. "I'm not sure I understand what I've written. I know the judge talked about the defense arguments related to the Peace Agreement and equality and justice. All I've noted is, 'no basis to dismiss charges.' I guess he meant the Peace Agreement and the Troubles aren't relevant to this case."

None of the jurors respond. Anne turns to Marta. "What do you think about Paul's observations, Marta?"

Marta carefully measures her response. "I think he's right. The judge doesn't want us to make a decision based on our emotions about the defendant. However, I don't think the judge really said anything about the Peace Agreement. He just made a decision that the Peace Agreement gave no basis to dismiss the charges against the defendant."

She pauses to gather her thoughts. "When I say the defendant isn't guilty, it's not a matter of sympathy . . . although, God knows, she has suffered incredibly. I just agree with the defense. How can the Peace Agreement not apply to this case? If it weren't for the Troubles, if it weren't for the Fountain Street bombing, we wouldn't be here. Actually, if it weren't for the Peace Agreement, we wouldn't be here."

"But that's not for us to decide," Paul argues. "That's for the judge, and he has made a decision. Our job is to decide one thing and one thing only. Is Gráinne O'Connor guilty of the murders of Sullivan and O'Neill based on the facts that have been presented to us?"

"I understand," Marta responds, "but those facts include the reality of the Fountain Street bombing. Those facts include the reality of the Peace Agreement, for it was the Peace Agreement that abrogated what the justice system provided when the Fountain Street bombers received their original sentences. Think about it. How can we even consider such an important element as motive if we don't acknowledge the relevance of the Peace Agreement to this case?"

Once again, silence permeates the room, but the shell shock experienced earlier has subsided. Anne says, "I think we need Judge Sinclair to help us here. Maybe we should put the issues on paper and ask him for guidance. However, I'll need your help to word them so he understands the problems. Maybe Marta, Paul, and I can prepare a draft and then we'll all review it."

It takes over an hour to write the issues to everyone's satisfaction. Anne has a headache. She feels drained and suggests they adjourn for the day. "I hope Judge Sinclair will respond to the three questions in the morning so we can resume our deliberations." She asks the other members to think through today's discussions. She hands the questions to one of the jury keepers and asks him to deliver them to Judge Sinclair.

At home, Anne thinks about what she heard today. She knows from the discussion that Paul, Tricia, and Philip are the only ones who believe O'Connor is guilty on both counts. The three of them, Anne, and one other believe Gráinne's guilty of the murder of Kevin O'Neill. For the first time, Anne realizes each charge may spawn a different verdict.

She's surprised five people are undecided in both cases. Imogene admits she's unsure. Helen's struggling with the concept of reasonable doubt, so she probably is undecided. Agnes has said little. She's probably undecided. Anne feels Samuel may have opted to handle the flip chart to avoid sharing his opinions. If she's correct, then Marta, Marcella, Valerie, and Mark feel the defendant isn't guilty in at least one of the cases.

It wouldn't surprise her if at least three of the five jurors who are undecided are women. We tend to be less decisive, at least initially, she thinks. However, she'll have to wait for the first show of hands.

Judge Sinclair is surprised when the jury keeper hands him three notes at the end of the day. He's not sure how to interpret this. Are the jury that close to a decision or are they horribly at loggerheads?

17

September 28, 2005

ANNE DOESN'T SLEEP WELL. On Wednesday morning, she wakes up with a migraine and wishes she didn't have to go to court. She takes two Panadol and makes herself a round of toast. Over breakfast, it dawns on her that she's not responsible for getting a unanimous verdict or, for that matter, any verdict. Her only responsibility is to chair deliberations. When she arrives at court, the jury keeper hands her the responses from Judge Sinclair. To get a clear picture of what everyone is thinking, she decides to take a quick poll before sharing the judge's answers.

"Let's go around the room and share where we stand at this point in time." She remembers Paul's complaint that she never leads. "I'll begin. I vote 'not guilty' on the charge of murdering Sullivan, but 'guilty' on the charge of murdering O'Neill."

To no one's surprise, Marta says "not guilty" on both counts, as does Mark. Agnes, Helen, Samuel, and Imogene indicate they still are undecided on both counts. Paul, Philip, and Tricia vote "guilty" on both counts. Marcella and Valerie split their vote, "not guilty" on the murder of Sullivan, but "guilty" on the murder of O'Neill.

Anne's surprised there are still four jurors undecided on both counts. However, the positive sign is that there has been some movement, albeit small. She feels optimistic that some level of consensus is developing and hopes Judge Sinclair's responses will help the process.

Anne asks one of the jury keepers to make copies of the judge's responses for each juror. She then reads the judge's responses. "On the question related to a unanimous decision, I want you to work hard so there is a unanimous verdict. Don't be rigid. Be willing to let others convince you.

"On the definition of reasonable doubt, reasonable doubt is a standard LESS than certainty. So what is the level necessary to convict? It's the level where, after exercising your best judgment by applying common sense to the facts you've heard, you're reasonably sure the defendant is guilty. If you're not reasonably sure, then you should find the defendant 'not guilty.'

"The issues of how the 1993 Fountain Street bombing and the provisions of the 1998 Peace Agreement apply to the 2002 and 2003 murders of Eamon Sullivan and Kevin O'Neill are beyond the scope of this trial. I understand and accept that the Fountain Street bombing and/or the Peace Agreement had a direct bearing on the actions of the defendant. However, whether that brings the actions of the defendant under the umbrella of the Peace Agreement provisions isn't something I can answer.

"Further, I don't believe this court should interpret the provisions of the Agreement. Even today, not all the provisions of the Agreement have been fully implemented. For that matter, the parties to the Agreement haven't interpreted all of the provisions.

"The laws that apply to criminal cases are complex. However, certain basic principles apply. I want you to take these principles, apply them sincerely to the facts that have been presented to you, and come to a unanimous verdict.

"The defendant is charged with murder. Let me reiterate what constitutes murder. Murder is unlawful killing with malice aforethought, that is, with premeditation. Put as simply as I can, you are being asked to decide whether the killings of Eamon Sullivan and Kevin O'Neill were unlawful and whether the defendant is responsible for their deaths and, in this case, had the intention to have them killed. Put another way, the killings were not an accident and were not incidental to some other objective."

Anne asks the jurors whether they have any comments or questions.

"I think the judge's responses are very clear," Paul says. "It looks like we should concentrate on answering the questions of the four people who are still undecided."

"That makes sense," Anne agrees. "However, before we do that, yesterday Marta explained why she feels the defendant isn't guilty. I would like to give Mark the same opportunity, if he wishes."

"Okay, I will," Mark says. "I guess, like Marta, I believe the defendant's testimony. It's not an issue of the Fountain Street bombing or the Peace Agreement. For me, I believe Mrs. O'Connor when she says she didn't ask Hugh Barr to kill the bombers. I think she probably was overcome with despair when the bombers were released early from prison. She didn't know what to do. It was no longer within the jurisdiction of the courts, so she just sought out someone who would do something. Maybe she was careless or cavalier in how she communicated what she wanted. But there was no intent to kill. As I said, she was in a state of despair. She just wanted justice. Actually, she still wants justice."

Mark hasn't spoken much. He tends to giggle nervously when asked to comment. But Anne is impressed with the clarity of his explanation. Once he gets over his nervousness, he's an excellent communicator.

"I'm not sure it was despair," Paul argues. "I think it was anger."

"Maybe so," Mark says, "but anger and despair aren't the same as revenge. Anger and despair are emotions. Revenge is an act. As I said, I think her motive was to get justice. I don't think she thought through the consequences of what she was asking Hugh Barr to do."

"I wish I could agree with you," Imogene says with a sigh. "But she continued to hire Hugh Barr, even after she knew he'd killed Sullivan. I can understand 'not guilty' in the case of Sullivan, but not in the case of O'Neill."

Marta tries to clarify the point. "The testimony we've heard clearly shows the last two payments to Barr by the defendant were in response to blackmail and had nothing to do with the original contract. When she made payments to Barr prior to the murder of O'Neill and prior to Barr's suicide, she did so under duress. Her motivation derived solely from the fact she was being blackmailed. Remember, unlike the situation with Sullivan, she didn't contact Barr prior to the O'Neill killing. He contacted her. That makes the situations very different."

"That may be," Paul says, "but she showed a callous disregard for life. Even if all you say is true, O'Connor initiated the original contract, and as a result of that contract, Sullivan and O'Neill were murdered. She's like the driver of the getaway car. She's guilty by association."

"But she's not guilty of murder," Marta insists. "The killings were incidental to her objective to make the bombers suffer. They were murdered by Hugh Barr for whatever reason. In his response to our questions, the judge specifically says intent is important. It's not murder if the killing is incidental to some other objective. I don't think it was her intent to kill. She wanted to make their lives miserable. Hugh Barr went too far."

"Okay," Anne says. "Now that we know Judge Sinclair's responses, I think we need to redo our poll on each charge."

"Is that really necessary?" Philip asks.

"Yes, it is. Judge Sinclair has clarified the law. He has answered our questions, so we need to factor his input into our judgment," Paul explains.

"Let's do a quick vote," Anne says. "Then we can decide what we need to do. Sam, for clarity, will you record our vote on the flip chart?"

He turns to a new page, lists the jurors in the order they're seated, and makes a column for each of the charges.

"Let's begin with the first charge, the murder of Eamon Sullivan," Anne says. The jurors split 8–4 with Anne, Marta, Agnes, Marcella, Helen, Valerie, Imogene, and Mark voting "not guilty." Simpson's surprised by the result. She hadn't expected three of the four undecided jurors to vote in the negative. Perhaps Mark and Marta's arguments are bearing fruit. She's glad everyone has a definitive position on the issue.

"Now, let's vote on the murder of Kevin O'Neill."

The vote is 7–5, but this time Marta, Agnes, Helen, Imogene, and Mark are the only ones to vote "not guilty." The result is more in line with what Simpson anticipated. She doesn't expect Marta, Agnes, or

Mark to change positions. Helen and Imogene may or may not be convinced to change their vote.

Given the outcome, she asks Agnes, Helen, Imogene, and Samuel to share what moved them from "undecided."

Imogene speaks first. "I feel the defendant should have known O'Neill might be killed, once Sullivan was killed. I don't see it makes a difference whether O'Connor paid money because of blackmail or due to the contract. However, when she first hired Barr, I'm not sure she knew, or even thought, Barr would kill Sullivan. I guess I'm prepared to believe her and give her the benefit of the doubt. In other words, I'm not reasonably sure she intended to commit murder."

Agnes and Helen's viewpoints are similar to that expressed by Imogene. Samuel indicates he finds it difficult to split his vote. He feels O'Connor is guilty of the murder of O'Neill, and if she's guilty of one, then she's guilty of all.

Anne feels they're making progress and suggests they break for lunch.

By the end of the day, Anne wonders whether they're really at a point of impasse on the verdicts. The afternoon's four hours of heated discussion bring minimal movement. But just before she calls it quits for the day, Philip, who tends to speak without thinking, stuns the room with an unexpected observation. With deliberations going nowhere, he throws up his arms and asks, "Does it matter if we find her 'not guilty' in the Sullivan killing? As long as we find her 'guilty' of murdering O'Neill, finding her 'not guilty' of murdering Sullivan isn't going to make one whit of difference to O'Connor's sentence. Really, it's not. She's going to get her due whether we find her guilty of one murder or two."

Anne and Paul are appalled at such a perspective. Marta seethes with anger. They argue principle shouldn't become the victim of expediency, but Philip is pleased with his new notoriety. He maintains his argument is logical. He suggests they go home and think about his observation. At 5:30 p.m., Simpson adjourns discussions for the day.

On the evening of the jury's second full day of deliberations, Gráinne calls Pascal to find out what's going on. He explains that he has no access to the jury deliberations, but from his perspective, the longer the jury is out the greater the likelihood there's disagreement among the jurors. He sees this as a positive sign.

"But what happens if they can't reach agreement?" she says.

"Then we may be in for a retrial, and that probably favors your long-term acquittal."

"But I don't want to go through another trial," she emphasizes. "I just want it to be over."

18

September 29, 2005

AS SHE DRIVES TO THE COURT, Anne wonders how the jury members will react to Philip's comment. She doesn't have to wait long to get her answer. When she asks them whether one more night's contemplation has changed anyone's mind, only Philip indicates he's prepared to vote "not guilty" on the Sullivan murder charge. Tricia, Paul, and Sam stick with "guilty."

Anne asks Samuel to conduct one final poll on both charges for the record. This confirms the 9–3 "not guilty" vote on the Sullivan murder charge. The vote on the O'Neill murder charge is 8–4 in favor of "guilty." Only Imogene switches her vote.

Marta's pleased with the steady movement toward a unanimous "not guilty" verdict in the Sullivan case. However, she's troubled that, each time they vote, one more juror moves to the "guilty" side in the O'Neill case. She senses if she's going to stop and reverse this trend, she must intervene strongly.

"I know this may be an uphill battle, but I want to restate why I feel we shouldn't find the defendant guilty on either charge. Even though Gráinne paid money, except for Tricia, Paul, and Samuel, we don't believe Mrs. O'Connor knew Hugh Barr was going to murder Eamon Sullivan. Isn't that right?"

"That's how we voted," Anne says.

"Well, it doesn't logically follow that just because she continued to pay money, she believed Hugh Barr might kill again. She testified the second and third payment had nothing to do with the original agreement. She made the payments because she was blackmailed."

"It doesn't matter why she made the payments," Paul argues. "She made them, and Kevin O'Neill got his brains blown out."

An awkward silence fills the room. Anne is about to intervene, but Marta addresses Paul. "Do you know what it's like to be threatened by the IRA?" She waits for an answer. When there's none, she continues. "Well, I do. In 1979, the IRA accused my brother of being a tout. He denied it, but one night a gang of young volunteers stripped him, tied him to a lamppost, and tarred and feathered him. Then, they knee-capped him. He has walked with a limp and a cane ever since. Apparently, he screamed and screamed, but no one went near him. No one admitted who'd done it. That's what it means to feel threatened. That's what it means to be afraid.

"I have one question for each of you. Do you know beyond a reasonable doubt it wasn't fear of the IRA that caused Gráinne O'Connor to make those final payments?"

"Not beyond a reasonable doubt," Helen says.

"Then how can we find her guilty of murdering anyone?"

In spite of Marta's plea, no one offers to vote differently. When further discussion fails to achieve consensus, Anne asks the jury keepers to communicate to Judge Sinclair that the jury is ready to render its verdict.

A little after ten o'clock, the twelve jurors file into the jury box. None of them look toward Gráinne, so she finds it difficult to anticipate their decision. She feels tightness in her stomach muscles, her lips are dry, and her palms clammy. She crosses her legs and clasps her hands around her knees but can't get comfortable. She shifts and reshifts her body. She's glad when Sinclair stops playing with the papers on his bench and addresses the jury. "Would the forewoman please rise?"

Gráinne fights for breath. The agony of the unknown is excruciating.

Anne stands. She runs her tongue across her lips. She quickly glances at the information on the page she's holding.

"This is case number 4052. In the matter of count number one, the murder of Eamon Sullivan, have you reached a verdict on which you are all agreed?" the clerk asks.

"No, My Lord, we've not," Anne says.

The judge nods at the clerk.

"In the matter of count number two, the murder of Kevin O'Neill, have you reached a verdict on which you are all agreed?"

"No, My Lord, we've not."

Gráinne tenses at the thought of a retrial. She wonders what will happen next. Judge Sinclair quickly answers the question. "Members of the jury, you've deliberated steadily for a little over two days. The prosecution, from the beginning of this trial, indicated the nature of the trial was complex. I'm not surprised it's taking time to reach consensus.

"However, the best of all outcomes is a unanimous verdict. Therefore, I'm asking you to continue your deliberations until you've reached a unanimous verdict. There may come a time when I can accept a majority verdict. I reiterate that to find the defendant guilty as charged, you must be satisfied beyond any reasonable doubt. Review the facts. Listen to each other. Continue to work diligently."

"His Lordship doesn't want much," Tricia says, when the jury members return to their room.

"We'll be here all weekend," Philip says.

Anne tries to address the deflated spirits. "Look, we've worked hard. When we started, we were divided, pretty much fifty-fifty. Discussion has moved us closer to consensus. I don't know if we can get there, but I sense the judge may accept a majority verdict. We need to do this for the Sullivan and O'Neill families and for the defendant. We owe it to them to do the best we can to provide justice. Let me try to summarize where we are."

Mark interrupts her. "What do you think he means by a 'majority verdict'?"

Paul responds. "I believe it's a verdict on which at least ten of us agree. I know it's not a simple majority."

"That would be too simple," Mark says and giggles.

There are a few smiles. Anne realizes it's Mark's way of releasing nervous tension, the disappointment of having to continue deliberations. She takes control. "Okay, let's begin with the murder of Eamon Sullivan. We all agree Hugh Barr killed Sullivan after Mrs. O'Connor asked him to help her get justice. We all agree she paid Barr. The issue is whether O'Connor meant Barr to kill him. Let's go round the table and share what we believe. Marta, will you begin?"

"There's no issue for me. Mrs. O'Connor is a victim. She lost everything: her husband and her only child. After she found closure with the conviction of the bombers, the old wound was ripped open. It was like a dagger plunged in and twisted slowly, every waking moment. That's what she wanted for Sullivan and O'Neill. Not death, but a constant reminder of their unfathomable cruelty. She's not guilty of murder."

"Agnes?" Simpson asks.

"Not guilty. I don't believe she wanted him to die."

Marcella, Helen, Valerie, Imogene, Philip, Anne, and Mark agree in quick succession. Tricia feels the pressure. "I guess if I've to choose who to believe, I'll go with O'Connor rather than McArdle. I'll vote 'not guilty.'"

"That's a girl," Marta whispers. Paul and Samuel stay silent.

"Well, boys?" Anne asks.

"Okay, I'll go with 'not guilty,'" Samuel says.

"Not for me," says Paul. "I don't believe McArdle, but I look at the preponderance of evidence: the meeting with a known UVF member, the payment of money, the fact she did nothing after Sullivan's murder to help the police and continued to pay money. For me, she's guilty."

Anne asks Samuel to record each vote on the chart. This confirms the 11–1 "not guilty" vote. "Thank you. Let's take fifteen minutes, and then we'll tackle the Kevin O'Neill case."

Anne resumes the discussion. "If I'm correct, when we last voted, all of us, except Marta, Agnes, Helen, and Mark, think the defendant's guilty of the murder of Kevin O'Neill. Why is that? If O'Connor's not guilty of the murder of Eamon Sullivan, how can she be guilty of the murder of Kevin O'Neill? Let's go in a different order. Sam, we'll begin with you."

Samuel blushes. He didn't anticipate going first. "The difference is the defendant, even if she didn't want Barr to murder O'Neill, knew this was a risk after he killed Sullivan. She continued to pay money. She even paid after O'Neill was killed. It's too difficult to distinguish between the original contract and the subsequent events. It was the original contract that led to the death of O'Neill, not the blackmail."

Philip, Paul, Anne, and Tricia concur. Mark retains his "not guilty" stance. "I don't understand how she can be innocent of one and guilty of the other," he argues. Anne's not surprised, since Mark has voted "not guilty" on all ten votes.

Imogene, Valerie, and Marcella maintain their "guilty" vote. Simpson knows Marta will stay with her "not guilty" position. She looks at Agnes and Helen.

Helen says, "I've struggled with 'reasonable doubt,' but I see Samuel's point about the payments. I'm willing to go with 'guilty.'"

Agnes hesitates. She hates to go against Marta. Paul sees the vacillation. He wastes no time. "Well, Agnes, you can vote 'guilty' and we're finished or 'not guilty' and there'll be a new trial." It's enough to persuade Agnes to change her vote.

"On count number one, the murder of Eamon Sullivan, have the jury reached a verdict on which they are all agreed?" the clerk asks when the court reconvenes.

"No, My Lord, we haven't," Anne says. There's a slight murmur from the public gallery.

"Have the jury reached a verdict on which at least ten of them have agreed?"

"Yes."

"What's the verdict?"

"Not guilty."

An audible gasp rises in the court. The clerk requests silence. Gráinne tries to stay controlled. She steals a glance at her parents and looks quickly at Pascal. For the first time, she feels hope. The clerk's voice interrupts her thoughts.

"In the matter of count number two, the murder of Kevin O'Neill, have the jury reached a verdict on which they are all agreed?"

"No, My Lord, we have not."

"Have the jury reached a verdict on which at least ten of them have agreed?"

"Yes."

"What's the verdict?"

"Guilty."

Gráinne's mother lets out a loud "no!" and begins to sob.

The clerk asks for silence. "What is the split?" he asks.

"Ten to two," Anne says.

Sinclair's amazed at the findings of the jury. The verdict isn't one he considered. The betting among his colleagues was reputed to be even for conviction on both counts and even for acquittal on both counts. He doubts anyone bet on a split verdict.

When the buzz subsides, Judge Sinclair continues. "The jury having found the defendant guilty of the murder of Kevin O'Neill, I hereby sentence Gráinne O'Connor to life imprisonment. It's now my responsibility to decide the tariff, or minimum period of imprisonment, the defendant must serve. I'll consider the evidence presented in this case and the law that governs this and similar cases and make a decision as rapidly as possible."

Before dismissing the jury, Sinclair publicly thanks the members for giving up their personal time to support the judicial process, their attentiveness in court, their patience with the resolution of legal issues and, most of all, for the hard work involved in delivering an acceptable verdict. He tells Anne Simpson he's indebted to her for her leadership as forewoman and her work to achieve the necessary measure of unanimity.

This is the moment Gráinne's parents have dreaded: waiting to face their only daughter after a "guilty" judgment. Her mother is overcome with grief. Her father tries to stay strong for her mother's sake, but he's not sure if he can keep his emotions in check once he sees Gráinne.

From the day Gráinne had told them about her problem, they had ceased to live for themselves. Everything they did was designed to show Gráinne their unconditional love. Not a day passed without at least a phone conversation. When they were alone, they speculated incessantly about why this had happened, about what they could've done differently to stop it happening. How did they not know? Why did they not suspect something significant had changed in their daughter's life?

The months leading up to the trial had been a roller coaster, hope climbing as Pascal explained the case was circumstantial, there were no witnesses, and his optimism that Brendan McArdle would not testify, eliminating the so-called confession. But just as their optimism crested, they had to face the gut-wrenching decision by the DPP to give McArdle immunity. Everything seemed upside down. The person who had planned the Fountain Street bombing that killed their son-in-law and only grandchild was being treated with kid gloves, while their daughter, who had lost everything, now faced life in prison.

Pascal helps Gráinne into the defense chambers. He's accompanied by Herschel Solomon and William Litton. Her eyes are red, her skin pallid. She sits down immediately and rests her head and arms on the table. She closes her eyes. Her mother puts her arms around Gráinne, but says nothing. She doesn't know what to say.

Solomon breaks the silence. "First of all, I'm sorry for this outcome. It's not what we wanted. But amid the disappointment, I feel there's a ray of light. I know it's faint and flickers with uncertainty, but it is there, nevertheless. The 'not guilty' verdict on the Sullivan charge is huge. To be found 'not guilty' of one charge and yet be found 'guilty' on the second charge raises all sorts of issues that we'll address on appeal. So please don't give up hope. All three of us will continue to work tirelessly for a better outcome."

Gráinne lifts her head and rubs her eyes with her fingers. She searches for Solomon. "Herschel, I want you to know you did a wonderful job. I've nobody to blame but myself. I made choices, and now I must bear the consequences."

She forces a smile. "I was so excited when I heard the 'not guilty' verdict. I couldn't believe it. I think it confused my thinking. For some reason, I just expected the second verdict to be the same as the first. When it came down 'guilty,' I was devastated. I just felt numb. At the moment, it's hard to comprehend. I can't think about what this means."

Pascal speaks. "Unfortunately, Gráinne, it means some more time in prison. It will take the judge one or two months to decide on the tariff; that's the minimum time you must serve before being eligible for parole. But as Herschel said, we'll begin the appeal process immediately."

"Can Gráinne get bail pending the appeal process?" her father asks.

"That would be unusual in a life sentence. I'm not optimistic we can get that."

"What do you think the minimum sentence will be?" Gráinne's mother asks.

Pascal had been dreading this question, for most tariffs in life sentence cases are twelve years and up. He decides to hedge. "That's not an easy one to answer, for the process is quite complex. The judge has to review the evidence; he'll look at what has happened in similar cases, and he'll consider whether there are any aggravating or mitigating circumstances. I'll meet with you in the next few weeks and share with you what I think may happen. I'll give you my best guess."

"Thank you, Herschel. You've been so supportive."

19

October 2005

FOR THE NEXT FOUR WEEKS, Sinclair works steadily to document the verdict. He carefully reviews the charges, the evidence presented by prosecution and defense counsels, and the witness statements. He studies case law and the advice of the Sentencing Advisory Panel to the Court of Appeal. Sinclair hasn't any doubt that however he handles the sentencing phase, there's likely to be an appeal by defense counsel.

On Monday, October 24, he issues the formal trial verdict. There's been much speculation among the public, since the "guilty" verdict, as to whether he'll sentence Gráinne O'Connor to jail. In the legal community, the speculation's not whether O'Connor will go to jail, but how Sinclair will decide the minimum period of imprisonment for an adult mandatory life sentence prisoner. Most betting says the sentence will be at the lower end of the spectrum, typically in the range of twelve to fourteen years.

Once again, the public, family members, and the press pack the courtroom. Gráinne notices Eamon Sullivan's parents aren't present. She doesn't see Sean Lynch or Brigid Maguire. She doesn't feel as on edge as she did waiting for the jury verdict. Pascal has briefed her on what to expect.

Sinclair provides copies of his judgment to legal counsel.

IN THE CROWN COURT IN NORTHERN IRELAND
REGINA -V- GRÁINNE O'CONNOR, CASE NO: 4052

SINCLAIR H

[1] Gráinne O'Connor was acquitted at Belfast Crown Court on 29 September 2005 of the murder of Eamon Sullivan following a trial lasting approximately three weeks.

[2] Gráinne O'Connor was convicted at Belfast Crown Court on 29 September 2005 of the murder of Kevin O'Neill by a 10–2 verdict of the jury. The evidence presented at trial identified that someone using a 9mm Browning automatic murdered Kevin O'Neill on the Lower Limestone Road. Mr. O'Neill died from injuries caused by two wounds to the head. In his evidence at trial, Detective Inspector Rory Higgins advised that a Mr. Hugh Barr killed O'Neill in March 2003, just as he had previously murdered Eamon Sullivan in March 2002. Higgins testified that Barr subsequently committed suicide sometime in 2004 using the gun he'd used to kill both Sullivan and O'Neill. A forensics expert confirmed the use of this gun in all three deaths.

[3] Evidence given at trial, including the testimony of the defendant, proved that Gráinne O'Connor paid Hugh Barr to harm both Eamon Sullivan and Kevin O'Neill. The question the jury had to decide was whether the defendant knew that "harming" the victims might mean their death. If so, the defendant, Gráinne O'Connor, would be just as guilty of murder as the triggerman, Hugh Barr. The jury was unsure whether the defendant knew that Barr would murder the first victim, Sullivan. However, with the second victim, O'Neill, the jury decided that, based on her knowledge that Barr had already murdered Sullivan, the defendant knew it was possible, and in fact likely, that Barr would murder O'Neill or one of the other Fountain Street bombers. The jury, therefore, decided the defendant is guilty of the murder of Kevin O'Neill.

[4] Following the conviction of the accused by the jury, I imposed upon her a sentence of life imprisonment, which is the only sentence

available to the court. The court must now determine when the release provisions that govern life sentences shall apply to Mrs. O'Connor. That means, in effect, I must set a minimum term of imprisonment, which she must serve before she may be considered for release. At the expiration of this period, it shall be for the Life Sentence Review Commissioners to consider whether release is appropriate. Even if released, the accused will be subject to supervision, and her subsequent actions will determine the need for a recall to prison for the rest of her natural life.

[5] The minimum period of imprisonment must satisfy the requirements of retribution and deterrence, having regard for the seriousness of the offence. There has been much debate by the legislature, Lord Chief Justices, and the Sentencing Advisory Panel in its guidance to the Court of Appeal as to what is the proper minimum term to be served by a mandatory life sentence prisoner. Since about 2000, in order to meet the requirements of retribution and general deterrence, the minimum term to be served by a person convicted of murder has generally been set at 14 years. However, in 2002, the Lord Chief Justice of England and Wales issued a Practice Statement replacing the fixed 14-year starting point with a normal starting point of 12 years and a higher starting point of 16 years. The higher starting point applies when the crime is especially serious, such as when the killing is a contract killing, the killing is politically motivated, the victim is a child, or the offender committed multiple murders. These starting points are then increased or reduced due to aggravating or mitigating factors. While Northern Ireland is a separate jurisdiction from England and Wales, the Practice Statement is of enormous practical significance in Northern Ireland courts.

[6] Aggravating factors can include the fact that the killing was planned, the use of a firearm, dismemberment of the body, and the offender's prior record. Mitigating factors can include the intention to harm rather than kill, a lack of premeditation, the offender's age, and clear evidence of remorse.

[7] I come now to deal with the application of these principles to

the case of Gráinne O'Connor. Great weight must be accorded to the views of such distinguished authorities as the four judges of the Crown Court of Northern Ireland, the Lord Chief Justice of England and Wales, and the Sentencing Advisory Panel. It also is my responsibility, as far as I can, to ensure consistency in the application of the principles outlined above.

[8] In the case of *Regina v. Graham*, McLaughlin J wrote: "For my part, I believe Northern Ireland should set suggested minimum periods which are significantly higher than those suggested in England and Wales in order to reflect the continuing sense of despair and revulsion voiced in the community by the families of victims whose lives have been destroyed by those who kill deliberately or do so as a result of inflicting grievous bodily harm on others. It is incumbent on the courts to recognize that for many families, the death of a loved one at the hands of another creates pain and disruption to their well-being often for the remainder of their lives. The prospect, or reality, of seeing the killer freed, or seeing the freed killer, in 12–14 years in some cases is considered an affront and brings the criminal justice system into disrepute in many quarters."

[9] I, too, am concerned that a lenient sentence, in the case before me, will send the wrong message—a message it's all right to take the law into one's own hands or that murder is justified if the offender is motivated by the desire to get revenge (or justice). Imagine our already violent society if we permit the victims of the Troubles to kill those responsible for their suffering, without consequences. I cannot allow the desire for justice to become the justification for murder. Considering the fact that the murder of Kevin O'Neill was a contract killing, the higher tariff of 16 years is applicable as a starting point.

[10] However, that's merely the starting point. The term must be varied upwards, or downwards, to consider aggravating or mitigating features. The fact the killing was planned and the use of a firearm are certainly aggravating factors. But, given this was a contract killing, I believe that the higher starting point of 16 years already incorporates these factors.

[11] In this case, the key issue is whether there are mitigating factors and, if so, to what degree they should modify the starting point. I don't see any evidence of remorse, and the offender has maintained a position throughout the trial that she's not guilty of the offence. However, two disturbing and significant ironies have emerged during testimony.

[12] The first is that Mrs. O'Connor is clearly a victim of the Troubles. In fact, there isn't a more perfect example of a victim than Mrs. O'Connor. To paraphrase Judge McLaughlin, those who kill deliberately have destroyed her life. As noted by McLaughlin, "It's incumbent on the courts to recognize that for many families the death of a loved one at the hands of another creates pain and disruption to their well-being often for the remainder of their lives."

[13] The second irony is even more troubling to me. Again, I reference Judge McLaughlin: "The prospect, or reality, of seeing the killer freed, or seeing the freed killer, in 12–14 years in some cases is considered an affront and brings the criminal justice system into disrepute in many quarters." Mrs. O'Connor is experiencing that reality. In fact, she has seen the killers of her son and husband freed, not in 12–14 years, but after only six years. To add insult to injury, the architect of the bombing that killed Mrs. O'Connor's son and husband has served no time and will not serve any time for his crimes. She has not only experienced the reality of seeing the killers freed, but also she has experienced the affront of seeing the killers of her husband and son sitting in court in front of her as free people every day during this trial. This irony is a direct result of the Peace Agreement. Such, one might say, is the price of peace.

[14] I'm faced with setting the minimum period of imprisonment for Gráinne O'Connor. Given the early release of the killers of her son and husband after six years, and the fact that the architect of that killing won't serve any time in prison for the killings, there's an argument that Mrs. O'Connor shouldn't serve any more than six years. However, the jury found Mrs. O'Connor guilty of murder, and that verdict requires punishment and retribution at a level that will uphold the value and sanctity of life and deter anyone else who might think of copying

Mrs. O'Connor. As I stated during the trial, I do not believe it is the function of the Crown Court to interpret the Peace Agreement and, in particular, to determine if the early release provisions of the Peace Agreement have application to this case. I am well aware my decision may be a ground for the defence to appeal both the verdict and the sentence. Mrs. O'Connor has been sentenced to life imprisonment, and I order the release provisions will not begin to operate for 12 years. This, I believe, balances the need for a deterrent with the mitigating factors to which I've referred.

[15] Before I conclude, I wish to commend both prosecution and defence counsel for the professional manner in which you have executed your responsibilities. In particular, your handling of the legal issues on how the Peace Agreement applies to this particular case properly recognizes these issues must be addressed by a higher court.

A general silence greets Judge Sinclair's decision that life imprisonment will require Gráinne to serve a minimum of twelve years in prison before she can be considered for release. However, as soon as Sinclair vacates the bench, the noise level rises to a crescendo as the public pushes for the exit doors, and reporters scurry to call their offices and stations with the judge's decision. Gráinne looks in vain for her family. They're hidden in the melee of bodies. Two prison officers take her back to the offices being used by defense counsel. Pascal has arranged a brief consultation with his client before she's driven back to prison to resume her sentence.

Gráinne's pleased to see Pascal and her parents. Her mother and father hold her tight as they fight back tears.

"Well, Gráinne, it's over. How do you feel?" Pascal asks her.

"I'm okay, I guess. You prepared me well for what to expect. It could be worse. When Judge Sinclair set the initial bar at sixteen years, I was afraid I was in for a much longer sentence."

"You're right. However, the significant recognition of mitigating factors by the judge is good. It gives me hope our appeal will be successful.

To be honest, I had hoped he might go for something closer to six or eight years, but Judge Sinclair isn't one to rock the boat. He doesn't want to be reversed on appeal. Unfortunately, the appeal itself is likely to be a lengthy process. I doubt there will be any quick decision on how the Peace Agreement should apply to your case, if at all. I expect the appeal may go all the way to the House of Lords. Politicians wrote the Peace Agreement, so it is likely politicians will have to interpret it. However, we should get an answer in a lot less than twelve years! I'll visit you as soon as we settle on an appeal strategy."

In the prosecution's chambers, Martin Mulligan and David Ingram meet with Marie O'Neill. Mulligan and Ingram had expected a minimum sentence of fourteen years, but twelve years is close enough for them. Mulligan asks O'Neill how she feels about the terms of the sentence.

"I guess I'm all right with it. I would like it to be longer. To me, she's a traitor. She killed one of her own, someone who spent his life fighting for a free Ireland. However, she's going to jail. It's what she deserves, although she'll have it easier than Kevin did in the Maze. Just don't let her win the appeal."

"We won't," David Ingram assures her, but Mulligan is less certain than his young understudy. He understands O'Neill's anger and pain. She has lost her husband. But he's bothered by her total lack of compassion for O'Connor. Why is O'Connor's loss of her husband and son any less than O'Neill's loss of her husband? Is what Kevin O'Neill did less heinous than what O'Connor did? He doesn't think so.

Brendan reads about Gráinne's sentence in the *Irish Times*. He reads the article repeatedly. He's both relieved and troubled. He's glad she's off the streets. He, Sean, and Brigid are safer. But his thoughts return to the troubled Gráinne he met in Newcastle. He replays the walk along the beach, the confession, and his words of comfort. The words of comfort predominate. A feeling of pride assuages the guilt of deceit, pride in how well he did what he had to do. For Brendan, this is the bottom line. This is what matters.

Pascal's optimistic that the House of Lords will hear an appeal eventually. For this reason, he's interested to see how the leading English papers report the sentence. Most simply give a factual account of the outcome of the trial, without comment, but to his delight, one newspaper leads its editorial section with a headline in bold print, "UNEQUAL JUSTICE UNDER THE LAW."

The editor poses the question, "Do we not have equal justice under the law?" He answers this with a chilling critique of *Regina versus Gráinne O'Connor*. It's the first article Bourke puts in his newly created appeal folder.

20

November 2005

Gráinne's taken to Hydebank Wood Prison for in June 2004, all women prisoners previously held at the Mourne House, Maghaberry, were transferred to Hydebank. Women prisoners now reside in Ash House. The reception process goes smoothly and, knowing what to expect, Gráinne isn't as intimidated by the strip search.

The prison is smaller than Maghaberry. There are four landings with fourteen cells on each landing. The cells are similar to those in -Maghaberry, but with one disturbing difference. There are no toilets in the cells. Each landing has a separate shower room with toilets and washing facilities. During periods of lockdown, toilet access is controlled by an electronic unlock system. When a prisoner presses a buzzer, it registers on a panel in the control room. Security then unlocks the cell door. To Gráinne's dismay, only one woman is allowed out of her cell at a time. She wonders what happens if there's a genuine multiple emergency. The reception officer tells Gráinne this deficiency will be corrected in 2006.

Because she could be in Hydebank for a considerable time, Gráinne is more interested in the rules than she was when she arrived at Maghaberry. She eagerly studies what she's allowed to have in her cell, the daily routine, the visitation schedule, the recreational facilities, and whom she will be allowed to mix with. She's surprised to discover her fellow inmates have been convicted not only of serious crimes like murder and drug-related offenses, but even for something as simple as nonpayment of fines. Their ages range from eighteen to sixty. Even more surprising, thirty percent of the inmates are foreign nationals.

Most prisoners wear tracksuits, casual trousers, or jeans. She's allowed sixteen tops, eight bottoms, and two jackets, three sets of nightwear, a dressing gown, and underwear. She isn't allowed hoodies, vest tops, baseball caps, or gel-filled bras, and her belts must be no larger than one inch. She cannot have her own toiletries, perfume, or makeup. These, including sanitary towels, are provided by the prison. She's allowed to wear trainers, slippers, or flip flops. She can have a watch, a limited amount of jewelry, and whatever money she wants to use on phone credits or in the prison shop. However, she cannot hold the money on her person—it's kept in a personal account.

Gráinne finds the first few days are like starting school or a new job. Under the induction process, she gets quick visits from the prison governor, a nurse, and even a probation officer. She thinks the probation officer visit is odd; given her sentence, she's unlikely to need a probation officer anytime soon. However, she quickly discovers that almost half the residents are in custody awaiting trial and that the majority of sentences for inmates are less than four years.

She finds the atmosphere more relaxed than she had expected. The majority of the guards are women, and they don't wear a uniform. Almost every member of the staff she interacts with asks her what she did to end up in Hydebank. She's pretty sure they already know, but it's a way of initiating conversation. They take time to tell her what education courses and recreational opportunities are available. Each landing has a dining and recreation room. So far, although there is a multi-choice menu, Gráinne hasn't found the food great. A staffer explains that, after about four weeks, she'll move from the committal landing to another landing.

The most disappointing news for Gráinne is that she may have only one family visit per week. She can keep in touch with family and friends by writing letters or by phone. So far, she finds the days long. Her cell is unlocked for about ten hours during the day, but she's not sure what to do with this time.

Herschel Solomon, William Litton, and Pascal meet to discuss the grounds they'll argue in their submission to the Court of Appeal.

Pascal speaks first. "I think we could try to argue that none of the evidence proves Gráinne had the intent to kill O'Neill when she hired Hugh Barr. However, the jury didn't buy this, maybe because she admitted in testimony that she wanted Hugh Barr to harm O'Neill. She talked about tarring and feathering and kneecapping. I think the court may rule that she meant to cause grievous bodily harm, and that's enough for her to be guilty of murder. It's well established in case law that the act or omission of the defendant need not be a substantial cause of the death of the victim for the defendant to be held guilty of murder. The prosecution only has to show the acts of the defendant significantly contributed to the death."

"I follow and agree with your line of thought," Litton says. "But couldn't we argue that the O'Neill killing had nothing to do with Gráinne's original contract with Hugh Barr? She didn't contact Barr at all after the Sullivan murder. She didn't follow up to see why nothing was happening to the other bombers. I think this is significant. It was Barr who approached Gráinne and, in effect, made a new contract by blackmailing her. There's a significant difference between paying money to have someone harmed versus paying money to avoid being harmed. In considering the two murder charges against Gráinne, the court failed to recognize this subtle but important change in circumstances, and the judge failed to properly instruct the jurors."

"I think that's an important argument if we challenge the conviction," Solomon says, "but there's an even more important ground for appeal. Judge Sinclair failed to give direction to the jury on the issue of manslaughter. Particularly with the jury struggling to find consensus, the jury should have been instructed that they could find the defendant guilty on a lesser charge of manslaughter. The judge not only didn't explain this to the jury, but he pushed the jury to find consensus. That's where your argument is relevant, William. If Gráinne were to be found guilty of manslaughter, and the judge accepted that the payment made prior to the O'Neill killing was in response to blackmail and not a continuation of the original contract, he might sentence her to one to four years. That's a lot less than twelve years. Of course, if he doesn't accept that argument and rules the killing was barely indistinguishable from murder, he could sentence her to eight to fifteen years."

"I agree the manslaughter option is the way to go," Pascal says.

"What about appealing the sentence as well as the verdict?" Litton asks.

"I think that's also worth doing. We should argue that the provisions of the Peace Agreement do apply to this case. Even though O'Neill was killed after the date of the Peace Agreement, I don't see how anyone can say this case has nothing to do with the Troubles, and, in fact, what developed after the Peace Agreement was the direct result of the Agreement. Judge Sinclair acknowledged the likelihood of an appeal to a higher court. I don't know if he thought it was a good basis for an appeal, but I believe this is where we stand our best chances of getting the sentence reduced. I understand how Sinclair arrived at twelve years, but it just doesn't seem fair. I think the problem is rooted in the right to equal treatment under the law."

As her solicitor, Pascal has more opportunity to visit Gráinne than her family, and he is her first visitor from outside Hydebank.

"I want to keep you informed," he says. "I'll try not to inundate you with too much legalese, but I want you to understand what we are doing and why we're doing it. First, you just can't appeal a conviction or sentence because you feel like it. If that were allowed, everyone would appeal. The various acts that govern appeals state they must be based on questions of law and fact, and an appeal will only be allowed with leave of the Court of Appeal or, in your case, if Judge Sinclair grants a certificate that the case is appropriate for appeal. From the trial, you won't be surprised to hear he has already indicated he's willing to issue a certificate."

"That's good news. So what happens next?"

"Before I go there, let me share our thought process. We believe we can appeal both the conviction and the sentence. Obviously, it would be preferable for the court to throw out the conviction, but our best chance may be to get your sentence reduced.

"The rules for appeal provide that only certain types of evidence may be presented. For example, we can't retry the case on evidence already presented to the jury. However, the court will hear any evidence which wasn't adduced in the trial and where there's a reasonable explanation for the failure to present this evidence at the trial. We believe the judge erred in not advising the jury that they could make a verdict of manslaughter instead of murder. I don't want to go into all the technicalities, but the good news is a manslaughter verdict usually carries a lesser sentence. However, the bad news is there would be a new trial, and the new jury could bring back a verdict of murder. Anyway, what's important at this stage is to get the current conviction quashed, for the prosecution may be willing to accept a plea rather than go through another trial."

"I don't want to go through another trial."

"I understand. Let me share our thoughts on appealing the sentence, that is, the twelve years. We believe the Peace Agreement should have been applied to your case, but Judge Sinclair ruled that the Agreement, or more precisely the interpretation of the Agreement, was beyond the authority of the Crown Court. He was quite happy to punt the issue up the line. If the Court of Appeal accepts the Peace Agreement is relevant to your case, we are hopeful the sentence might be substantially reduced."

"When will this happen?"

"That's difficult to project because once the court accepts the appeal, we'll have to argue our case before the court, and the prosecution will argue against us. As you know, it takes time to prepare arguments, but we've submitted our appeal. Now we must wait and see what happens. I'll keep you informed."

Pascal asks Gráinne how she has settled in and if there is anything he can do for her or her family. He assures her that Solomon, Litton, and he will do all in their power to expedite the appeal.

21

December 2005

ALTHOUGH THE AFTERNOON is bitter, rivulets of sweat trickle down Mrs. Sullivan's chest as she enters Hydebank Wood Prison in South Belfast. She tries to shut out memories of her visits to Eamon in the Maze Prison and concentrate on the purpose of her visit. She has come early, knowing she'll have to enroll in the visitor system.

She shows a copy of her driving license to the security officer, has her photograph taken, and her index finger scanned for future proof of identity. She's not sure she'll ever need it again. The officer hands her a pass that shows her photograph and identifies Gráinne O'Connor's name and number. It also gives the number of the table she will use in the visitors' room. He gives her a token for a locker and asks her to place all personal belongings such as wallets, purses, and keys in it.

Mrs. Sullivan enters the visiting area through an electronically controlled door, and a metal detector before a female officer gives her a quick body search. Then, to her surprise, she's instructed to stand on a mark on the floor while a dog checks for illegal substances. Finally, after the guard verifies her pass against details on a computer screen, she's admitted to the main visiting room.

Gráinne's happy to have a visitor. Hydebank isn't as comfortable as Maghaberry, and she finds the days long. There's limited access to the library, and it has only one computer with no access to the Internet. She feels this has a lot to do with her lack of motivation to resume writing her novel. She's very surprised to see Mrs. Sullivan.

"I hope you don't mind me visiting you," Mrs. Sullivan says as

Gráinne shakes her hand and sits across the table. "I was at Mass on Sunday, and Father talked about a season of new birth. Now that the trial's over, I thought about this maybe being a time of new birth for my husband and me, to put Eamon's death behind us, and to move on with our lives. Then I started to think about you and realized you'd be spending your first Christmas in prison."

Mrs. Sullivan tries to collect her thoughts. She notices Gráinne listening intently. "Gráinne, I want you to know I bear no ill will toward you. I don't know if you intended Hugh Barr to kill Eamon, and I don't want to discuss it. What I know is that you're as much a victim of the Troubles as I am. The Fountain Street bombing changed all our lives. It put Eamon in prison for six years, and you lost your husband and son. And while the Peace Agreement brought freedom for Eamon, it made a mockery of the justice system for you. To be honest, I find it hard to understand justice. It's like what you asked on the stand: 'What is justice?'"

This comment brings a flicker of a smile to Gráinne's face as she remembers Judge Sinclair's admonition. "I'm so glad you've come, Mrs. Sullivan." Her voice falls to a whisper. "I'm sorry." She puts her hands on her face. Tears dribble slowly through her fingers. She raises her head and looks directly at her visitor. "I'm sorry I caused Eamon's death. It was wrong."

"I want you to know that Eamon was a good person," Mrs. Sullivan says. "Although he represented IRA volunteers in court, he was never a member of the IRA. I don't know why he sheltered Kevin O'Neill and Sean Lynch. He probably had no time to think or couldn't say no. It doesn't matter now. I realize I have to move forward. I hope we can both move forward and experience this season of new birth. I know, because you're in here, it'll be harder for you. But I think the new birth Father was talking about has little to do with our outward circumstances. It has to do with our hearts and the peace our Savior brings us."

Gráinne notices the small silver crucifix around Mrs. Sullivan's neck. She senses it's more about faith than fashion. "Thank you. I'll try. It means so much to me to have your forgiveness. I need to work on developing that spirit within me. I know it in my head, but I don't always experience it in my heart."

"You will. It took me a while to realize healing's a choice. Like your Peter, Eamon was my only son. I've a choice to allow bitterness, grief, and anger to eat me up or allow Christ to heal me. I don't understand it all, but I know my willingness to forgive is part of the healing process. I'll begin a novena for you this evening. I'm certain God will meet your needs."

Mrs. Sullivan's surprised the one hour passes quickly. She returns her pass and has her finger scanned as she leaves the visiting room. She's glad she made the decision to visit Gráinne.

"How are you, Gráinne?" Father D'Arcy asks. He tries to visit her once a month.

"I have a surprise for you, Father. I had a visit from Eamon Sullivan's mother. It was so good. She told me she has no hard feelings against me. You can imagine what it's like to feel forgiven. It's like a burden lifted from me."

"I'm so glad. Now I want you to think about what it means to Mrs. Sullivan to forgive you. Think of the burden she has given up. In the Lord's Prayer, we ask God to forgive our sins as we forgive those who sin against us. I believe Christ asks us to forgive because he knows we hurt ourselves when we hang on to anger and resentment. I believe there's such a thing as justifiable anger, but sometimes even though it may be justified, anger can harm us."

Father D'Arcy smiles before continuing. "Gráinne, there's an old Chinese proverb that says, 'The one who seeks revenge and refuses to forgive needs to dig two graves.' What it's telling us is that not only is it good to be forgiven, but it's healthy for us to forgive. I'm sure that's what Mrs. Sullivan is experiencing, and I hope this Christmas season you'll think about not only what it means to be forgiven, but the tremendous healing power that's available to us when we forgive."

Another smile crosses his face, and Gráinne wonders what's coming next. "To forgive isn't as easy as pressing a button on a water fountain to immediately quench your thirst. It's a long-term process, more like an addict living a day at a time. You have to work at it daily. Maybe for some, healing comes like a flood; but more likely you'll receive it a drop at a time."

When Father D'Arcy leaves, Gráinne thinks about his little sermon. He always has a little sermon. Her eyes moisten. She removes a handkerchief from her sleeve and wipes away tears. She knows Father D'Arcy has a way with words, and he gets to the point with a habit of gentleness. For the first time, she wonders if the price of her personal peace is a willingness to forgive.

22

January 2006

SINCE THE NEW YEAR, Gráinne has tried to focus on setting goals and establishing some order to her daily routine. It's something she does every year, but this year is different. She's no longer free to do as she wants. Even worse, she faces spending the next twelve years in prison. It's difficult to be upbeat, but her parents and the prison staff tell her a thought-out routine is necessary if she's to cope with the daily challenges of prison life. In setting her goals, she thinks about Mrs. Sullivan's visit and Father D'Arcy's words.

She decides to get up every morning in time for breakfast and to spend each morning trying to enrich her mind. She'll make sure she has lunch with the other prisoners and try to exercise each afternoon. Maybe she'll take an art class. The evening will be her time for watching television, listening to music, writing letters, and making phone calls. Although she's not motivated enough to resume work on her novel, she decides to keep a daily journal. She'll do this in the evening before she goes to bed.

She had asked Father D'Arcy to recommend something she could read about forgiveness, and he brought her two books and some pamphlets. It doesn't take long for Gráinne to realize that forgiving won't be easy. It's not really a process of mental gymnastics. It's more concrete. It'll require a conscious decision on her part to let go of her anger toward the bombers. This is huge, she thinks, because she'll have to be willing to accept what happened, look past it, and move on. She wonders if anyone can truly forgive and forget.

Father D'Arcy assures her that she can find the grace to forgive. He cautions her that forgetting may be more difficult, for even if she can stop holding grudges and let go of her anger, there almost certainly will be reminders of what happened: anniversaries, old photographs, all the things that jog memory, a retrial.

That night, she writes in her journal, "Forgiving is an essential part of healing. I may not be able to forget, but I will get to the point of forgiving." She underlines the last eight words.

On his next visit, she asks Father D'Arcy how she'll know she has truly reached the point of forgiveness.

"You'll know," he says to her.

"But how will I know?"

"You'll know because the Holy Spirit will have transformed your soul. This isn't some airy-fairy thing. It's not mind games. It's real. You and others will see the change in you. There'll be no anger, no hatred. The hardness of your heart will be replaced with love. Your thoughts will be about the positive and not the negative. For example, if you find yourself praying for each of the bombers, you'll know you have forgiven them. I can't tell you how long it will take. But it will happen if you want it to happen. I know this to be true, for I see it every week in my pastoral care. Just look at Eamon Sullivan's parents. If they can find grace, you can find grace. It's not a matter of willing it in your mind. It's surrender to the only one who can change you."

Gráinne's parents visit her every week. She talks to at least one of them every day on the phone. At first, she would ask them about life outside the prison. But as the days stretch to weeks and the weeks to months, she finds she has less interest in the world outside. The weather just doesn't matter. All she's interested in is how they are doing. What's happening in their lives? She keeps them informed about her day. She tries to assure them she's coping fine. She knows it was the most difficult Christmas of their lives.

Now, with her goals in place for the year, she broaches a subject everyone in her family has been sweeping to the back of their minds.

"Daddy, what do you think I should do about the house?"

"What do you mean?"

"Well, if I'm going to be here for twelve years, is there any point keeping it? Why incur rates, insurance, heating expense? It's in good shape. I'll be sixty when I get out of here. Now may be the best time to sell it."

"Gráinne, we don't know you'll be here for twelve years. I'm confident the Court of Appeal will reduce your sentence, particularly given the Peace Agreement. Let's keep hope. It's too soon to think about selling. Let's get through with the appeal process."

23

April 2006

DESPITE MAINTAINING HER REGIMEN, there are days Gráinne struggles to get out of bed. She has been moved from the committal landing to the landing that houses the few prisoners serving lengthy sentences. All units now have in-cell sanitation, and there's talk of a new progressive landing that will give long-term prisoners greater freedom. But for Gráinne, it's not the facilities and staff that depress her; it's the thought of living like this for twelve years. Often, all it takes is the release of another prisoner. During Easter week, two prisoners on her landing are released, and just when Gráinne feels she can't take it anymore, she has another visit from Mrs. Sullivan.

"I guess I'm starting a habit of visiting you on the big holidays, but I want to see how you are doing."

"You couldn't have come at a better time. I've been doing okay, but this week for some reason I'm tired, depressed, unmotivated. I'm sorry you find me like this, for I've been doing really well. I think every time someone completes their sentence, it makes me realize how long I have to go."

"What's the status of your appeal?"

"It's been filed. We're just waiting for a court date."

"Do you know when that might be?"

"Not exactly, but Pascal says it's on the calendar for October. The wheels of justice grind slowly."

"Tell me what you've been doing to keep your sanity."

"I've been reading and thinking about forgiveness and have had some great discussions with Father D'Arcy. I keep a journal. I think I'm getting there but at times forgiveness is like trying to square a circle."

Mrs. Sullivan laughs. "I love your simile. I can see why you're a writer. I hope you'll soon get back to working on your novel. I enjoyed your first one. You are very talented. As for your analogy, the only way you can square the circle is if the circle isn't fixed, it's flexible, has a lot of elasticity. That's why forgiveness is difficult. It requires radical change. But the problem is that if we don't forgive, we will always be victims. We will always be nourished by resentment."

Before she leaves, Mrs. Sullivan asks Gráinne to keep her informed on the appeal. She would like to support Gráinne any way she can.

That evening as she prepares for bed, Gráinne thinks about Mrs. Sullivan. She wishes she could be like her. As she says the rosary, her thoughts wander to Eamon Sullivan. She didn't know him. She only saw him in court during the trial of the Fountain Street bombers. If he were alive, he'd be in his early forties. She'd seen his name in the paper often, representing Republicans charged with terrorist crimes. He was popular in Republican circles, a thorn in the flesh of Loyalists. He was Mrs. Sullivan's only son. Gráinne's eyes moisten. She closes them, clutches the rosary tight in her hands, and brings them to her lips.

"Our Father, who art in Heaven, hallowed be Thy name. Thy kingdom come, Thy will be done on earth . . . in my life . . . Give us this day our daily bread, and forgive us our trespasses . . . forgive me for causing the death of Eamon Sullivan. Forgive me for the pain and suffering I've caused his family. Have mercy on his soul. Let him enjoy eternal life . . . as we forgive those who trespass against us and lead us not into temptation . . . Thank you, Father, for your forgiveness. Thank you for the forgiveness of Mrs. Sullivan. Father, help me to forgive, in Jesus' name."

In her journal, Gráinne writes, "It's a start. Help me, Jesus; help me, Mary."

24

October 2006

THE COURT OF APPEAL SITS at the Royal Courts of Justice on Chichester Street. The architecture was designed to convey the dignity and tradition of the law. The first three stories are articulated by giant Corinthian columns freestanding at the porch. The outside façade is faced with Portland stone, the external steps and curbs with Irish granite. The central hall is paneled from floor to ceiling in Italian travertine marble.

Herschel Solomon and Pascal Bourke enter the building by the Court Funds Office. The Lord Chief Justice, Basil Robinson, will hear Gráinne's appeal along with two Lord Justices of Appeal. Martin Mulligan and Graham McIlhenny appear for the Crown.

The Lord Chief Justice speaks first. "On 29th September, 2005, the applicant, Gráinne O'Connor, was convicted of the murder of Kevin O'Neill following a trial before His Honor, Judge Sinclair, and a jury. She was sentenced to life imprisonment. The conviction was by a majority of ten to two. On 24th October, 2005, the learned trial judge fixed the minimum term to be served in accordance with Article 5 of the Life Sentences (Northern Ireland) Order at twelve years. He granted leave to the applicant to appeal the court's decision. The applicant is appealing both the conviction and sentence. Mr. Solomon, are you ready to present the grounds for appeal?"

"Yes, M'lord. Let me first present the basis of the applicant's appeal against conviction. Simply put, the learned trial judge failed to give direction to the jury on the issue of manslaughter. Such direction would have been appropriate, and its absence deprived the jury of an important alternative verdict.

"The Court of Appeal in Northern Ireland in *Regina versus Shaw and Campbell* in 2001 made clear the duty of the trial judge to direct the jury on manslaughter if a jury might reasonably return such a verdict based on the whole of the evidence. By omitting to mention manslaughter, the judge made the law seem more rigid than it is by representing that the jury had only a choice between murder and acquittal with no alternative position. The risk here is the jury convicts out of reluctance to see the defendant get away clean or acquits merely because they cannot be sure the defendant is guilty as charged. Both results are unacceptable, and our system guards against them by requiring the judge to explain the law of manslaughter to the jury.

"As Lord Tucker so aptly concluded in *Bullard versus The Queen* in 1957, 'Every man on trial for murder has the right to have the issue of manslaughter left to the jury if there is any evidence upon which such a verdict can be given. To deprive him of this right must of necessity constitute a grave miscarriage of justice, and it is idle to speculate what verdict the jury would have reached.' The failure by the judge to give this direction in this case is a material misdirection in law, and in accordance with section 2(1) of the Criminal Appeal Act 1968, the appellate court should quash the conviction, for, by reason of the misdirection, the conviction is unsafe."

The Lord Chief Justice asks Martin Mulligan if he wishes to respond.

"My Lords, in *Regina versus Maxwell* in 1990, the House of Lords held that in cases where the judge fails to leave an alternate verdict with the jury, before interfering with a verdict, the Court of Appeal must be satisfied that the jury convicted the defendant out of reluctance to see the defendant escape some form of justice. In the case before you, there is no evidence that occurred. The requirement to place an alternative verdict before the jury does not apply in circumstances where giving such direction does not serve the interests of justice. It's unfortunate that we don't know Judge Sinclair's reason for not bringing an alternate verdict of manslaughter to the attention of the jury, but it seems reasonable to assume the learned judge made a conscious decision that it was best not to introduce an unnecessary complication and one that would not change the verdict of the jury.

"In effect, Judge Sinclair properly directed the jury on a more serious offense, and since the jury convicted the defendant of that more serious offense, the failure to introduce the lesser offense of manslaughter does not of itself render the conviction unsafe."

The Lord Chief Justice asks Solomon if he wants to comment.

"I do, M'lord. You are aware from the transcripts of the trial that the jury had considerable difficulty in reaching a consensus and, in fact, were unable to render a unanimous verdict that the defendant was guilty of murder. There is no way we can know what discussions took place among the jurors, but it's reasonable to conclude that had the option of manslaughter been given to the jury, they may have convicted the defendant on the lesser charge of manslaughter.

"To quote Judge Callinan in *Gilbert versus The Queen* in 2000, 'The appellant was entitled to a trial at which directions according to law were given. It is contrary to human experience that in situations in which a choice of decisions may be made, what is chosen will be unaffected by the variety of the choices offered, particularly when, as here, a particular choice was not the only or inevitable choice.'

"My Lords, I think it's clear in the case before the court. You are aware the defendant was charged with two counts of murder. In both, she was accused of paying a third party to commit the murders. But the jury found her not guilty on the first charge and guilty on the second charge. What is significant to this appeal is that there was no contact between the defendant and the third party in the period from the first killing until the third party started to blackmail the defendant. So, if she was 'not guilty' of the first killing, how could she be 'guilty' of the second killing when she didn't initiate any contact with the third party? I think the answer is the jury felt the defendant had some culpability for the second killing but they were left with no choice. It was either guilty of murder or acquittal. In reality, Judge Sinclair should have given the jury the option of a manslaughter verdict. Instead, he instructed them to find consensus on the murder charge. With a 'not guilty' verdict in the first killing, I have to believe the jury would have rendered a 'manslaughter' verdict in the second killing had the judge given them the manslaughter option, as he is required to do under law.

"I am certainly unable to say that if given a direction on manslaughter, the jury would nevertheless have convicted the appellant of murder. I think accordingly the verdict is unsafe and should be quashed."

"Mr. Mulligan, would you like to respond?"

"Yes, My Lord. Whether the third party blackmailed the defendant or not, she confirmed in testimony that she made another payment to the third party and, therefore, under law is responsible for the actions which followed as a result of the payment. One could argue that if she hadn't made the payment, the third party would have had no motive to harm the victim. The second payment was identical to the first payment. The jury found the defendant not guilty of the first murder. They could have found her not guilty of the second murder, but that second payment convinced the jury that the defendant did have a clear responsibility for the second killing, the murder of Kevin O'Neill. Even if the jury had been given the alternative of manslaughter, we are certainly unable to say they would not have found the defendant guilty of murder."

Having heard the arguments on the appeal of Gráinne's conviction, the Lord Chief Justice adjourns the session for lunch.

Gráinne returns to her cell after lunch. She wonders how the appeal is going. She feels conflicted. Even if the appeal is successful, the thought of having to go through another jury trial is almost as daunting as the thought of being in jail for another eleven years. She wonders if she's getting used to this new way of life, a routine where she's secure, provided for, has so little responsibility her biggest decision is whether to stay in her cell or socialize with her fellow inmates. A simple reduction in her sentence would be her preferred outcome of the appeal.

"Now, Mr. Solomon, let's hear your arguments against the sentence that the defendant serve a minimum of twelve years."

"M'lord, the learned trial judge followed the established process to determine the minimum period of imprisonment for a defendant who had been found guilty of murder. He set the starting point, sixteen years, at the higher end of the norm because the murder was a contract killing, and he wanted to make an example of the defendant so that others, particularly victims of the Troubles, wouldn't be tempted to take the law into their own hands. He felt that there were no aggravating factors not addressed by this starting point.

"The trial judge then considered mitigating factors, and it is here that I believe he erred grievously, although I recognize that this may have been the result of a conscious decision to exclude the Peace Agreement from his consideration. Perhaps this is not surprising, for there are no decisions that I'm aware of that could properly be described as guideline cases for sentencing in a case so influenced by the Peace Agreement. Now the Crown may argue that application of the Peace Agreement to this case is beyond the jurisdiction of the court. If so, which court should rule on the application of the Peace Agreement to this case, for it is clear the Peace Agreement, at worst, usurped the power of the judicial process, or to be gentler, the Peace Agreement became an integral part of the judicial process?

"How did the Peace Agreement do this? Well, it established a new category of crime: those that are politically motivated. More significantly, it redefined the punishment for politically motivated crimes. Let's look at the application of the Peace Agreement to politically motivated murders.

"Under the terms of the Peace Agreement, Kevin O'Neill, whom Mrs. O'Connor has been found guilty of murdering, had his sentence of thirty years reduced to six years for murdering Mrs. O'Connor's husband and son. Sean Lynch, who also had been convicted of murdering Mrs. O'Connor's husband and son, had his sentence reduced from life to six years under the Peace Agreement. Even more astounding is the case of Brendan McArdle, who testified against Mrs. O'Connor. If today he could be charged with the murder of Mrs. O'Connor's husband and son, and if he were found guilty, under the Peace Agreement he would serve two years maximum. Because he was given immunity to testify, he actually will serve no time.

"And let's understand what constitutes a politically motivated murder. In the case of Kevin O'Neill and Sean Lynch, it is placing a bomb in the middle of a crowded shopping center for the purpose of killing and maiming as many innocent men, women, and children as possible. The victims don't even have to oppose the political views of the bombers; they may well have the same political views as the bombers. All that's required is that the bombers attach some political motive to their crimes.

"Now the issue is whether the terms of this Peace Agreement should apply to Mrs. O'Connor. What does the Peace Agreement say? Let's look at this. The Peace Agreement says, and remember the Peace Agreement is now a historical and integral part of the judicial system, 'We must never forget those who have died or been injured, and their families,' and, 'It's essential to acknowledge and address the suffering of the victims of violence.'

"The appellant is someone who lost her husband and son in the Troubles due to a bomb abandoned indiscriminately by the person she has been found guilty of murdering, a person who served six years out of a sentence of thirty years because of the Peace Agreement. Six years. The Peace Agreement looked at the mitigating factors—political motivation—and reduced the sentence by twenty-four years. How much did Judge Sinclair reduce Mrs. O'Connor's sentence by when he looked at mitigating factors? He reduced it by four years. Is that acknowledging and addressing the suffering of the victims of violence? What about the vision of equality and justice foreseen in the Agreement?

"My Lords, I'm not sure how to make a distinction between the murder of a husband and child in the commitment of a robbery and the murder of a husband and child in the commitment of a political act of terror. The result is the same. The wife is left without her husband and child. What I know is the Fountain Street bombing in February 1993 is regarded as a political act. I know Kevin O'Neill was one of the bombers, and our justice system sentenced him to thirty years in prison. I know the bombing killed five people, including the appellant's husband and son. I know the 1998 Peace Agreement reduced Mr. O'Neill's sentence from thirty years to six years. I know that the appellant's actions that resulted in the death of Mr. O'Neill stemmed from the Peace Agreement, particularly the provision that reduced Mr. O'Neill's sentence from thirty years to six years.

"When I look at cause and effect, how can I say that the actions of Gráinne O'Connor do not attach to the political act of Kevin O'Neill? I can't. Although they occurred after the signing of the Peace Agreement, they are as much a part of the Troubles as anything that occurred in the period 1968 to 1998. Gráinne O'Connor is as entitled to the justice and equality provisions of the 1998 Peace Agreement as Kevin O'Neill and the hundreds of prisoners released under the Agreement.

"My Lords, the trial judge erred when he didn't apply the terms of the Peace Agreement to this case and, in particular, in refusing to consider what those early release provisions of the Agreement mean for justice and equality. If Brendan McArdle can serve no more than two years for the murder of Mrs. O'Connor's husband and son, I respectively argue that it's improper for Mrs. O'Connor to serve more than two years. This concludes our arguments on behalf of the appellant."

Lord Chief Justice, Basil Robinson, looks at his watch. "Mr. Mulligan, I expect the Crown will have counterarguments. How much time do you anticipate needing?"

"Actually, Your Lordship, our response will be quite brief."

"Then let us hear it."

"My Lords, as Mr. Solomon has noted, there simply is no precedent in the courts that guides us on whether the 1998 Peace Agreement has or has not any application to this case. I must congratulate learned counsel on arguing such a strategy. I'll resist using the term 'concocting,' for he has raised an issue that I for one am glad I don't have to answer.

"I don't think any of us know whether the framers of the Peace Agreement intended the prisoner release and the inherent reduction in prisoner sentences to be a once-and-for-all event, similar to an amnesty. I suspect they did see it as a one-off event, but that's not for me to determine. Leaving aside the application of the Peace Agreement to this case, something which I believe Judge Sinclair handled correctly, it is the Crown's contention that the sentence of twelve years was generous. We agree with the starting point of sixteen years but feel there was insufficient ground to reduce the starting point by four years, particularly as the defendant has never shown remorse. Unless there is something in the Peace Agreement that we do not understand, it is our position that the sentence of twelve years is fair and just."

The Lord Chief Justice addresses both parties. "Before we adjourn, I want to thank both counsels for the way you have handled the arguments. I will consult with my two colleagues and make a ruling as expeditiously as possible. The court stands adjourned."

25

February 2007

IN THE FIRST WEEK OF February, the Court of Appeal issues a decision on Gráinne's appeal. She's surprised when she sees Herschel Solomon sitting beside Pascal in the prison visitor room and nervous when she realizes a decision must have come down.

"I guess you have good news or bad news," she says, as she shakes their hands.

"Gráinne," says Pascal, "I believe you will think it good news. I hope so."

Solomon refers to the paper in his folder. "The Court of Appeal has quashed the conviction of the Crown Court and ordered a new trial."

Pascal sees the color change in Gráinne's face. She puts both hands on her chair seat and adjusts her position. "Don't panic," he says, "just listen to what Herschel has to say."

"What's important, Gráinne, is the reasoning behind the ruling. The court ruled that Judge Sinclair should have instructed the jury that they could return a verdict of manslaughter instead of murder. Now, this ruling puts the Crown in a dilemma. You have already been found not guilty of the murder of Eamon Sullivan. You cannot be retried for that charge. The Crown is faced with going forward with a retrial for the murder of Kevin O'Neill but with a very important difference. Even if you are charged with murder, the Court of Appeal has ruled that the judge must explain manslaughter to the jury and direct them that they can find you guilty of manslaughter or murder. In cases where the jury are divided but don't feel they should acquit, the manslaughter verdict is often a more palatable option."

"What is the sentence for manslaughter?"

Pascal explains. "It can range from one to four years for an unlawful act, such as asking someone to physically harm another person, or eight to fifteen years where, for example, substantial violence is shown to the victim."

"In your case," Solomon says, "the new jury will be faced with the same issue as the first jury—did you intend the victim to be killed? The Crown knows the first jury acquitted you of a similar charge with respect to Eamon Sullivan, so we know they are concerned with going through another lengthy trial and risking an acquittal or a manslaughter verdict. Add to that, the Court of Appeal decided not to address your appeal against the length of the sentence imposed by Judge Sinclair until after the retrial. So the Crown knows that even after a retrial, it is likely the Court of Appeal or the House of Lords will be asked to rule on our argument about the application of the Peace Agreement."

"But here's the best news," Pascal says with a broad grin. "Given the situation Herschel just described, the Crown is prepared to consider a plea to manslaughter provided you serve six years (the same as the bombers) and indicate your remorse."

Gráinne smiles at Pascal, and her eyes water. He sees the tension leave her small frame.

"What do you think?" she asks.

"It's better than twelve years," Solomon says, "and you would avoid another trial, which I know you don't want."

"Gráinne, we don't want to give you false hope. We will try to do better than this. We're in the early stages of discussions, but in any plea negotiations, we need our client's concurrence."

"You have mine," she says. "I don't know how to thank you. I'll do whatever you recommend. I've only not followed your advice once, and that was a costly mistake. It led the police to Brendan McArdle and his testimony against me."

"Very good," Pascal says. "We'll continue with our negotiations and keep you informed."

"Can I tell my parents?"

Pascal looks at Solomon.

"Yes, but it shouldn't go any further until everything's bottled up. I know you understand."

"You have my word."

Martin Mulligan decides to meet alone with Marie O'Neill. It's a meeting he wishes he didn't have to conduct, but it is his duty to consult the family of a victim before considering a plea agreement with the defendant. He explains to David Ingram that a smaller audience is more likely to keep Marie from going ballistic, although he can't be certain.

"Marie, I want you to know the Court of Appeal has ruled on Gráinne O'Connor's appeal against her conviction. The appeals court has decided that she must be retried for the murder of Kevin. The reason for this is that in the court's opinion, the judge should have instructed the jury that manslaughter was an alternative to murder as they considered guilt or innocence."

"What are you telling me?"

"I'm saying the verdict of the Crown Court has been quashed, and the Department of Public Prosecutions must consider where to go from here."

"What do you mean? Aren't you going to retry her for murdering Kevin?"

"The problem we face, Marie, is that having listened to the evidence, the jury acquitted Mrs. O'Connor of one murder and found her guilty of Kevin's murder, but the verdict was not unanimous. We have to weigh the likelihood of getting a murder conviction now, with the alternative of manslaughter clearly on the table and explained to the jury. To be honest, I don't feel we can get a murder conviction."

"So what are you saying?"

"If we take Mrs. O'Connor to trial—"

Before Mulligan can finish, Marie interrupts. "What do you mean, 'if we take Mrs. O'Connor to trial'? You're not saying you're not going to prosecute the bitch?"

"Marie, I want you to listen to me very carefully. If we charge her with murder, it is likely the jury will find her guilty of manslaughter, but it is also possible they may find her not guilty of anything and she will walk free. Remember, this time she won't be charged with the murder of Eamon Sullivan, so it's unlikely the jury will be allowed to hear much, if anything, about the original contract with Hugh Barr. What they'll hear is that Hugh Barr threatened her and blackmailed her into paying him money and that after receiving the money, he killed Kevin. The risk of an acquittal is significantly greater now than it was in the first trial."

"I don't understand. Are you saying you intend to charge her with manslaughter instead of murder?"

"Not exactly, for if we charge her with manslaughter there's still the possibility the jury will acquit her. We believe the best option is to try to work out a plea agreement under which Mrs. O'Connor will plead guilty to manslaughter and be sentenced accordingly. That way, she will serve time in prison."

Marie stays silent. Mulligan imagines the cells churning in her brain. He knows what is coming.

"How long will she serve?"

"Our recommendation is that we go for four years."

"Son of a bitch, you can't be serious. She's going to do less time than Kevin. That's unacceptable."

"Would you prefer two years?"

Marie stares at Mulligan. "What do you mean?"

"You know that had Brendan McArdle not been given immunity, the most he could serve if found guilty of murdering Mrs. O'Connor's husband and son is two years. The defense is going to argue strongly that justice and equity dictate two years—first, because Brendan won't serve any time and, secondly, because Kevin served six for murder, and this is manslaughter, which usually, although not always, results in a lesser sentence. So the choice is: I think I can work a plea deal for a firm four years, or we can take the risk that the judge may give her two years, or the jury may acquit her."

To Mulligan's surprise, Marie stands up. It's clear from the way she snaps her purse shut that she's about to leave.

"I should've known better than to think for one moment I'd find justice in a British court. It's a sad day for Irish Catholics when someone who murdered an Irish hero can escape justice."

Mulligan is tempted to remind her that in the course of the Troubles, more Catholics were killed by the IRA than by the British Army, RUC, and Protestant paramilitaries combined. But before he can put his thoughts into words, she slams the door shut and is gone.

When David Ingram asks Mulligan how his meeting went, Ingram shakes his head and says, "It could've been worse."

Pascal and Herschel enter the Department of Public Prosecutions with optimism. They feel they're in a strong position and can do better than six years. But they know the DPP will have met with Marie O'Neill, and she may have demanded the Crown go for nothing less than twelve years.

As negotiations go, the meeting is unusually brief. Mulligan says he will accept a plea deal of six years provided the defendant pleads guilty to manslaughter and shows some evidence to the court of remorse. Herschel counters with two years and a statement of remorse. They quickly agree on four years.

26

April 2007

MARTIN MULLIGAN IS RELIEVED to see that Marie O'Neill is not in court. There are a handful of reporters but nothing like the coverage of the original trial. Gráinne's parents are present. Mulligan is surprised to see Mr. and Mrs. Sullivan sitting beside them. When the proceedings convene, the judge says to Mulligan that he understands a plea deal has been reached in the case against Gráinne O'Connor.

"Yes, My Lord. The defendant will plead guilty to a charge of manslaughter in the death of Kevin O'Neill on March 2nd, 2003. The Crown recommends that the defendant be sentenced to serve four years in prison. I understand the defendant wishes to make a statement if Your Honor concurs."

"You may do so, Mrs. O'Connor."

"Your Honor, I've had a long time to think about the pain and suffering I caused when I asked Hugh Barr to get me justice for the death of my husband and son. I want to apologize to Mrs. Barr and to Mrs. O'Neill for my role in the deaths of their husbands. I wish they were in court this morning so I could apologize directly to them. I'm glad Mr. and Mrs. Sullivan are present, and again I apologize to you both for my responsibility in the death of your beloved son, Eamon.

"My remorse is not the result of a plea deal. Shortly after I entered prison in October 2005, Mrs. Sullivan came to Ash House in Hydebank Wood Prison to visit with me. I was greatly surprised, for I was responsible for the death of her son. She told me she bore no ill will against me and hoped, as Christmas approached, I could find new life and the peace of Christ. I will not say I found this easy, but as I searched my soul and read more and more about forgiveness, I began to realize that to really experience the forgiveness of Mrs. Sullivan, I had to forgive. For the first time, I began to understand the Lord's Prayer. Today, I can say that I forgive Eamon, Kevin, Sean, Brigid, and Brendan, and I'm working hard at forgetting."

She turns to face the Sullivans. "Mr. and Mrs. Sullivan, thank you so much for coming today. Thank you for your gift of healing. You've changed my life."

She turns back to face the bench. "Thank you, Your Honor, for allowing me to address the court."

The judge reviews the papers on the bench in front of him. "In the matter of the Crown versus Gráinne O'Connor, the court accepts the guilty plea of the defendant to the manslaughter of Kevin O'Neill and sentences Mrs. O'Connor to serve four years in Her Majesty's Prison. The time the defendant has served since October 2005 will count against the term of four years. I understand, Mr. Solomon, the defense will not appeal the conviction and sentence of this court and will withdraw the outstanding appeal against the original sentence of twelve years."

"That is correct, M'lord."

"I have to believe there are a lot of scholars in the Court of Appeal and the House of Lords who are relieved to hear this. The court is adjourned."

Later that month, Gráinne and the other prisoners serving longer sentences are moved to the newly constructed landing, known as Ash 5. The unit can hold up to ten prisoners at a time. Gráinne is delighted, because the new landing is self-contained and located on the ground floor. This allows easier access to the outdoor exercise area. This grouping of women serving longer sentences also should reduce the amount of coming and going among inmates and provide a greater sense of community. To her surprise, Ash 5 has communal cooking, dining, and living areas, and the prisoners are permitted to carry the keys to their rooms. She feels she can handle this for another thirty months.

27

January 2009

IN HER CELL, GRÁINNE TURNS on the six o'clock news. According to the newscaster, proposals dealing with the legacy of Northern Ireland's Troubles have created a firestorm among politicians and victims' groups alike. This is because the recommendations include a plan to pay the nearest relative of each person who died in the conflict a £12,000 "recognition payment." But the proposed payment includes relatives of paramilitaries killed in the Troubles. This is not acceptable to the victims. Gráinne wonders how anyone who has experienced the pain and loss associated with the Troubles could make such a recommendation.

The newscaster goes on to note that none of the thirty recommendations propose an amnesty for crimes linked to the conflict but recommend that a Legacy Commission make a proposal on how "a line might be drawn." She's pleased to hear people at least are talking about the impact of the Troubles in a broader context than the Peace Agreement. She has only nine more months to serve, so, if and how the line is drawn, it is unlikely to affect when she will walk free.

She thinks back to a discussion between Herschel Solomon and Pascal Bourke the day the court accepted the plea agreement. Pascal had asked Herschel what he thought the Court of Appeal would have ruled had they been faced with determining if the Peace Agreement applied to her case.

Herschel just smiled, shrugged his shoulders, and said, "We'll never know."

AUTHOR'S NOTE

IT IS NO COINCIDENCE that the first quote I use in this book comes from Senator Mitchell. This is because the novel, although fiction, has its roots in the Northern Ireland peace process. Just like the Middle East peace process, the Northern Ireland process was fraught with significant challenges that threatened at any moment to derail the talks. For many months, it was two steps forward and one back. But unlike the Middle East process to date, the talks in Northern Ireland produced the 1998 Peace Agreement, an agreement that for the last fourteen years has allowed the people of Northern Ireland to live in a semblance of normality and begin healing. It is not an understatement to say that Senator Mitchell's perseverance was pivotal to the achievement of the successful outcome.

This story is not, in any way, meant to take away from the importance of the Peace Agreement and the enhanced quality of life experienced by the people of Northern Ireland subsequent to the Agreement. But it tries to show that even peace has a price, a price that raises significant questions about justice, and the relationship of justice to peace and forgiveness in the lives of the individual. I hope these questions will resonate with readers regardless of where they live, for justice and personal peace have universal application.

I was born a Protestant in East Belfast. My wife was born a Catholic in North Belfast. Both of us lost close friends in the civil unrest; some killed in bombings, some in shootings. When we left Ireland for North America in 1974, we could not foresee an end to the Troubles, so the 1998 Agreement was a milestone event. But as I read the terms of the Agreement, my heart ached for the families of victims of the Troubles. In July 2000, all of the prisoners sentenced for terrorist crimes would be released. For some of these families, this had to be the hardest day of the peace process.

Almost without exception, when faced with the death and injuries of loved ones, families would plead that there be no retaliation. But, almost without exception, those families sought closure through their faith in the justice system. Even when they were able to forgive, they expected the perpetrators of violence to be brought to justice.

As I read the reactions of victim families to the early release of prisoners, my thoughts increasingly focused on the meaning of justice. A father who lost his son described the releases as an affront to his son's memory. "These people can walk away from prison, walk away from their sentences. We can never leave our sentence behind." A woman orphaned in a bombing said she felt let down and the victim of another injustice.

I began to ask if there is such a thing as justice. If so, what is it? I wondered whether justice is for the living or for the dead, and out of such thoughts, *The Price of Peace* was born.

On one level, the novel is simply a work of fiction; a legal thriller that pits prosecution and defense in a chess match with an uncertain outcome and the risk of a stalemate. But on a deeper level, my hope is that the story will encourage the reader to think about the meaning of justice. Is justice merely the punishment for breaking a law? Or is it more akin to acceptable, legalized, revenge? How critical is justice to a family's process of closure? What are the relationships between justice, personal peace, and forgiveness?

There are a myriad of potential answers to these questions and throughout history they have been the subject of legal, philosophical, and theological debate. But, when I think of justice, two characteristics predominate: one is fairness, the other is equity. In the novel, I believe that is all Gráinne asked for.

About Celtic Cat Publishing

Celtic Cat Publishing was founded in 1995 to publish emerging and established writers. The following works are available from Celtic Cat Publishing at *www.celticcatpublishing.com*, Amazon.com, and major bookstores.

Regional
Appalachian Tales & Heartland Adventures, Bill Landry

Poetry
Exile: Poems of an Irish Immigrant, James B. Johnston
Marginal Notes, Frank Jamison
Rough Ascension and Other Poems of Science, Arthur J. Stewart
Bushido: The Virtues of Rei and Makoto, Arthur J. Stewart
Circle, Turtle, Ashes, Arthur J. Stewart
*Ebbing & Flowing Springs: New and Selected Poems and Prose
    (1976-2001)*, Jeff Daniel Marion
Gathering Stones, KB Ballentine
Fragments of Light, KB Ballentine
Guardians, Laura Still

Humor
My Barbie Was an Amputee, Angie Vicars
Life Among the Lilliputians, Judy Lockhart DiGregorio
Memories of a Loose Woman, Judy Lockhart DiGregorio

Chanukah
One for Each Night: Chanukah Tales and Recipes, Marilyn Kallet

Young Adult
Voyage of Dreams: An Irish Memory, Kathleen E. Fearing (April 2012)

Children
Jack the Healing Cat (English), Marilyn Kallet
Jacques le chat guérisseur (French), Marilyn Kallet
Twins, Tracy Ryder Bradshaw (April 2012)

End of Life
Being Alive, Raymond Johnston